SO-CAA-350

The tall shadow materialized right before his eyes

It was as if the battle smoke had breathed the armed figure forth from the night. Braxton hesitated for a split second, as he found his stare riveted on the icy blue eyes framed in the black-streaked face. Eyes that seemed more like orbs of pure fire than anything human.

But there was something about the man Braxton thought he recognized, or maybe it was the stare that burned back, telling him something about himself, as if the shadow had known him all along.

And he was judged.

The distance was twenty yards, nothing too great to overcome, but where he hesitated in bringing his assault rifle to bear, Mack Bolan's M-16 was already shooting flame.

Don Pendleton's Mack **Bolan**®

FORCE LINES

A GOLD EAGLE BOOK FROM

W❂RLDWIDE®

TORONTO • NEW YORK • LONDON
AMSTERDAM • PARIS • SYDNEY • HAMBURG
STOCKHOLM • ATHENS • TOKYO • MILAN
MADRID • WARSAW • BUDAPEST • AUCKLAND

If you purchased this book without a cover you should be aware
that this book is stolen property. It was reported as "unsold and
destroyed" to the publisher, and neither the author nor the
publisher has received any payment for this "stripped book."

First edition January 2007

ISBN-13: 978-0-373-61515-5
ISBN-10: 0-373-61515-9

Special thanks and acknowledgment to
Dan Schmidt for his contribution to this work.

FORCE LINES

Copyright © 2007 by Worldwide Library.

All rights reserved. Except for use in any review, the
reproduction or utilization of this work in whole or in part
in any form by any electronic, mechanical or other means,
now known or hereafter invented, including xerography,
photocopying and recording, or in any information storage
or retrieval system, is forbidden without the written permission
of the publisher, Worldwide Library, 225 Duncan Mill Road,
Don Mills, Ontario, Canada M3B 3K9.

All characters in this book have no existence outside the
imagination of the author and have no relation whatsoever to
anyone bearing the same name or names. They are not even
distantly inspired by any individual known or unknown to the
author, and all incidents are pure invention.

® and TM are trademarks of the publisher. Trademarks indicated
with ® are registered in the United States Patent and Trademark
Office, the Canadian Trade Marks Office and in other countries.

Printed in U.S.A.

The brave man inattentive to his duty, is worth little more to his country than the coward who deserts her in the hour of danger.

—Andrew Jackson,
1767–1845

It's gotten so these days that it's sometimes hard to tell the good guys from the bad. Honor, in some cases, seems to be a thing of the past, integrity just another word. But justice will not fade away, and shall prevail. Judgment is waiting. I consider it a duty.

—Mack Bolan

FORCE LINES

PROLOGUE

"They're here."

Hamal Amarshar acknowledged his lieutenant's grim pronouncement with a flip of the half-eaten oblong date, plunging it into the fire barrel before taking up his AK-74. The sudden current of tension through the cave told him his fighters were braced for the worst, whereas he had to maintain, at the very least, the appearance that he anticipated the best of all possible news. Had there been a significant boost in numbers of Americans or a noticeable upgrade in their hardware, he would have been forewarned, his scouts in the hills keeping the vast wasteland at the eastern edge of the Dasht-e-Kavir under constant surveillance for those on the other side foolish enough to stray outside the arrangement.

He briefly pondered the words of the man who called himself Black Dog, spoken at their first meeting.

"Hey, if I wasn't here to deal straight with you, my

friend, if I wanted your scalps in a bag as trophies—and collect enough bounty on your hides in the process that would set me up for my golden years—it would be no large feat for me to bring down a Tomahawk or a bunker buster or two on your heads."

That much may well be true enough, he supposed, having already done the math in terms of geography, as best he could, without, that was, the advantage of the enemy's high-tech wonder toys. Their hideout was a dozen or so meters up, weathered out by time and the cruelty of the desert in the side of a low-chain of rock that had aeons ago broken off from the Payeh Mountains. Between U.S. Navy warships stationed in the Gulf of Oman, roughly seven hundred kilometers due south—with Kabul about eight hundred kilometers east as the eagle flew in what was a major surrounding area of occupation by the enemy—there would be enough cruise missiles and fighter jets on hand and within striking distance to blow him to Paradise—or seal him up in the side of the mountain.

Amarshar considered both the moment—hopefully the gift his guests would come bearing, as promised— and the future. The Iranian listened to the rumble of engines, the squeal of timeworn brakes, saw the thinning spool of dust that rose from the floor of the wadi, as doors opened and closed and shadows began to filter up through the gritty sheen of harsh sunlight. It was a bizarre affair, to understate the matter, this striking a bargain with the devil, but an alliance that placed him at the crossroads of destiny. Just what the future promised—both immediate and long term—remained to be seen.

He struck a pose of calm defiance, legs splayed, assault rifle cradled across his chest as they filed in. He restrained the smile when two of them stepped forward, holding the large black box by thick straps before they carefully set it down in front of him. At the risk of appearing too eager, Amarshar took his time, scouring the faces, hidden behind dark sunglasses and partly swathed in keffiyahs that matched their buff-colored fatigues. It was either a testament to their courage, he thought, or their own greed and ambition that Black Dog and his armed canines even dare stray across the border. They were U.S. special operatives, was about all he could say, and that came from two former SAVAK agents who had originally come to him with the proposal to do business with the Devil.

Amarshar watched as Black Dog, the M-16/M-203 combo pointed at the ground, waved over his shoulder. Three operatives stepped forward and deposited black nylon bags on the ground, then fell back, hard, sun-burnished faces wandering over the Iranians hugging both sides of the cave.

"The CD was left with your SAVAK buddies back near the border," Black Dog said in near-perfect Farsi that drew a few eyes of admiration mixed with suspicion from the newer warriors.

Amarshar felt the scowl harden his features at what he considered no less than a breach of contract, a grotesque inconvenience at best. He gestured for his men to open the merchandise all around. "Without the operating instructions, then what you brought me is useless," he said.

"Just a precaution, you understand, until we're safely back in Afghanistan."

"A precaution? Or…"

"There's no 'or.' If you don't like it, you have a radio, call one of them, if you're worried. The operating procedures are so basic, your people could walk you through it in under two minutes."

True enough, perhaps, and he wanted to openly question that, but he was turning his stare toward the merchandise as two of his warriors knelt beside the black box. Amarshar blinked twice at the strange insignia painted on the lid.

As he took a step forward, bending at the neck, he thought at first it was some kind of joke. Then he began to slowly discern what it was he thought he saw. Those were four faces of what appeared a lion, a human, a calf and an eagle, staring him back. Only half of each face was connected to the next creature, so that they were four distinct faces but appeared as one. Surrounding them were what, at first glance, appeared to be six wings above and beneath each face—twenty-four in all, he counted upon further scrutiny—and circling them, with the faces appearing to come straight out of a roiling cloud of fire, with numerous black dots all over the faces, which he supposed passed for eyes.

Amarshar looked at Black Dog who, adjusting his

shades, simply said, "They would be the Four Living Creatures you're gaping at."

"From the Christian Bible," Amarshar said as he felt several pairs of eyes look his way, puzzled. "The Book of Revelation, I believe."

Black Dog smiled. "Give the man a gold star. Supposedly they surround the throne of God. The Four Living Creatures, the strongest, wisest, swiftest and most noble."

"And which would be you and your men?"

"I didn't say that. You did."

"And they represent, as I recall, the coming of the Day of Judgment?"

"I believe your Koran holds some similar version regarding the Day of Reckoning."

"Indeed. Where the unbelievers will be separated from the faithful and cast into a lake of fire for all eternity."

"Something like that, if, that is, you choose to believe."

"I take it you believe in something else."

"I believe in what I can see and touch in the here and now. Like money—for starters."

"Ah, but, of course. You wish to be like your Donald Trump perhaps."

"Not hardly. I'm all man, all warrior. I don't need to hide behind money or flaunt it because I have nothing else going for me."

"I see. Still…this insignia of the Four Living Creatures…"

"Hey, I couldn't tell you exactly who did the artwork, but mine is not to question my own higher and invisible authority."

Amarshar wanted to push the matter, certain the infidels were trying to warn him about personal doom, but sensed the sudden elevation in tension before one of his men, staring at the keypad, demanded to know the access code. As one of Black Dog's operatives began to rattle off numbers and one of his lieutenants punched the sequence into a personal digital assistant, barking at him to slow down, Amarshar watched two of his men zip open the other nylon bags. Long slender tubes of gunmetal gray displayed, Amarshar stared at the eyeless face of Black Dog. In the corner of his eye, noting the bubbled helmets and spacesuits being hauled out and unfolded, he said, "I hope you'll understand if I contact my men first and confirm what you have told me."

Black Dog looked set to curse as his lips parted to bare clenched teeth. "Yeah, okay. But make it quick."

Amarshar shut down an image of this man tied down and going under the heated blade of a knife that would skin him alive. The unmitigated arrogance of the infidel never failed to both amaze and enrage him, but he maintained an even tone as he said, "Then you'll understand, also, that I have some concerns regarding what you have delivered."

Black Dog scowled. "And they would be?"

"It is my understanding that the agent before us," Amarshar said as his lieutenant finished punching in the last numbers on the keypad and he heard a soft click that told him the lid was unlatched, "may not be as potent as you have previously indicated."

"How's that?"

"High explosives tend to incinerate the agent before it can be fully, effectively dispersed."

Black Dog chuckled, glanced over his shoulder at his men as if he were stuck in the presence of a fool.

Amarshar bristled, his grip tightening around the assault rifle. "You find what could potentially prove a colossal waste of money on my part amusing?" he growled as one of the operatives, his cheek swollen with chewing tobacco, spit on the ground.

"Fear not. The charges have been shaped—engineered, if you will—to prevent just what you fear from happening. What you'll get is a muffled pop, not much more than a smoke bomb going off, but with just enough force to disperse the agent in a vapor that is nearly undetectable to the naked eye. As advertised, I may add. Now, before your men there," he said as Amarshar noticed the lid opening to reveal two neat rows of what appeared to be aluminum canisters, "start fooling around with that stuff like it's nothing more than a handful of dung patties, I suggest you make that call, so me and mine can be on our way. One more thing."

Amarshar turned as one of his men hustled forward with the portable sat link. He held out a hand, a silent gesture that stopped the warrior in his tracks.

"For the full desired effect, I suggest you figure out

which way the wind is blowing before you go lobbing around those canisters." Black Dog chuckled. "And I'd strongly urge jumping into one of those HAZMAT suits before you go much further examining that merchandise. They're sealed up good with some state-of-the-art alloy I've never heard of, but you never know."

Amarshar shook his head at the men peering his way. They stood quickly, nearly jumping back two or three feet as if they'd just stumbled onto a nest of vipers.

"That's right, jump back, Jack. That stuff," Black Dog said, "is virulent enough to maybe kill every man, woman, child and camel in this country. And, once again, my Iranian friend, that's just as advertised."

"So you had previously mentioned. Which leads me to my next concern. What about the vaccine?"

"Well, as I also previously mentioned, once my own agenda is accomplished you'll get your magic fix."

Amarshar snorted. "You'll forgive my suspicion and my impatience in that regard, being as I have already delivered into your hands fifteen of my own warriors."

Black Dog had to have sensed he was stepping toward the edge of an invisible precipice as he glanced at the armed Iranians taking a step or two closer to his left flank. "Take it easy. You're asking me when will it happen?"

Amarshar glanced at his men, smiled. "The man is a mind-reader," he said.

Black Dog's voice turned to glacier ice as he said, "Soon. It will happen real soon. That's about all I can tell you. So, I would suggest you keep in touch with your chat room in Mashhad and inform them they'll want to stay glued to al Jazeera for breaking news."

Amarshar paused, fighting down his rising anger, wondering just how far he should push this contest of wills. He nodded, grunted, hoping both the gesture and noise came across as a man in charge but who could accept the enemy's terms in a show of mercy. In truth, he found himself trusting the infidels even less than their first meeting, even less certain now which direction precisely the future as he envisioned it would take, and what that future was. Yes, they were on his hallowed ground, such as it was, they had come to him via cutouts, granted, and he had agreed, more or less, to their terms, but...

But what?

Was he afraid for his own personal safety, now that they had delivered what they had promised, at least in terms of the agent? That much made sense, as he considered how they were holding out on what could eventually prove the ultimate lifesaver, if and when, and where and how he chose to release the agent, and on whom.

Amarshar decided to let the immediate future take care of itself, one way or another, and snapped his fingers for the sat link to be brought to him.

"CRYING RACISM has become the hoped-for trump card of the coward."

"Who you callin' a coward!?"

"The race card has become the last refuge of the

wicked and the guilty in this age of spineless political correctness and where near everyone in this society seems to be running around bewailing how they are victims of even the smallest perceived slights."

"Who you callin' wicked!? Who you callin' guilty!?"

"You dare on national television inquire about cowardice? You dare ask about wickedness and guilt?"

And Jason Hall groaned, more out of pain from the increasingly persistent nausea and burning knots in his guts than revulsion over the fireworks just getting touched off on "The Bigger Picture." Some other night, and the former U.S. Marine would be front and center, planted in his easy chair, glued to the television set for the full hour as the moderator, Jim Bright, danced through his charade as peace-maker while upholding his image, the modern King Solomon on the side of right and just, as he nightly self-anointed his role before lighting the fuse to loose cannons on both sides of the political fence. Or, in this instance, lobbing grenades down both sides of the racial-social spectrum.

For another few moments, Hall watched, despite his best intentions. As usual, the thought occurred to him that America had become a land of endless, needless babble, ranting and raving, on and off the television. Fanning the flames of division and hostility by rumor, gossip, detraction and slander, not to mention who could shout the loudest, had become something of a national sport, so much so that it was a rare piece of pure gold when Hall stumbled across one man in a thousand of civil tongue. As a decorated war hero Hall's personal creed was, "Speak little, endure all."

Ah, but where to be found such a pillar of decency and courage these days? he wondered. True, it was perhaps easy enough for him to keep in fine-tuned character, living as he did, alone, at the east edge of Flathead Lake, far removed from the bustling tourist traps at Polson and Bigfork. The two-story stone-and-wood home had been built from scratch, due in no small part to his father's inheritance. No circling buzzard where inheriting the hard-earned life savings of blood was concerned, and unlike several roustabouts he'd known from the service and who had squandered the small fortunes of inheritance on fast-and-loose living, he had charted another, and what had looked to be a wise course.

A personal crusade, in fact, he anticipated would any night now bring the wolves baying to his doorstep.

Hall listened to the wilderness beyond the deck overlooking the placid waters. He thought he heard something, a faint, distant noise that wanted to set off warning bells in tried-and-true instincts. Anything—man or beast—could be out there, he knew, both real and mythical. Something like 128 miles of wooded shoreline, Flathead Lake was the biggest body of fresh water his side of the Mississippi. Rumors abounded in these parts about the Flathead Nessie, in fact locals dedicated lengthy cult ceremonies to this alleged relative of the Loch Ness Monster, though no one had yet to make a sighting of the creature, much less catch even a fleeting shadow of the thing on film.

He shut down his laptop, picked up the Colt Commando assault rifle leaning against the side of his desk, but didn't budge from his chair. He reached for the remote control, one eye and ear still trained on "The Bigger Picture," the thought crossing his mind that he was daring fate by not scrambling to his feet, malingering as he listened to the verbal Hellfire barrage.

They were here.

What remained to be seen was exactly who "they" were.

The shorter version of the M-16, bought at a local gun show and modified by his own hand for fully automatic, was up and leading his charge a second before the light show hit the roof. Braking in midstride, he didn't hear the familiar whirlwind of rotor wash until a few heartbeats later.

Somehow he moved and found the gas mask at the edge of the desk, tugged it on. The suddenness and sheer audacity of the attack told him nothing less than black ops were hitting the roof, as he made out the running drumbeats of combat boots above. Squinting, he slipped the open nylon satchel around his shoulder, the bag stuffed with spare clips and an assortment of flash-bang, tear gas and fragmentation grenades he'd likewise recently collected across a state that had proved itself an arsenal that could just about match anything the United States armed forces had on hand. The rotor wash finally descended, full blast in his ears, providing nasty silent penetration, as it all but covered the enemy's moves.

At least by sound.

Three, then four shadows, framed against the curtains and armed with subguns clearly nozzled with fat sound suppressors, were crouched and hustling down the deck when Hall hit the trigger and raked the moving silhouettes with a long burst of autofire. For an angry second, as the shadows dropped out of sight, he wondered if he'd only blasted out the windows, shredding fabric. A moment later failure was confirmed as the canister sailed into the study, trailing a fat dragon's breath of billowing smoke.

He turned about-face, moving for the open door, adjusted his body to hose down the visible armed breaching point to his left wing, thinking about cover, when he sensed their approach from the living room.

Hall had to get the truth out to the world at large. It was something to fight for.

And he would do it his way, the Jason Hall version.

He determined the entertainment stand with stereo and giant speakers made for as respectable cover under the circumstances as he could hope for. He was delving into his war bag for a frag bomb, swinging his aim toward the living room and capping off three or four rounds when something speared deep into his left arm.

He held on, shooting for the ceiling on the fall, bellowing out a curse even as he knew he was finished.

It could have been two seconds or two hours, but he felt the mask ripped off, the weapon and war bag stripped away by angry hands.

So much for his way.

Shadows and voices swirled around him as Hall stared through the mist.

"Where did you find it?"

"Behind his Bible, where you said it would be, sir."

The CD. They knew, but somehow he'd already suspected as much. Given the sudden disappearance of the others, recalling before their vanishing acts their own dire predictions and suspicions, how all of them were aware what the defenders of national security were capable of…

He was shuddering up on an elbow, ready to fire off a battery of questions when the fever seemed to balloon behind his eyes like a living fire, a sickness so sudden and shocking it was all he could do to manage to hold back the greasy spears of molten liquid ready to burst, one end to the other orifice. He fell on his back, outstretched in a sloppy crucifixion, a groan of pure misery floating away into the white light.

They were still talking, when he made out a pair of black boots and matching pants, heard a lighter clacking, smelled the cigarette smoke. Something then rattled and was dumped on his chest. It was his rosary.

"You've got about thirty minutes before what's in your bloodstream burns out your brain, ten minutes, unfortunately, before you're swimming in your own waste. Still, that's plenty of time, Mr. Hall, pain and all the evil filth about to spill out of you aside, to say all five decades before the end."

Hall looked at his tormentor as a stream of smoke funneled his way from the hole of the mouth behind the black hood.

"Who are we, you ask? You wouldn't believe me, if I told you. Why are we here, you ask? Well, Mr. Hall, you should have kept your mouth shut, but a few of your jarhead buddies found that out the hard way, but I'm sure you've already figured out as much when you discovered your Web sites zapped then began your nightly armed recon around this stretch of Flathead Lake. Yes, you guessed correctly. You have been under constant surveillance. Okay, moving on. Instead of you accepting a chance to expiate your own guilt and treason, you turn down a reasonable offer to work for your country on a classified counter-bio warfare project, but you decided to stick to your lingering rebel nature. It wasn't enough you came home from the first Gulf War and incited the whole of the U.S. Senate and Congress about what you thought you and a lot of other vets had fallen ill from over there."

"You're going to kill me because I told the truth?"

"The truth was, more or less, already out there, Mr. Hall. Pyridostygmine was supposed to have been a vaccine to prevent the effects of any nerve gas Saddam might have thrown at the troops. Then some snippy Congressman whose panties you got all twisted up did some investigating—or more to the point—had somebody else do the work for him, and he comes out claiming before God and the whole world to hear that somehow the vaccines were contaminated by the AIDS virus. Just to clue you in, the so-called Gulf War Syndrome bore, more to the truth, similarities to the West Nile virus, but the AIDs claim was what got the hue and cry sounded."

Bile squirted up Hall's throat. The fog was thickening in his eyes, or had he been hit by another wave of smoke? He struggled for breath that felt like flames in his throat as he said, "We were used as guinea pigs."

"Maybe, maybe not. If you were test subjects, then let's say it was for a just cause, being as Gulf One may have been the first time our troops were threatened by the mass deployment of chemical or biological weapons. In other words, our side needed to know something in order to engineer a preventive measure. Unfortunately, the experimental vaccine didn't pan out as hoped. But, your mouth, that was strike one."

"Men who fought for this country died…"

"Strike two was refusing the offer. Strike three was putting out on the Internet to all your former comrades-in-arms and any other conspiracy fruitbasket who would listen to what little you thought you knew but which, by your crusade, might have well placed national security at grave risk nonetheless."

"So I die. You can't kill us all."

"And that would be you blustering it out until the bitter end?" The black hood chuckled. "Now then. What's killing you, you ask? To my knowledge—which, I may add, in this particular field is extensive—there are fifty-one known toxic warfare agents." He shrugged, smoked, then quickly added, "Actually there are sixty-five, but that's when I count those agents not even those in the sanctified realm of U.S. intelligence know about between our side, the Russians, several Mideast terror orgs and North Korea. But that's another story. Anyway, you have been stricken with, you guessed it, an experimental agent that is formed from the recombinant DNA of seven toxins. Botulin, anthrax and dioxin which, as you so boldly put out there, is an ingredient used in pesticide and which you believe was what caused GWS. But these are three of the seven you would be most familiar with, I'll leave the others to your imagination."

Hall watched as the black-clad executioner rose, staring at his watch.

"You have about twenty-five minutes now, Mr. Hall. Have a nice journey."

Hall watched the man as he stepped past before he was swallowed up into the white light.

He wanted to be angry over this treason, murdered, no less, by agents of the very government he had fought and killed for, outraged, terrified he was minutes away from dying...

But felt a calm peace settle over him. Still, this was no way for a warrior, he thought, to die, as he felt the first wave of white-hot pain knifing from head to toe. Still, there were those out there who knew something about the compound, who believed, and whom, he was sure, could count on to spread the truth. Or would they? Were there any even left to talk?

CHAPTER ONE

"What in the name of…"

Benjamin Dekel collapsed into the wall, aware that God had nothing to do with why he was about to die, had nothing to do with why he was burning up with maybe a 104 degree temperature, and climbing. Or why the pain in his chest was turning to a clenching fire that was seconds away from squeezing off the last bit of air to his lungs. Or why every last drop of bodily waste and liquefied organs was set to burst from both ends as his stomach and bowels caught fire. He was verging, he knew, on the edges of what they called "the liquid state."

Complete internal organ meltdown, followed by paralysis.

His voice struck his ears from a great distance as he heard himself croaking, "Help…someone…"

There was no answer, and he knew there was little time left now, perhaps down to a mere few minutes, since when the pain and nausea had finally driven him out of a deep sleep and he had heaved himself off the cot. And even if he reached the vault in what was called the Gold Room he was far from certain the Trivalent antitoxin derivative could be administered in time through the 20 ml IV vial, much less combat the effects of the hybrid strain he himself had taken part in creating.

With a sudden viciousness, he cursed the very day he'd quit Fort Detrick and accepted this post in what would now not only prove the middle of nowhere, but would be his final resting place. More money, they'd pledged, and delivered that much, and with talk among his colleagues about the possibility of a Nobel Prize…

His vision, he discovered, as predicted during the early stages of testing on African monkeys, was the first of the senses to start collapsing. Within moments, after the initial onslaught of the fractured maze with gray light webbed around narrowing peripheral vision, total blindness would descend. That would prove the least of his concerns, he knew, though it somehow might prove a blessing in disguise.

He stumbled, limbs turning quickly to boneless rubbery appendages, into the main corridor, gasping for breath, like the drowning man he knew he was. The stark white of the concrete walls seemed to drive hot needles through raw eyeballs, and served only to inflame the fire in his brain. Alternately hugging and sliding down the wall, it occurred to him one of several scenarios had taken place. The agent had either been accidentally released from the Hot Zone—the Black Room—or this was an act of sabotage. The contagion, he knew, could be spread by food, water and air. And he could have been infected as far back as six to eight weeks for all he knew. For that was just one of the insidious natures of the pathogenic mycoplasma they'd spliced and engineered into the whole hellish concoction. It laid dormant, evading the human immune system as the man-made bomb hid—no, vanished—deep inside cell nuclei, the lab-bred microbe near impossible to detect and diagnose as it ticked away, biding its time until it decided when it would strike. Then there was the other batch, able to act within minutes...

Which one?

It didn't matter, as he cursed himself for even entertaining such a foolish thought, as if that alone could bolster vain hope.

Beyond the terror of knowing he was dying on his feet, Dekel felt the strange vast emptiness stretching out before and behind him. In fact, nothing seemed to move, no sound anywhere, but that could just be his senses on the verge of meltdown as his brain became nothing short of microwaved jelly. Still, near forty personnel between the science staff, security and management and yet someone by now should have appeared. Or...

Were they, too, dying? Or already dead?

The vomit shot into his mouth then past lips, spilling off his chin, just as the strange notion struck him that the entire base felt as empty and lonely as an entire lifetime dedicated to the advancement of defensive biological-and-chemical warfare. The very idea there was anything remotely defensive about so-called pre-emptive advancements in the bio-chem theater of war was something of an obscene joke by itself, but he long since knew the United States had to play the diplomatic charade in accord with the agreement they'd signed with the Russians and their other allies many years back.

Was he now, thus, an ultimate dupe of what was an ultimate lie?

Where is everybody? he heard his mind scream. Was there anybody out there?

Was that a shadow at the deep south end?

"Hello? Help…me…"

He struggled to stay on his feet, saw the shadow grow, a figure slowly materializing around the corner. He wasn't sure what he saw at first, blinking away the sweat burning into his eyes, then…

The scream was on the tip of his tongue as he recognized the HAZMAT suit, the silver hose in its hand for what it was. The human, safe in his white cocoon, strode straight for him, moving with purpose, he believed was the common military jargon. And the moment was somehow made even more horrifying by the fact he couldn't see the face hidden by the black shield, as if by eye contact he could communicate the plea for mercy he heard building to a raging crescendo in the furnace of his brain. The distance was ten feet and closing when Dekel felt his eyes bulge in shock and horror, aware of what was coming.

And the shriek ripped from his mouth an instant before the silver hose burst forth its cleansing fire.

"YOU CALL THEM WHAT?"

"The Black Wizards. And that would be 'called them.'"

Mark Drobbler shot a sideways glance at what he privately called his tour guide. Despite his cryptic tone, the encrypted e-mails that had detailed their rendezvous and the night's subsequent jaunt in the Black Hawk helicopters—the first stop less than an hour ago to deal with a local rabble-rouser—the man in black hood and matching one-piece combat suit he knew openly as Infinity wasn't as much an enigma as the operative wanted him to believe. Drobbler was one of the few recruits of his organization who was a former U.S. government employee—what they called Storm Trackers—for the Department of Defense, but he had a feeling Infinity knew as much, if not more.

For nearly a decade, before putting in for early retirement following the collapse of his second marriage, he had a sizable hand in collecting and sorting out critical intelligence regarding homegrown terrorists operating under the guise of militias, and international terror cells that had established roots in the Continental United States.

Another lifetime, that was, without question. These days...

Well, these days it was a whole different game, a different outlook, an ideology that was in lockstep with the good fight against the signs of the times he and the others believed were leading to the Apocalypse.

Looking away from Infinity's penetrating stare, Drobbler felt a moment's gratitude he was both armed with a shoulder-holstered Glock .40, and was accompanied by two of his own people, but who were right then on-board one of the other four Black Hawks that had descended on the compound. As he had requested an aerial view of the clean-up task, he stood in the open doorway, the gunship hovering about a hundred feet up and to the south of the cyclone fencing.

It wasn't much, as far as classified compounds went. The compound sat on about five to six acres, with the squat one-story concrete block grabbing up an area about the size of a football field, the heart of the base tucked back in the dense pine forest of rolling hills. Over those hills, Lake Pend Oreille was the site of long-standing rumors, he knew, about a top secret Navy project named Cutthroat. In the recent past, he had seen from a distance the silver boxes that were set in a triangulation pattern around the second largest lake west of the Mississippi. They were called Horizontal Control Stations and Electronic Sites. The public had been told they were permanent lookout stations for the local forest rangers, but the whispers around these parts was that they were, supposedly, testing the kind of cutting edge satellite and electronic communications equipment that had spawned rumors all over the Panhandle. They ranged from UFO landing sites to technology that could harness and control lightning, which, in recent years, was believed to have been the cause of sudden and inexplicable wildfires that had devastated much of northern Idaho.

Which left him wondering, being as they were in such close proximity to another classified government facility, how they intended to hide the mess they were in the process of creating.

Infinity had referred to the night's outing as an invisible program of confirmation and cooperation, and Drobbler went back to watching what he couldn't see but had been told was happening inside the walls of the germ factory. There were no vehicles, now that the black GMCs had rolled through the main gate with their cargo of nylon bags, evidence seized, he suspected, that wouldn't leave behind any trace of what the Dormitory—as Infinity called the bio-chem compound—was all about. The small helipad was already chocked to capacity by the Black Hawks, and the men in spacesuits who had disgorged from those gunships had been inside for twenty-some minutes by his reckoning.

"I know what you're thinking."

Drobbler threw the man a sideways look. If Infinity did, then he might want to pull the HK MP-5 SD 3 subgun off his shoulder. Now that he knew what was happening down there, he wasn't sure he was all that keen on going the full distance. His attitudes, opinions, in short, his whole point of view about the dreadful and rapidly deteriorating state of affairs in the Western World were anarchist, to put it kindly, but he was a few short hours away from…

"Even with full cleansing of the Dormitory and the kind of plausible deniability we are able to erect around ourselves, we cannot safely determine at what point and how this will all warrant a closer investigation."

"Which is why the green light…"

"Further, it does not help our cause on two specific fronts. One, that your vaunted leader deemed it necessary to make himself a national television star. Attention is the last and most dreaded area we need to concern ourselves with at this late juncture. Two, that your organization was infiltrated."

Drobbler grimaced. "I thought you said you took care of that?"

"Be all that as it may, we still do not have absolute control over the United States Department of Justice, even from the deep shadows, even with all of our resources."

"The attention thing, right?"

"Very astute."

Drobbler fought to keep the scowl off his face, as he spotted a sarcastic twinkle in those blue eyes. He turned away from Infinity's laughing stare, just as he heard the wail ripping from the east edge of the main building. An icy shiver walked down his spine an instant before he saw the dancing shadows come flailing into the aura of spilled light. Infinity had the tactical radio in hand before the horror fully registered in Drobbler's mind.

"Infinity to Dragon leader!"

Drobbler heard the order barked for the door in question to be sealed, but it was too late. The human comet streaked onto open ground, ran on for a few feet, thrashing inside the fireball, as if it could somehow escape from that hellish cocoon. Then it seemed to wilt inside the shroud of fire, toppling in a slow-motion buckling of the legs. Drobbler had seen more than enough. But, even as he turned away and fell back into the fuselage, the screams of a man being burned alive—an employee of the United States government—echoed in his ears. He felt sick to his stomach. Suddenly, had it all been up to him...

But it wasn't. And, even if he could refuse to move forward, what he'd just witnessed, he was sure, was meant to serve as a warning.

He was onboard for the full ride, and began to wonder if it all was only just bound for Hell.

CHAPTER TWO

The man in black was a silent ghost, virtually invisible to the naked eye at that predawn hour, as he crept to the edge of the dense western exterior of pine forest. With the HK MP-5 SD 3 submachine gun and its integral sound suppressor, he knew it was a safe bet that he wouldn't be mistaken for some hunter who had lost his way, or some weekend warrior most notable for blustering through the local saloons of Montana's Glacier Country with tall tales of big game kills from a half mile or more out.

He was, though, in the strictest and most lethal sense, a hunter, and of the most dangerous game. Here, east of Flathead River and at the western edge of the Continental Divide, and now as anywhere then previous in his War Everlasting, Mack Bolan had no interest in bagging grizzly, elk or bighorn sheep to stuff and hang on his trophy mantel.

As for the warrior part...

The big, tall shadow hit a crouch at what he determined was the most secure scouting roost, as he spied his perch through the green world of his night-vision goggles. Concealed in a horseshoe of thick brush, the man also known as the Executioner took a few moments to get his bearings, review, assess, upon giving his six and flanks another thorough scan.

No warrior, he knew, no matter how good, how often he'd been tested in the fires of combat could ever rely on the bloody glory of yesterday's victories to carry him through the next engagement. That would be foolishness. But it was something often overlooked by the arrogant, the proud, the bully, those who believed all they had to do was to show up for the fight and fearsome reputation would take over, all but send a foe scurrying to hide under his bed.

There was, Bolan knew, always a David out there to every man's Goliath.

That in mind, the lone wolf operative for the ultra-covert Stony Man Farm couldn't say, one way or the other, if the two FBI agents who had gone undercover to infiltrate the Sons of Revelation had been careless and sloppy, falling back on their own hallowed and sanctioned law-enforcement status, which, of course, no sociopath, no armed reprobate ever respected anyway. Whatever the case, they were found, beaten to a pulp in an abandoned log cabin up near the town of West Glacier, before, that was, they'd each been shot once in the head. Since the FBI fell under the jurisdiction of the

United States Department of Justice, and considering the nature of their shadow work and the group believed to have executed them, Hal Brognola had offered Bolan the assignment.

Looking back, Bolan should have declined—murder investigations were somebody else's job description— but Brognola was a high-ranking official at the Justice Department who also headed up the Sensitive Operations Group at the Farm. Beyond that, and notwithstanding he was the soldier's longtime friend, Brognola was liaison to the President of the United States, the Man being one of the few in the loop about Stony Man's existence, and who also gave the Caesar's thumbs-up or -down to each mission. That the murder of a federal law-enforcement agent fell under the statute of capital punishment was serious enough to give Bolan second consideration, but there were other factors involved that had seen the soldier give the man from Justice the final nod. Aside from the fact that both agents were leaving behind grieving widows and children, stoking the natural fires of Bolan's sense of justice, both men had managed to pull together enough loose threads of a general conspiracy, one that allegedly involved the import of foreign enemies of America, and who were believed associated with the radical militia group now in question.

Then the hunches, swirling around some big event the agents had tagged the Day of Judgment, though what the exact nature of the conspiracy had gone to the grave with them. With money, however, with the arsenal the enemy was alleged to possess—and there was no telling what other kind of firepower they had at their disposal—anything was possible, the soldier knew, even the sale or acquisition of a tactical nuke, a so-called dirty bomb, or chemical or biological agents. Throw the fuel of twisted ideology into the fire of one man's belief in his superiority to his fellow man, and that all but blazed his will to use violence and intimidation. From grim and countless personal experience, Bolan knew just such individuals would spare no extreme, would even view collateral damage—the murder and misery of the innocent—as the cost of their revolution, and to further their agenda.

The Sons of Revelation had more than a few former lawmen, ex-military and two ex-spooks that Bolan knew of among the bunch of armed malcontents. That alone raised a red flag in the warrior's mind.

Shedding the high-tech headgear, Bolan adjusted his trained night-stalking vision to the sheen of light that enveloped the compound. He took one last look at the PDA, found the coordinates—programmed into the palm-held cutting-edge computer by the cyberteam at the Farm, gleaned from Brognola's facts as the FBI knew them on the general vicinity—were on the money.

It was just under a mile hike from where he'd ditched the Ford Explorer rental in a wooded gorge. The big war bag with the heavier firepower, satellite link, spare clips and grenades was stowed in the back of the SUV, and may God have mercy on the man fool enough to venture forth with curious or felonious hands. The vehicle was rigged with a state-of-the-art zapper, voltage enough to dump a man on his back, out cold. Should some enraged vandal witnessing a comrade's initial failure then smash out the windows, the war bag was armed with sensors, primed to cut loose with enough sulfuric acid to melt its contents into a molten puddle, and in the meantime cook off some rounds and frag bombs to send the more brazen and stupid running for cover. Should a local cop or state trooper pose a problem, then Bolan was armed with his bogus Justice Department credentials that declared him Special Agent Matt Cooper.

All set, then, but for what exactly?

The soldier had a plan, but the more he thought about it he began amending the original blitz to include, above all else, the capture—or at the very least—the grilling of an SOR reprobate on the spot.

The stone-and-timber lodge and surrounding six acres was the sole property of the leader of the Sons of Revelation. He was a former Boise sheriff who had retired before suspicions of alleged corruption were brought to light. Two stories high, with veiled light striking against thick curtains on his side—the south end—the Stony Man warrior counted two sentries posted on the east and west edges, both armed with assault rifles. If timing was everything in life then it looked as if a full SOR gathering was underway beneath the roof. Strung out to the east and north of the lodge was a motor pool of SUVs, backwoods 4X4s, with a few classics to finish off the vintage car show. The late and lamented undercover men cited the rabble at forty to fifty strong, maybe more, depending on plebes undergoing initiation pains, the likes of which had also reached Brognola's desk. Then there were drifters, handfuls of other miscreants believed loosely affiliated with the right-wing vultures, local cops suspected of being buried deep in the group's coffers.

Dirty cops posed something a problem. In the beginning—a hundred lifetimes and a thousand battles ago—Bolan had vowed to never gun down an officer of the law. But with the changing times his personal philosophy could be altered enough to include a tainted shield, especially when it came down to them or him. In truth, the more he thought about it, a dirty badge was worse than the criminal they had publicly sworn to protect law-abiding citizens and their property from.

But he would take the savages, on either side of that thin blue line, as they came, as they called the play.

Evil was still evil, no matter the law, flag, money or mask of human respect it hid behind.

The soldier gave the narrow plateau another search, this time through small field glasses he switched to infrared. As he panned the wooded perimeter around the compound, he felt the combined weight of his walking arsenal hung from webbing, slotted in a combat vest. Given what little he knew, the soldier wondered if the mixed assortment of grenades, twenty pounds of C-4 with radio-remote primers, the spare clips for his subgun, the shoulder-holstered Beretta 93-R and the .44 Desert Eagle Magnum hung on his hip in quickdraw leather would prove sufficient.

So far, the EM scanner hadn't turned up any sensors and cameras. In truth, Bolan knew a den of Goliaths may be on hand, waiting for his special brand of scorched earth, but the Executioner wasn't about to take any man for granted.

The living ghost in black spied a narrow trail that snaked northward, marked it on the personal digital assistant, and set out to ring in the new day for the Sons of Revelation.

CHAPTER THREE

It was beyond insanity. And, he decided, when he weighed the truth and the rediscovered precepts of his own faith against the present, he now knew, beyond a morsel of doubt, that he no longer belonged, no longer fit.

That he was living a lie.

Or was he now simply donning the disguise of wolf in sheep's clothing?

Whatever the case, the strange state of utter and miserable aloneness he now found himself submerged, Mitch Kramer braced for the coming events. If the past proved true to form—and he had little doubt it would—the floorshow would be one part briefing, laced with the usual fire and brimstone about the ills of America and the coming Apocalypse, one part initiation. The latter already had him squirming in his seat, even as he tried to will away the first onslaught of revulsion.

They were gathered in what was called the Council of the Living Creatures. He was seated at the knight's table with the other so-called High Sons, while the regular army—just over thirty strong—was forced to take its place in the rows of metal chairs at the back of the hall, reserved for the grunts. Two of the big chairs were empty, and about twelve seats from the grunt gallery were vacant, but he had his suspicions, based on what little he knew about the Day of Judgment. Dear God, he heard his mind groan, what had he done? What had he involved himself in?

As he felt the anticipation build from without and the blazing furnace of disturbance heat up from within, he felt himself on the verge of a sudden and frightening revelation. For the first time since day one—when he'd allowed himself to become entangled through what he reasoned was the sheer loneliness and maddening isolation that was alcoholism and the final dirty vestiges of every vice attached to his old ways he had sought so desperately to shed—Mitch Kramer saw it all in a new and blinding light.

He had begun to pull himself together a few short hours ago and then the call had come from the First High Son, demanding his immediate presence. Reporting, then, to the SOR compound, he felt trapped, surrounded by living evil. In truth, his very participation in the events about to unfold would find him condemned by his faith, both in this world and the next.

From the far end of the knight's table, he watched as their leader took his chair, a mahogany throne, rather, with gold trim around the arms, on which protruded white marble cherubim and seraphim. Jeremiah Grant cleared his throat in a rumble that called them all to order.

The lingering silence seemed to carry a living force all by itself, as Grant sat, unmoving, glaring down the table, with the coat of arms of the Four Living Creatures seeming to roll out of the wall directly behind the man. With smoke clouds swelling the air from one end of the hall to the other, Kramer stole the dramatic pause to search each face in turn, and wonder about the madness of it all.

"Soldiers and Sons of Revelation, we are the chosen converts of the Almighty. As such, we are no longer 'of' the world, but are simply 'in' the world, a world, we all know, that is quickly succumbing to the dominion of the adversary. Our own country, once the land of the free and the brave, is being devoured with each passing minute by an army of infernal spirits who masquerade among us as human beings in the present day American society."

And thus Grant began, but in a slightly altered version of his usual preamble. It was all Kramer could do to stifle the groan. Suddenly, the vision wanted to flame back to mind, and he wondered why the .45 Glock grew heavy in its shoulder rigging beneath his sheepskin coat. He glanced at the leader, fearing he might be singled out for lack of rapt attention. He was pretty sure that sparkle in Grant's eyes was owed more to a shot or two of whiskey-spiked-coffee than any fire of fanaticism, though there was no question in Kramer's mind the man was deadly serious.

"In the name of God, we are prepared at what is the most critical juncture in the history of democracy to carry out His justice. We are at war, my friends, make no mistake, and we must stop the sons of Cain—the military-industrial-pharmaceutical complex of the United States shadow government and who uses the mass media as its propaganda puppet-slaves, but who control what was once a great and God-fearing nation. Yes, we know well who the sons of Cain are, my friends. They are the devil's vanguard. They dwell and claim seats of power and influence from the nation's capital to Wall Street, from the scattered and numerous classified military bases around the West and Southwest to the whoremongers and purveyors of filth of Hollywood, but this is our supreme hour. We must, therefore, take courage. And since we are on the side of God— and if God is for us, then who can be against us?—we will unleash what will be the breath of divine wrath on all those not of the elect and who would trample us to dust with every outrage, every vice, every blasphemy, every abomination. Nothing short of a vengeance that far exceeds anything that annihilated Sodom and Gomorrah in the blink of an eye is demanded."

And there it was, Kramer decided. For all of his next spiel about all of them renouncing their former ways, how there were no deathbed conversions among them and which was what made them all so real and heroic, doing what was right and true in the name of God's work without the terror of impending death forcing them to answer the call to divine arms, Kramer knew the very rottenness of their former lives and transgressions was what had led them all to this room.

To this moment in their lives where eternity would be decided.

"Before I get to the heart of our mission, I would like to remind you men of the simple facts of life, lest you feel your backbone begin to lose some of its iron."

Kramer glanced at the small black file in front of him. Each of them had been given their marching orders, detailed, more or less, on the CD-ROM inside each packet. He reached out and picked his intel package up, then spotted the tremble in his hand. He realized the other hand had suddenly somehow moved toward his coat lapel, just inches below the hidden semiautomatic pistol. Quickly, he dropped both his hands in his lap, one ear tuned to Grant, as his own voice seemed frozen in the blackest of midthought, shocked at what he realized he was prepared to do.

By slow degrees, he became aware of the doors opening, a shabby naked figure being marched forth, hustled toward the shower stall near the east wall, midway down. He heard the snickers from the grunt gallery, as one of the soldiers twisted the knob and water hissed from the nozzle. It was just about all Kramer could endure. As they held the plebe by the arms and whose hands covered his crotch and who wore the despair and horror of a condemned man he recalled his own agonizing rite of passage into the Sons of Revelation.

It was Grant's version of baptism, only these waters were scalding hot, and the only stain they purified was the surface dirt and grime.

With the concrete walls spaced just far enough apart to allow a man to squeeze between, there was no escaping even a few drops.

Kramer could already feel the man's pain. Every second in that cramped cubicle, he recalled, felt like an hour, as what seemed like no less than liquid fire wanted to eat the flesh right off the bones. A man quickly forgot about the shame of his nakedness.

As if reading the grim confusion on a few of the faces of the High Sons, Grant explained that this was penalty for failure, only it would be eternal.

And Kramer could believe it.

"Put him in," Grant ordered.

Kramer felt sick to his stomach as the figure was shoved ahead, all but vanishing into the thick billows of steam. At the first scream, Kramer was rising from his seat. He glimpsed the victim trying to fight his way out of the watery hell but, as part of the price for such a display of cowardice and timidity, he suffered vicious blows to the head and stomach that drove him back, his so-called guardians shouting curses in his face. Of course, he could quit, holler as much, but there would be no money, and he would be sent packing, warned to never return or speak about what happened and under the most severe penalty. When it was over, when he was freed—or sometimes collapsed from pain and shock— every inch of skin would be raw, his flesh like living coals but that burned inward. There would be blisters the size of thimbles all over, a relentless maddening itch from head to toes that would last for...

Kramer suddenly realized he was heading for the door, as Grant's voice boomed and shattered the sense he was a disembodied figure slogging through a bad dream.

"Where are you going?"

"I need to take a leak."

It was not altogether a lie, but he was surprised at how easy, how quick the words left his mouth, then how Grant seemed so ready to accept his excuse, the man nodding, then returning to the torture show.

Mitch Kramer somehow forced himself to move, slow and steady, even as the screams of pure agony flayed his ears and hit his back like invisible fists.

THE PLAN CAME to Bolan, walked straight toward him, in fact.

Opting for the sound-suppressed Beretta, he was settling into a low crouch, poised to launch from a half circle of bramble and hanging ferns, the last of four-pound blocks just planted and primed when the first of the bone-chilling screams, muffled as they were by the wall, struck his ears. The fireworks were staggered, every third or fourth vehicle, the shaped charges just inside wheel wells closest to the few gas caps he discovered lacked the modern era necessity of locks. He counted the headwinds as another small blessing, whatever fumes meant to be ignited by the initial blast wave carried away from the sentries.

The lean figure in sheepskin coat was ambling away
from his two militia pals, both of whom were chuckling and hooting about his lack of nerve while Sheepskin turned and shot them the middle finger salute. He
was hollering back something about a little privacy,
when the soldier judged the hang-dog expression that
struck him as akin to depression, or regret. Bolan considered himself better than a decent judge of character—though the darkest corner of the human heart and
mind was capable of hiding the worst of evil and treachery—and as Sheepskin shuffled closer he made a sudden decision.

A choice that would either burn him down before the
mission was even out of the gate, or lead him through a
back door, hopefully to step on the tail end of the vipers.

The next moment turned even brighter for Bolan.
Sheepskin got the privacy he demanded, as the soldier
watched the sentries vanish around the far south end.
For a heartbeat or two, the warrior analyzed the look,
weighed his next move against the pluses and minuses
of the hard probe.

Sheepskin, the bulge beneath his coat warning Bolan
he was packing, stepped onto the narrow path, took a
few more strides his way, unaware of the problem ready
to spring on him from little more than an arm's length
away. He put a cigarette on his lip, shook his head about
something, scowled, reached for his fly. That was dis-
gust, contempt or the expression, the warrior decided,
of a man in search of a new future. Clearly, he was

pondering some deep thought that had left him spooked, some far-away glaze to the eyes that Bolan would have sworn was the face of a man who had just seen a ghost—or his own death.

Just as he was torn between lighting his cigarette and tugging at his crotch, Bolan rose and surged forward. Sheepskin became aware, too late, of the dark menace boiling out of the brush. He was turning, as Bolan slammed an overhand left off his jaw and sent man and cigarette flying.

IT WAS BEYOND the point of no return, and this was only the start of the very beginning.

As Mark Drobbler trailed Infinity to the keypad on the steel door of the oversize black barn a mental picture flamed to mind, out of nowhere. He saw himself doing a rapid about-face, washing his hands all the way back to the Black Hawk. But, then what? He was too old, too tired, too set in his ways. There was nothing but an empty mobile home in the deepest bowels of the remotest wilderness to return to if he bolted. Four walls, inside of which he could sit, swill beer and whiskey and pass the time watching cable television or hang out in the local tavern for yet more drinking and mental gnawing on all that could have and should have been while...

Right. While opportunity passed him by. And if the others didn't outright hold him in contempt for bailing, all but branding him a coward and a traitor, he would never know a moment's peace for whatever the remainder of his days. Not without looking over his shoulder.

Not without sleeping with his assault rifle set on full-auto under the covers.

Infinity was punching in the sequence of numbers, then Drobbler found those lifeless chips of glacier ice were looking back at him, as if the black op was having second thoughts about something.

Drobbler broke the stare, scanned the dark wood-line. He was sure that hidden cameras, motion sensors were all over what was another classified U.S. government compound. Up to then he'd only heard a word or two about what waited inside the black barn, aware that the bulk of the matériel had only been shipped by van and military transport with U.S. government plates two days ago.

The door opened on a soft pneumatic hiss.

"After you, Mr. Drobbler."

Without hesitating, lest that stare turn even darker, Drobbler was past the man. Three steps inside the sprawling makeshift factory and he caught his breath, braking to an abrupt halt. The walls, he reckoned, were soundproof, had to be since the noise of hydraulic drills driving home bolts and the hiss and spray of blowtorches assaulted his senses, and would have carried clear to town, a short distance away.

A look to his side and Drobbler found the twelve handpicked Sons of Revelation. They were grouped around a large steel table, poring over what he knew were blueprints, computer-enhanced specs, to a man as grim as death. Two men in black raid suits with shouldered HK subguns were hovering behind them as they ran down mission logistics and parameters.

The drills suddenly ceased. Two figures in face shields stepped back from the rear of the bus they worked on, the blue-orange flames from blowtorches shrinking as Infinity rolled out to the middle of the floor. He was all award-winning actor, that one, eyes beaming as he claimed the spotlight. It was his world, no question, and this was his stage.

Drobbler took a few steps toward Infinity, one eye running the length of the leviathan. It was painted black, and for the life of him he couldn't tell where the windows began and ended. Eagle Charters was painted in bold white letters above where a cargo hold would have been. The single door to the front portside was open, with three steps leading up to a walled-in cubicle where the driver sat.

"There it is, Mr. Drobbler. Attila. In just a few minutes, it's all yours."

Drobbler saw Infinity motioning for him to step his way, then the black op slipped the subgun off his shoulder.

"Coming your way inside, gentlemen!" he called, then cut loose with the subgun.

Drobbler flinched as the first few rounds scorched the hull, his ears spiked as those bullets, muzzling at what he believed was 400 meters per second, marched a line of sparks down the side. Ricochets went screaming toward the nose end, the wall beyond and beside the entrance door absorbing more slashing steel-jacketed hornets. Drobbler felt a flash of gratitude that Infinity had seen fit to pull him away from Attila at the angle he now stood. Infinity shifted his aim, drilling some rounds where Drobbler suspected the windows were positioned. A split-second pause, then the black op burned out the clip, the final rounds pounding the rear tire with a peculiar loud thud.

Infinity was all smiles behind the rising cordite as he said, "You like it?"

Drobbler examined the bus, stem to stern, top to bottom, but couldn't spot the first nick, dent or scratch. Without a close-up inspection, though...

"Well?"

"Let me guess. The tires are reinforced by Kevlar?"

"And the hull is all titanium-plated. Double-layered where the driver sits. Nothing short of a cruise missile will knock him out of his seat. Hubs, axles, the whole chassis is reinforced steel with, again, a titanium coat."

"Windows are bulletproof, I gather?"

"Better. Right around your gun revetments and the driver's half of the window it's diamond layered."

Drobbler took another long hard look at it, their beast of burden. "Nothing short of a cruise missile, huh?" he muttered.

He had to admit he was impressed, but if he was supposed to be grinning like a school kid and jumping up and down...

The black op rolled past Drobbler and dumped the large nylon bag at his feet. He zipped it open, and Drobbler beheld the down payment. Three million dollars, rubber-banded stacks of hundreds, stared him back. He was about to bend, thinking he should touch a few stacks, just to make sure it wasn't too good to be true, when Infinity took a step toward him.

"You can count it on your own time, Mr. Drobbler. Right now, we have work to do and not much time to do it in before you and your men ship out."

"THE CHOICE IS REAL SIMPLE."

The voice was graveyard, icy, with no room for compromise. It matched the coldest set of blue eyes he'd ever seen. Those eyes, framed in the black-face of combat cosmetics, told stories all by themselves.

Bad stories. Real stories. Stories about death and pain and misery, and, Mitch Kramer could damn well believe, more given than received. This was not some weekend local yokel stumbling about the woods, playing paintball grab-ass with a few drunken morons.

This was the real deal. This, his gut screamed at him, was Death in human flesh.

Something hit his stomach, and Kramer saw it was his wallet. He was told to get up, wondering if he moved fast enough for the man's liking, but it was all he could manage just to get his legs back on the ground. He rubbed his jaw, worked his mouth, tongued his teeth. All there. The big man knew, then, about applying just the right amount of force where it didn't go too far, break something, put a guy in a coma or in the ground. Cop stuff. Or military training?

On second look, decked out in commando gear with slung sound-suppressed HK subgun, with all the right bearing, all the right attitude, the commandeered Glock now snug in his waistband, maintaining a nice distance where he could fire at will with his sound-suppressed Beretta before he could cut the gap in a quick rush…

The stranger was examining something in his hand. Kramer gathered his bearings. He had been dragged a few more yards deeper into the woods. He was wondering if the two SOR clowns posted as sentries had heard the ruckus, how long he'd been laid out when the big guy spoke.

"You come with me, cooperate as my prisoner, answer my questions."

Kramer was almost afraid to ask for the alternative, but said, "Or?"

"I'll send you back."

Why did that sound not only too easy, too good to be true, but no choice at all? Who the hell was this guy?

"You take option number two, be forewarned. When I bring the walls down on the Sons of Revelation, I spare no one. There will be no second chance."

Just being in the man's presence, Kramer could believe as much. "You know, you may not believe this, but I was looking for a way out."

The stranger held out what he'd been examining. Kramer took it and smiled even though it hurt. Somehow his laminated daily prayer card to Saint Rita had been dislodged from his wallet. During the fall, or the frisk? And did it matter? Glancing at the first few lines—"O powerful Saint Rita, rightly called Saint of the Impossible, I come to you with confidence in my great need"—and Kramer thought he might lose it. This was it. This was the moment, the deciding point in the fork of the road. He was a wretch, beaten, whipped, broken, defiled his whole life by his own hand. He was the vilest of worms, deserved nothing less than sudden death and instant justice, and yet...

He was tucking the card away, as the big man, holding up a small black box with a flashing red light, told him, "I even catch the whiff of a problem from you, and you'll have less than a second to call on that holy lady."

Kramer didn't need convincing, but he knew what was coming. The motor pool was maybe forty, fifty yards away, but to Kramer it sounded like the trumpet blast of Judgment Day, calling forth the living and the dead. He held his ground as the fireballs tore through the vehicles, pulped the classics that were worth, he'd heard, a combined quarter mil. There was shouting and screaming and cursing next as the wreckage pounded the east and north walls. Something told him, as he was ordered to get moving, this was only the beginning of the end for a whole bunch of bad men.

CHAPTER FOUR

"We're creatures of habit, Mr. Radfield. Each one of us is, to some greater or lesser extent, predictable. We wake up at the same time for the same job. We drink the same brand of coffee and the same amount before we drive roughly the same route to our place of employment that expects us there at the same time, five days of the week. We drink the same brand of beer, watch the same brand of movies, listen to the same brand of music. We go to the same church at the same time on Sunday and sit in the same pew, on the same side. We…"

Paul Radfield got the gist of it. And still he went on with the infernal litany, until Radfield had the urge to bellow at the guy to shut his damn piehole. But that was just a wishful thought. He'd been stalked and kidnapped, and was now cuffed, blind, and God only knew where.

How they'd done it—and who they were—was beyond him, but he had some general suspicions.

He stared at the pitched blackness, listening to what he began to think of as the Voice. It was smooth, educated, white, a taunting ring to the words, and why not? The SOB held all the right cards, and in his roundabout infuriating superior way was letting him know all about it. There was no Texas twang or Southern drawl he could make out, no accent of any kind, and that made him just about any man from Anywhere, U.S.A., with the possible exceptions of New England and New Jersey. As for where he was? Talk about a shot in the dark. There was something like 367 miles of Gulf Coast— 624 miles of tidewater coast when he threw in all the lagoons, swamps and bays and with the longest chain of barrier islands to be found anywhere on the planet— so he could be anywhere, even south of the border. Or maybe he was out on the water, only there was no discernible rock and roll that would come with even the most gentle of swells. And, for all he knew, once he'd been hit with the dart in the garage of his suburban enclave southeast of Houston, recalling how he'd glimpsed the dark shadow rising from beside the free-weight jungle gym, it could have been one hour or one day since he'd gone under. A little bladder gauging, however, told him it was the former, give or take.

Where then? And what about…

"We make love to the same woman the same three nights of the week, but, to one man's credit—that would be you, Mr. Radfield—rarely in the same position, though Cynthia—or Kit, as she likes you to call her when in the throes of passion—seems to like Thursday nights a little more than the others. That is, if I judge the sound of her voice and the way she cries your name correctly."

Radfield felt the blood pulse into his eardrums like a molten war drum. The bastard had bugged, worse, maybe installed hidden mini-cams all over the house, but he wasn't surprised. He felt his face flush next, as hot as live coals, wondering if the rotten SOB had maybe videotaped their passion for his own personal viewing pleasure. Get a grip! Shame was the least of his woes, he knew, as he then smelled his breath, sucked back in on his sweaty face, thanks to the tight confines of his hood. It was still ripe from the previous night's veal and pasta, those three whiskey and waters and a glass of red wine, with the residue of the morning's three—predictable three—cigarettes swirling up in his nose. He also took a whiff of the first tainted aroma of something else.

Fear.

Then he felt the sweat run cold down his face, slithering up under his jaw and chin, but where it ended suddenly, as the hood had been cinched—or noosed?—tight around his neck. The faceless human viper chuckled about something but the cold steel bit into his wrists as he felt his fists clenching, so hard his knuckles popped off like pistol cracks.

Impotent rage was not a feeling he was used to.

The former United States Special Forces captain

knew how to keep his cool, though, and under the worst of conditions. These—as it next turned out to his mounting horror—were worse than dodging Iraqi bullets and sniffing out chemical and biological stashes for a little known black op during Gulf One called Operation Specter Run. And his heart began to beat like a jackhammer, harder than before, if such a thing was possible, as the Voice recited, chapter and verse, the daily routines of his wife and two sons. Their likes, dislikes, habits. Right down to the type of music Ben and John both listened to, Kit's favorite television programs and which room she preferred, which sealed it that the house had been wired for visual spying. Then their movements, and by the hour, the eateries and friends they visited after school, when, where and who, down to the same time his wife hit the same health spa after work, and which housewives and where she had two dry gin martinis at her favorite bar, and which two days of the week. Son of a…

Stay cool, breathe slow, he told himself. Instinct told him nothing had happened to his family—yet—and he kept hope alive.

There was a long pause, during which Radfield wondered if his captor had left the room, the building, the boat, wherever he was.

"I have yet to hear the usual questions, Mr. Radfield. Even for a Medal of Honor winner, you're too cool and collected."

"Okay. I'll bite. Who are you?"

"Wrong first question. Unanswerable anyway."

"Right. If you told me, you'd have to kill me. You want something. What? And if I don't agree, then what happens to my wife and sons?"

"What happens?" The Voice made a noise somewhere between a chuckle and a snort. "Do I actually have to say the words?"

Radfield ground his teeth, steadied his breathing some more. No, the bastard couldn't see him sweat, but he had to control his own voice. "Yeah. You do."

"They'll be killed. Very quietly, very efficiently."

"Are they safe?"

"For the moment, they're going about their daily routine."

"What do you want?"

"How do you like Miami, Paul?"

Friendly like, confidence growing, the hook was in.

"Too hot, too much crime, too phony."

"Agreed. Not to mention there's something vaguely disturbing about an entire city built right over a swamp." The Voice chuckled. "It's almost as if the fools who live there are begging for some natural calamity to happen, between a giant sinkhole swallowing them whole and hurricanes blowing them clear out to the Everglades. Anyway…be that as it all is, it's the business you perform as part of your duties for your company out of Miami that will require an immediate attitude readjustment on your part."

And there it was. But the punch line, he suddenly knew, was merely part of the irony of his predicament.

His captor knew as much, and went on to tell him,

"As chief of security for Manexx PetroChem, you designed certain safety procedures at the Trans-World Bank of Miami."

"Okay. And?"

"Hasn't it ever struck you as odd that you are required every three months to escort the same three men donning the exact same black sunglasses and wearing the same three-piece black suits and who you, of course, do not know but provide security to and from the WBM and to and from their posh hotel suite, and who literally have the same briefcases chained to the same wrists? That for all of their public mantras about the need for this country to tap into new oil reserves that there are all of two—count them—two Manexx platforms out on the Gulf and with no plans in the foreseeable future to expand? That when you designed their off-shore security there was virtually no mention of deep-sea drilling, with just the basic equipment and skeleton crews necessary to maintain appearances?"

Radfield had, in fact, wondered about all of that, among a few other items not yet mentioned. As he had some nagging idea where this was headed, he felt the first itch of nicotine craving coming on when—

Fingers like iron rods twisted up the hood around his mouth. He heard something metallic—the snap of scissors?—then raw combat instincts flared. There was fire in his limbs, sudden anger to strike back coiling him. He was an inch or so off the seat when the gun muzzle was shoved against his temple. He barely heard the snip against the metallic click of the weapon's hammer as a section of hood was sliced away from his mouth.

"Here, have a smoke."

It was placed on his lip and lit.

"Now. Sit down, relax and listen. Should you even for the flash of an instant again think about fighting back you will be shot dead, dumped in the Gulf and…well, you can imagine the next regrettable step. Or, rather, three steps."

The weapon fell away, the second presence melting back. That left his captor, right in front of him. Two, then, at least, and his hands were cuffed in front of him, as he lifted them to work the cigarette. If not for his family…

"Are you with me so far, Paul?"

"I'm listening."

"We know that you suspect fallen comrades under your command in Gulf One were infected by our side in a vaccine program that was meant to combat the effects of what is now commonly referred to as Gulf War Syndrome."

"But which, was, in fact, our guys contracting the effects of a nerve gas agent and an unknown bio agent that was covered up by Washington after we blew up a couple of depots and were infected by subsequent fallout and which we were never told what was in said depots."

"Or everyone in the area in question was stricken by undetermined biohazards relating to Saddam's torching of those oil fields when his soldiers were sent packing from Kuwait."

"Or both."

"Or both. Correct. You made something of a spectacle a number of years back, but, as is the case of general public apathy when it comes to the military and the running assumption out there in America that national security is, in fact, 'secured,' and how it gets done is none of their affair as long as their lives go happily on in blissful ignorance, you kept up contact with certain men in the armed forces. Most of whom, I need to inform you, are no longer among the living. You were fanning the flames from the shadows, Paul."

"I was looking for the truth."

"The truth. You want to know about the truth, Paul?"

"I bet you're going to tell me, 'I can't handle the truth?'"

The Voice turned cold. "That stash you came across in southern Iraq was some of the most virulent bacteria before then known to man. Those three mobile labs you seized? Those bioagents were confiscated and shipped back to America for analysis."

"For upgrade and potential deployment, you mean. Unless some of those late comrades of mine you mentioned missed their guess, they were cultivated in germ factories in Idaho and Montana—recombinant DNA, altered genes and so forth—and for the advancement of a secret biological-chemical warfare scheme."

"Of which you and the others had nary a clue as to what it was—is—really all about."

Radfield pulled on his cigarette, blew a stream in what he suspected was the general direction of his tormentor. "Really? So, our theory that a general conspiracy about a shadow government within our government engineering a controlled genocide program and running experiments on live test subjects without them knowing it is a bunch of nonsense?"

"Not necessarily. What you suspect has been done before. Pesticide spraying in New York, New Jersey, Miami, for instance."

"Where there were so-called mosquito infestations that were spreading the West Nile Virus? Except the only areas being sprayed were the black and Hispanic neighborhoods? That conspiracy?"

The Voice chuckled. "You're getting warm. Think of a circle, Paul. Think of how the past somehow all circles back to the present."

Radfield felt his hand freeze as he put the cigarette on his lip.

"That's right, Paul. Manexx PetroChem."

"You're telling me…"

"I am, indeed. You work for a classified Homeland Security operation that is involved in producing both counter and offensive biological and chemical weapons, the likes of which would be catastrophic if they were unleashed. Only there is far, far more involved."

"Homeland Security?"

"That's right, or, rather, a recent and covert arm known only among the few elite as National Security Military Intelligence. Paul, you were chosen, you were groomed, and specifically for this moment in time. Think of it as destiny calling."

Radfield was inclined to believe the man, all of it. There were secrets, things—black ops—the United States government did in order to protect, secure and maintain the country's vested interests, both at home and abroad. Even if he were a nonmilitary citizen, reason alone would tell him the United States was number one in the lion's share of global weapons sales. That, all by itself, informed even the most unsuspecting and naive that America was, by and large, using its vast wealth to either thwart the expansion of rogue nations and terrorism, or seeking to foment chaos and plant their own lackey criminal regimes in countries of interest in order to keep the United States on top of the world heap. At the forefront of that list were the oil-producing nations. Then there were various strategic nation states that could serve as buffered armed outposts where attack could be launched with the quickest of ease...

Then it hit him.

Now he knew who and what the Voice represented. Now there was no choice how he left what was, without question, the hot seat.

"I can almost hear your thoughts, Paul. Play ball, save your family or—I would at least allow you the dignity of making your peace with God."

"What do you want me to do?"

"Go to your office. Proceed with the day as you normally would. You will receive an e-mail that will give you step-by-step instructions on the access codes we require. Your movements for the immediate future will be detailed, and monitored. You will obey?"

"Do I have a choice?"

"There's always a choice, Paul."

"I'll go with the program."

"Then, not only will I spare your life and the lives of your family, but I assure you that when this is done you will be more than adequately compensated. Both in terms of money, and the truth you seek."

And he was abruptly dismissed, as the cigarette was knocked off his lip and a viselike grip hauled him to his feet. There was no point in counting paces, direction and time from there on, but instinct took hold. It was roughly a dozen yards before a door opened and the sense of sound and smell began to give him some clue as to his whereabouts. There was a faint but sickly taint of sulfur in the air. There was no other smell like it he knew of, and it was more than noticeably noxious in certain areas around Galveston Bay where the waters around the island city were still yellow from ships spilling the infernal toxin from years gone by. He heard seagulls, caught a whiff of shrimp and diesel fuel, figured he was in the general vicinity of Seawall Boulevard, named so for the ten-mile, seventeen-foot-high wall built after the 1900 hurricane had all but wiped the fledgling town off the map and dunked it in the Gulf. He was three steps, smelling and listening, when a hand he figured could palm two basketballs dropped over his skull, bent him at the head and shoulders and shoved him ahead where he crashed into the soft padding of a long seat.

"Don't move."

By God, he wanted to spring at the new voice, would have if it had just been himself he was looking to save. Before he knew it the cuffs were gone, the cinch around his neck loosened. The hood was whipped away, but just as he began adjusting his eyes to harsh sunlight the figure was a blurring shadow, slamming the door in his face. His temporary home, he found, was the well of a limousine, with, of course, the windows blacked out from the inside. Hunched, he moved to the other seat, discovered the driver's partition was likewise blackened, and, most likely, shatter-proof. As he picked up the small black file on the seat beside him, a voice patched through the intercom and told him, "You are to read and memorize that and leave it on the seat when you leave. Do what you are told, Mr. Radfield, and you and your family will be fine."

They were pulling away, smooth and slow, when he picked up the file. No sooner had he opened and looked at the first sequence of numbers than Paul Radfield felt his stomach wanting to roll over. He wasn't one hundred percent certain what they wanted, but judging by what they wanted him to do—at least initially—a dark cloud settled over his thoughts.

Conspiracy and treason leaped to mind.

And which he was now part of. With three innocent lives he cared about more than his own life he was along for the full ride.

Stuck.

No way out.

CHAPTER FIVE

23:59:59.

It was T-minus now, and it was all Donald "Brick" Lawhorn could do to keep the smile off his face.

He was moving for the curtained balcony—hitting a button on the side of his Rolex watch, making the instant readjustment with a quick depression and scrolling reset on the digital secondhand display—when he heard the groan.

"Where are you going? What time…"

There was some purred question about why the clock was ticking backward as 50 flashed to 49.

Pulling an ice-cold Heineken beer from the small fridge, cracking it open, he looked back over his shoulder. She was a perfidious little courtesan, straight out of the Yellow Pages under Sweet Dreams Escorts, self-centered, self-indulgent, as vain as the night had been long. She had served his needs well enough, he supposed. That was when he could get her face out of the coke and shut her mouth long enough for her to stop talking about herself. She was supposedly working her way through some local college, doing porn on the side, telling him with a smirk as wide as Biscayne Bay beyond the balcony she got off thinking how other men would abuse themselves while looking at her naked body, all the legions of perverts and family men out there who could only ever have her in their inflamed imaginations, her spreads stoking their evil fantasies and leaving them suspended in frozen burning desire for her while she, on the other hand, could pick and choose who was worthy enough to even breathe the same air as her. Briefly, he pictured his hands around her throat, staring into eyes that silently begged him to spare her life. Any other time…

He gave her a look he hoped would send her diving under the covers. Instead, the overpaid trollop reached for the tray of white powder on the bed stand.

He slipped on the dark sunglasses, rolled his shoulders, enjoying the weight of the shoulder-holstered .45 Para-Ordnance P13. When she finally took a breath to deem him interesting enough to inquire what he did for a living, he had told her was head of security for a major computer-telecommunication company, and the VIPs he protected were in a different arena than the usual stuffed suits, hence the weapon. That either sufficed her phony attempt to be curious or she just didn't give a damn, beyond, that was, collecting her thousand bucks.

As he brushed past the curtains and stepped onto the

pink coral balcony, harsh sunlight, mirrored off the Bay and the Atlantic Ocean beyond the Art Deco enclaves and hotels of North Beach, glinted off stainless steel. He decided the morning sun felt good, another taste of paradise, in fact, as it beat down on bronzed naked flesh that was chiseled to lean, sinewy muscle. He was scarred around the torso and shoulders from ancient war wounds, and that had, indeed, caught her curious, anxious eye, trophies warning her that she was, indeed, sleeping with a lion.

The real thing.

At the balcony, picking up his cigarettes, shaking one free and lighting up, he stared down at the inline skaters, the lovebirds and the early morning breakfast crowd gathering under the thatched-roof cabanas, lounging poolside.

Oh, how he loved Miami, but it was more of a love-hate relationship now that he thought about it.

South Florida, he thought, was the East Coast's answer to the shallow, superficial and spineless PC asylum that was Southern California. They partied, drank, drugged the nights away in South Beach. They drove the newest, hottest cars, looking good and outfitted with the latest fashions at the top of the list of their concerns. At the number-one slot of all things vain—they had to be "seen" in all the right and trendiest clubs, these hyena wanna-bes craving to rub elbows with all the vile film and recording and sports worms that had in recent years oozed down here in their silken, bejeweled, perfumed snakeskin carcasses when careers were usually circling the bowl and they had to find a way to keep their faces out there.

Beyond his general contempt, outside of New York City, some of the most atrocious, senseless crimes—fueled, in large part, by a drug scourge that had never really gone away—had become so commonplace they were little more than the most fleeting of sound bites on the local news.

As he took a sudden gust of hot breeze in the face and drank deep, the big man's words rang through his thoughts.

"Picture this. Five hundred fall suddenly, mysteriously ill. Two hours or so later another five hundred or so are staggering into emergency rooms in yet another city, burning up with fever, puking and crapping all over themselves. Two or three hundred suddenly die. By the following morning it's a thousand, two thousand. By noon another American city sees it citizens dropping like the proverbial sprayed flies. One, then two more cities find their citizens croaking, and from clear across the other side of the country as walking contagions board planes, trains, buses, or simply drive to the next town. It's found in the water supply. It's killing livestock, it's infected produce, wheat. It's in the air, the water, maybe even the ground they walk on."

Shivering, as he killed the man's voice behind the rest of his beer, Lawhorn became aware the sweat was running off his chin in fat, thick drops. Twenty-four hours. And after that? he wondered. Would there be enough time? Say if even one of them became stricken, then what?

There was international travel to consider. There was the rabble doing the first leg of the dirty work for them. There was the fact that once they left the country...

He stabbed out his cigarette, but lingered as he still smelled her from where he'd done her for the fifth time, mashing her face into the railing.

The evil creature disgusted him.

He found her huffing away, her voice on the petulant side as she informed him it would be another thousand dollars if he wanted her for the day.

Lawhorn grabbed another beer. "Shut up. Get dressed and get out of here. Take the garbage with you. On second thought."

Before she could squawk or even blink, Lawhorn had the mirror in hand. He hurled it across the room, scattering a snowstorm of four to five grams. She became the perfect nude model for shock and horror.

"Five seconds to beat it, and then I get ugly."

FORMER LOS ANGELES Homicide Detective Mitch Kramer was nowhere near the full reprobate package the soldier had expected. After the first round of blunt questions and when Bolan decided he had enough to proceed he'd learned something about the ex-cop's life, or, rather, lack thereof. The subsequent and toned-down Q and A was more to get a read on the man's character and motivations than simple idle curiosity, since Bolan was on the verge of launching total war. He was still in the process of deciding what to do with the man.

With a few possible exceptions, Kramer's tale of

woe was pretty much the same for veteran cops worn
out and broken down by the job. They were divorced,
friendless with the exception of other cops, more often
than not had kids who couldn't stand being around
them. They collapsed into all manner of vices, and more
often than was publicly reported they ate their gun. As
the years ground by on the job, their world shrank and
grew darker by the day, and a once-decent conscience,
beaming with good intentions and pointing the way of
truth and justice, was blunted and callused to the point
where a man became an angry loner, aware in some way
he couldn't quite define or understand that he had become contaminated by the very ills and crimes he used
to abhor and fight. Oh, indeed, human nature being
what it was—inclined to Self and its own needs and desires—the soldier could well imagine the eroding toll
of having to listen to lies and excuses and the flimsiest
justifications and even for the most heinous of crimes
around-the-clock. Of being feared and held in disre-
spect and contempt by a society that was rapidly becoming more plagued by crime and corruption and
where the bad guys were sometimes better armed than
whole SWAT teams. Where even far too many law-abiding citizens couldn't care less about a policeman, as
long as they were front and center when they were faced
with mortal danger or loss of money and property.

Bolan realized he was perhaps painting it with a
broad brushstroke of cynicism, but, for damn sure, it
took a special brand of man, a unique and iron self-con-
trol and discipline and courage to march out there, day

after day, shift after shift, year in and year out, and do what the average citizen couldn't or didn't want to do, or didn't dare dream capable of handling. Even with the most tenacious of moral resolve, a number of cops didn't make it, couldn't cut it. Used up, burned-out, staring over the edge of the grave and down into the waiting worms and maggots.

Kramer had fairly told him as much about himself, with a look and tone the soldier read as saying that a simple thank-you way back when would have sufficed to keep him chugging along with an eye toward a half decent tomorrow. But, Bolan, ever the realist, knew there were some professions where, if a man was looking for a pat on the back, promotion or glory, then he was in the wrong line of work. What was more—and even worse—he could never fully do the job.

Soldiers dropped into that particular category.

For the warrior on the front lines it was all guts and no less than steely commitment to duty, with no expectations, or they caved when it hit the fan, or ended up seething wrecks of whining recrimination, bitter regret and the kind of relentless self-pitying anger that rotted out the very soul itself.

The world was a tough place, but the soldier was more than acquainted with the bitter facts of good and evil, life and death.

Another look at Kramer, and Bolan wasn't sure what to make of the man. He was no angel, but he was damn sure fallen. At the moment, the ex-cop was on his haunches, perched up against the base of pine tree. The laminated card was in his cuffed hands. Figure he was praying to the Holy Lady of Desperate Cases, and, for some reason, that alone was pushing the soldier toward a decision that might well prove one of his worst to date.

Or would it?

Bolan left Kramer to what sure appeared penitent reflections and silent imploring of divine intervention and walked forward several feet. Crouched behind a thicket of bramble and ferns—M-16 with M-203 grenade launcher having replaced the HK subgun now that it was all leaning toward open-ground warfare—the soldier gave the lay of the land a second thorough scan, while scraping together the few shreds of a strategy, given the few facts and rumor the ex-cop had laid out. Between the PDA and the mobile GPS unit he had mounted to the dashboard of his Explorer SUV, he found the remote wilderness where the big event was supposed to go down.

To the north, the misty shroud above the snow-capped sawtooth peaks of the Swan Range was being cleared away by the early morning sun. A few miles west, at the opposite edge of the Flathead National Forest, the Swan River ran in a north-south parallel course to Highway 83. Somewhere to his back, the soldier made out the cries of geese, mallards and other winged creatures taking to flight or searching out a meal. East, across rolling grassland he imagined once teemed with legions of bison, the soldier made out the road as it humped up and spined its two-mile-or-so course to what Kramer informed him was a forest ranger station.

The wide, undivided but paved road was nowhere to be found on any map.

Using its own intelligence sources and renowned cyberhacking, the Farm—after the soldier had faxed Kramer's CD with what were believed encrypted marching orders—believed the ranger station was a front for a classified government facility, but for the life of them they didn't know what went on there. With cyclone fencing around a squat steel-walled compound, the cyberwizards learning the road was slashed out of the forest and grasslands a few years back by the Army Corps of Engineers, and after Bolan had seen from a distance through his field glasses...

Well, the posted warning at the far south end of the road had sealed it. No trespassing, property of United States Government, and authorized to use deadly force cued the soldier that, despite his prisoner's ignorance of the finer details, this was the right place where the wrong thing—and what that was remained to be seen— would go down.

According to Kramer it would all begin any time now. What the cargo the Sons of Revelation planned to hijack, well, Bolan could venture a sordid educated guess.

WMD, of some type, and the soldier hadn't brought along his HAZMAT suit for the lethal party.

And with Kramer mentioning something about two men in black he read as spooks gathering for two recent private meets with the so-called Highest Sons that he knew of...

Problems, all around, but Bolan was never short on the determination, skill and experience to work them out.

Then there were enemy numbers to consider, and which could range from anywhere to a known forty or fifty to another ten to twenty. If there were snakes wrapped in the Stars and Stripes and hidden among the spook convoy that was due to roll its way from the north, if an inside job was about to land a cache of biological, chemical or radiological matériel into the hands of the Sons of Revelation for reasons that included money, twisted ideology…

Bolan turned and dropped a long look on Kramer. The question hung in his mind, as the Stony Man warrior knew a moment of truth had painted him into a corner. "Who was she? Saint Rita."

A tired smile crossed Kramer's lips, his eyes telling Bolan he was reaching back into memory. He slipped the prayer card into a coat pocket, said, "I was in a motel room, real crumby part of Hollywood, which really isn't saying much. I was loaded, as usual, with some hooker. I wasn't two steps inside the room when her pimp, or boyfriend or whoever, drove a knife square into my gut. Another inch or so higher, if he'd twisted up some even, or ripped down…sixty-two dollars and forty-four cents is what they took off of me. Funny, you know, how a guy can remember something so damn trivial, exactly how much his life might have cost him…or the amount of money he was prepared to throw away on his soul.

"I remember the girl. One of these corn-fed Midwestern blondes who comes to Hollywood, thinking she's the next Marilyn Monroe, but ends up tricking and doing porn and looking like an eighty-year-old hag by the time she's thirty. She was cussing like a fleet of drunken sailors the whole time he's rifling my pockets, pissed because that was all I had on me. Here I am, bleeding like the proverbial stuck pig, holding in my guts, and all she's worried about is how much dope she's going to get from setting me up and seeing me eviscerated, all in a snit because it's not nearly enough she'd hoped for. Funny thing, I saw her kind more than I count, worked some of the worst murders when I was a cop, but when cold-blooded murder is actually happening to you like that, when you're helpless and your number is up… Anyway, she kicks me a couple real beauts like only a junkie whacked out of her gourd and dying for the next hit can, all that geeking rage and hate. She wants the knife to finish me off but her boyfriend wouldn't give it to her—why, I couldn't tell you. Funny. Miserable as I was, how often I thought about dying— you know, Dear Mother of God, won't you come and take me away from this vale of tears—when it's actually happening I was terrified and wanted nothing more than to live, more out of my conscience screaming at me that what was waiting on the other side was a whole bunch of accounting.

"Long story short, I crawled to the phone, reached up like my arm was shot out of a cannon. Knocked the phone down and along with it comes a Bible. Brand-spanking new. I remember that because the edge of the spine felt like a steel rod when it bounced off the side of my face. The thought hit me—why in the world do they keep Bibles out for the kind of people go there to do what they're doing anyway? God is the very last thing on their minds. Well, turned out, somebody was reading it. Out comes the bookmarker."

"Saint Rita."

"Yeah, Saint Rita. How it ended up in my pocket, how it was still there when I was released from the hospital." Kramer paused. "I don't know how long it was, but I entertained a wicked desire to use some cop buddies I still had in Hollywood. Track those two down. Payback, the likes of which I couldn't even imagine the Devil himself conjuring up. Then, for some reason I can't explain, I'm in a library, a nagging suspicion that as bad as my life was it could get a whole lot worse, when I stumble across an encyclopedia on the lives of the saints. Who was she, you ask? Saint Rita wanted nothing more than to go into a convent when she was a young girl, but it seemed her family had promised her out in marriage. She marries, they have two sons, but her husband was murdered. Her two sons then set out to avenge his death. She prayed that they would die before they could carry out their plan of cold-blooded murder, thus condemning themselves to eternal ruin. Seems her prayer was answered. They died, but no one knows the circumstances. After that, she entered a convent, like she always wanted, became an Augustinian Nun. Prayed to share in Christ's suffering and bore the mark of a thorn on her forehead until she died. Almost six hundred years ago, and her incorrupt body is still just like it was, resting in a basilica in Cascia, Italy. My little motel misadventure was no epiphany, but I've kept her with me ever since. I'm not sure I can explain why."

As Kramer fell silent, Bolan held the man's look, thinking about the story he'd related, weighing the sincerity behind the words. As much evil as the soldier had faced in his War Everlasting, as many near death experiences as he'd brushed up against himself, he couldn't help but wonder right then if maybe there was such a supernatural phenomenon as miracles, guardian angels, the guiding hand of a divine force that could hand out mercy to the repentant, justice to the wicked, but already knew the answer. The simple fact that he was prepared to always offer the ultimate sacrifice to keep the scourge of Evil from devouring the innocent and the peacekeepers was proof enough in his mind there was a God, a creator, an eternal judge. When the dust of battle always settled, and the living were separated from the dead, the wheat from the chaff, it was the only concept that made any sense.

The ultimate good was the only principal worth fighting for.

Bolan made the decision. He had crossed the point where he felt it safe to say it wouldn't prove a fatal mistake. Mitch Kramer was a man in search of new life, who needed redemption, however and wherever it came.

So be it.

The soldier picked up the small war bag, inside of

which rested the HK, with spare clips and a bevy of fragmentation, flash-bang, smoke and incendiary grenades. He went and removed the plastic cuffs off Kramer's wrists, dumped the small arsenal by his side.

"Chances are," Bolan told the man, "I'm going to need some help. Don't let me live to regret it. Fair enough?"

Kramer nodded. "More than I deserve."

CHAPTER SIX

"Bison One to Hammer Wheel."

The man's voice crackled around the cab of the Ford GMC, sounding as if it were reaching out from some cavernous echo chamber. He was alone, with only Grant's voice reverberating in his head, and he wondered if maybe that by itself wasn't the clue, the opening...

Mark Drobbler kept him waiting, staring out the windshield at the eye of the camera that was hidden behind some ferns. Had the spooks not done their job, he knew he would have been swarmed by men in black fatigues already. Or...

Either way, it was zero hour.

Which was why he found his hands shaking uncontrollably.

He took a deep swig of whiskey from the silver flask, for all the good he reckoned it would do to calm the firestorm of raw nerves and churning stomach. The grim chuckle he sounded against his will seemed to ring back, loud and insidious, in his ears, like a death knell. He was minutes away from venturing into what he suspected was no less than a dark world of hurt he couldn't begin to imagine.

There were a few simple facts to consider along that line of pessimistic thought. First, he knew how spooks operated, despite all of Grant's promises and reassurances they were aboveboard, and that coming from a man who had been little more than some backwater dirty badge with both hand and extra-marital tool out. Right. Mr. Fire and Brimstone, always preaching about the end of the world, how the elect needed to get busy scrambling to fight the good fight, and before the barbarians at the gate devoured the few standing God-fearing Christians. All this from a man who had his own agenda here on Earth, and that involved nothing other than big, quick and easy money, so he could coast through the rest of his golden years.

As for the spooks, they came to them, smiling sheep, pretending to be nothing other than simple government officials, but in this case, they came bearing gifts and promising Paradise on Earth—a cash ticket for Easy Street—for the Sons of Revelation. Drobbler knew their ilk. They were nothing less than snarling wolves behind the lamb's mask. The clincher, in his experienced mind, though, was the fact the spooks had actually told them who and what they represented.

Homeland Security.

Considering what was before them, that revelation was unheard of, tantamount, in fact, to professional suicide.

Or capture.

Assuming they were to be believed, there was the dilemma all of them were being marched into an elaborate Federal trap, hammered and cut to ribbons, and whatever rabble left to be scooped up would be branded as treasonous cutthroats in front of God, man and country. All this before they were even out of the gate. To compound what he couldn't deny was mounting horror and doubt, there was the attack at the lodge, right before daybreak. Car bombs, of all the maddening mystery—and planted under the very noses of watching sentries—though he thought of those guards in the loosest sense of anything close to resembling vigilant—had reduced to smoking rubbish what was a fleet of top-of-the-line vehicles, vintage classics a few of the less devout were still whining over, demanding immediate compensation, retribution, but, for God's sake, were up in arms and angrier than ever to follow through with the mission. To throw fuel on the fire of the mystery, there was no sighting, no sign whatsoever upon subsequent combing of the woods and general perimeter of some adversarial force that had up and vanished like a ghost.

To make matters worse still, one of the High Sons was missing, a former L.A. cop, gone to take a leak, ostensibly, but vanishing into thin air.

Hence—the missing cop—was another godforsaken riddle, and this, after they'd been infiltrated by the Feds there was no telling...

"Hammer Wheel! Respond!"

He felt his hand reaching out for the gearshift, but realized he needed to turn on the ignition first.

Stay or go?

How far to 83? Missoula? How close was the nearest town…?

"Hammer Wheel! Why are you just sitting there?"

Drobbler flinched. They were watching. That sealed him in.

He picked up the radio. "Yeah?"

"What the hell's the matter with you?"

"Nothing. I was just thinking."

"The thinking part's already done. Move out and assume your position."

Too late, but Drobbler had known as much, hours earlier. Whatever hope he'd clung to evaporated as he felt watching eyes somewhere in the forest. He grabbed up the Colt Commando assault rifle, the small nylon satchel with spare clips, shouldered out the door.

The trail was narrow, but he knew it by heart from prior walk-through. Originally, his role had been that of advanced scout only, which he was abandoning to now…

It was a short walk, and he saw it looming before his eyes, too soon, too sudden.

A beast of burden.

A monstrous thing of death and destruction.

The door was open and waiting. Drobbler climbed the few steps and dropped behind the wheel of Attila.

IT WAS T-Minus 21:48:47 and counting when Donald Lawhorn spotted them, and fought back the scowl before the look betrayed the murderous rage thundering in his heart. They were in the deep back corner, that section reserved for those fools under the delusion a few games of pool would stand them out as something more than the usual hyenas. The doors were barely open for business, and there they were, playing grab-ass with two strippers.

Cheap thrills he could understand, but this little floor show was beyond stupid.

Marching past the center stage, nary a glance at the blonde gyrating for a few suits he figured good for another round of beer and a handful of fives before scurrying back to work or wives, Lawhorn felt his pulse beat to the rhythm of the rock number blasting from the jukebox, the heavy-metal rifts and drums loud enough, he figured, to drown out every jumbo jet landing and taking off at MIA. Fire burned yet hotter behind his eyes, as he scoured two of the operation's foreign imports, head to toe. He didn't like what he found, to state the very least.

South Floridians didn't wear Don Ho shirts or sport deep tans that leaned more to raw sunburn that would soon bubble and burst and leave them looking like irradiated alien monsters. South Floridians didn't wear matching white pants, or alligator- or python-skin cowboy boots that rendered them walking neon signs. South Floridians didn't deck themselves out in gold Rolex watches and five pounds of diamond necklace that when hit by harsh sunlight could give sight to the blind. South Floridians, finally, didn't wear black Blues Brothers sunglasses indoors or Jimmy Buffet hats like they just stumbled off a banana boat.

Point being, they looked like tourists. Worse, they were easily enough remembered, and by the most apathetic citizen.

Closing, undecided whether they looked like "Miami Vice" or Pablo Escobar knockoffs, he glanced at the door directly behind them, six or seven paces, considered the moment. It led to the back alley, he knew, long but tight, stinking confines where the dregs and the wayward all congregated to drink, smoke crack, flop down to sleep it off. As he took in the fumes of cologne that left him wondering if they'd bathed in the stuff, he began feeling the weight of the Para-Ordnance beneath his cream-colored, nondescript windbreaker, shouldered on the left side of his black nondescript sports shirt. This was a tough part of Fort Lauderdale. Despite the city council's best efforts to march out the tour-mongering charlatans and tell the world Lauderdale had cleaned up its act, dope, whores and strip clubs were still the town's stock-in-trade. Gunshots were as expected as annual spring break.

The trouble was, it was too late in the game to change the roster.

He was moving on the back end of the table when the Chechen lined up his shot on the eight ball from the far side. There was a lot of green to go for the winning shot before it dropped into the pocket Lawhorn stood in front of. Despite the No Gambling sign, clearly posted and in full view behind the Iranian, there were three brand-new one-hundred-dollar bills on the rail. One of the two working girls, the brunette, wasn't too shabby, but even in bad light he could see the track marks, covered, as they were, by two or three layers of makeup.

The Iranian was glancing his way, cool, like he was in charge of something, the women tittering in whispers to each other, when the Chechen stroked his shot. He clipped the eight high, nice and easy, sent it rolling, smooth and kissing close down the rail. The eight ball was losing steam, but still rolling strong, inches from dropping in and with just enough force the Chechen could start to smile, when Lawhorn scooped it up.

Lawhorn issued the contact phrase. "Welcome to America. I can see that you are loving life."

One of the women gasped. Both the Chechen and the Iranian went rigid, and Lawhorn could tell at least one of them was thinking some pretty ugly thoughts. Likewise a thought crossed his mind to push it to the limit, but he knew the look in his eyes clearly warned them the nonsense was over. Just to make sure they understood, he plucked up the bills, thrust them at the women and said, "Beat it."

The redhead took the money but both of them held their ground, undecided.

"They're finished for the day."

They went, muttering something lost to the heavy-metal rifts and drums of the music.

Lawhorn followed the imported duo, Spanish nationals—as stated by their passports—to a table that was littered with several empty beer bottles, an overflowing ashtray and two full shots of whiskey. They were sitting, the Chechen reaching for his drink when Lawhorn beat him to it, and drank it for him. Just looking at their unmitigated arrogance, smelling their perfumed stink, aware of how much they hated a nation he once believed in and fought for, what they had signed on to do with a glee and eagerness that was beyond psychopathic, and it was all he could manage to stay his hand from grabbing his piece and blasting away. Orders. The operation first, then…

He took a piece of crumpled paper and flipped it on the table, then helped himself to the Iranian's shot. "Report to that address. They're expecting you. No delays. No stops except the one you'll make at your motel to change out of those costumes. Should I hear you made any more pitstops, should I hear you are en route and still walking around looking like cheap drug dealer scum, I will personally terminate your mission. If we are clear on that, get up and leave this instant. If not, sit there two more seconds like you are and give me those hard looks like you think you've got the balls of a lion, and I'll show you just what vile slimy little worms you are and how easy it will be for me to crush you as such."

They exchanged looks, some of the arrogance replaced by disbelief and anger, as the Chechen grunted and scooped in the paper.

"One…"

Lawhorn took two steps back and spread his legs. He

figured his present position gave him about a four-foot clearance to avoid blood spatter, visualizing point of impact right between their eyes. At that range half their brains would get blasted out the back of their skulls, all but obscure the No Gambling sign. He was opening his mouth, ready to form the number, when they got up and left. Without hesitation or a parting look their way, he claimed the Chechen's seat just as a leggy blonde in a string bikini and black pumps was on her way to take his order.

Lawhorn decided to turn on the charm as she slinked closer. He pulled out a wad of hundreds thick enough to choke a white shark, peeled off a bill and saw the spark ignite in her blue eyes. "Can you clear away this garbage those two pigs left, honey?" He checked his watch: 21:45:51. "I'll take exactly what they were drinking." He breathed in her fragrance, smiled into her eyes as she started gathering empties and said, "By the way, do you shoot pool?"

"What did you say to them anyway, made them leave like their pants were on fire?"

Lawhorn held the smile. "If I told you, I'd have to kill you."

She laughed.

CAPTAIN CLAY BENTON of the United States Army's Special Division of Bio-Chem Warfare felt the first wave of ice shoot down his spine. At first look from the shotgun seat through the one-way bulletproof windscreen of his customized black Ford GMC he thought the vehicle was one of theirs. It was black, all right, but it was a Ford Bronco. The windows weren't blacked-out, either like one of their specials, and those weren't the patented U.S. government plates. Definitely not one of their guys. Civilian, then, and broken down, now of all times. Twenty yards or so away, he made out Montana plates as a burst of sunlight broke through the clouds and hit the front end. Why it was parked at a slightly cocked angle across the road, as if the driver was undecided how much space to grab up—or block— and with no sign of life...

Upon further study, he spotted the flattened tread, rear starboard.

Benton didn't like it. It looked like what it was supposed to be—a stranded motorist—and that set off the first round of alarms in his head.

He scanned the broad, sweeping grasslands to both sides of a road that wasn't marked on state or national maps, and which all by itself sent up flares to the locals, but who could figure the way spooks thought. Trouble was, a complete and thorough scan of the countryside was impossible, since the prairie rolled and humped in broad areas, and just like the road out of there.

Which made him stare back at the Bronco, noting suddenly that it was abandoned at the very apex of the incline.

"Do you want me to hit the horn, sir?"

"No. Sit tight," he ordered Specialist Johnson, and, taking the M-16, exited the vehicle.

Easing ahead, assault rifle held out and set for single-shot, Benton looked back over his shoulder. The convoy was strung out behind his lead vehicle, engines idling as they sat and waited for him to do whatever he was going to do, and at the moment he wasn't sure of anything. Fourteen strong between four Humvees with mounted TOWs and .50-caliber machine guns, seven black GMCs packed to capacity with soldiers and a spook assortment, and with two troop transports he was platoon strength times three, maybe closer to four. It was the black armored vehicle next to last in line that was cause for sudden concern.

That, and the fact that those who were supposedly in charge of the operation had, for reasons unknown, sent them all on ahead at the last minute. But his orders were clear. The cargo was to be evacuated, transported to what was tagged a special pickup site outside Missoula, again for reasons not specified. Why, though, was he feeling the hackles on the back of his neck rise? What the hell was keeping the spooks who were supposed to act as both vanguard and scouts in the Black Hawks? The State Police, he knew, were ready and waiting to link up, just a few miles down Highway 83, beef them up as escort to clear local traffic at critical junctions and all the way into—

Benton thought he saw a figure move on the other side of the Bronco. He took a few steps forward, called, "Hey! You there! This is United States Army Captain Benton! You are on restricted government property."

"I know."

He knew!? Another wave of ice shivered down his back, warning Benton the guy wasn't trying to be cute.

This was trouble.

No movement on the other side, then Benton clearly made out a dark figure as it stood to full height, as if he'd been in hiding. Something smelled, for damn sure.

Benton grabbed the handheld unit off his belt, just as he made out the sound of an engine rumbling in the distance, coming, it sounded, from the other side of the rise, a vehicle, rolling his way, hard and fast. He hit the button to transmit the order for all hands to fall out but only static crackled back in response. He glanced down at what had all of a sudden become a useless piece of junk, spied the far door opening as Johnson began to disgorge.

A behemoth black rig rolled over the incline, materializing out of nowhere as if the road had simply split open and heaved it out. He wasn't sure which happened first, but the world seemed to erupt in a flash of weapons fire and rolling thunder in the same instant. The shadow blurred, a rush of movement around the front portside of the Bronco. Benton caught maybe a half-second view of the assault rifle flaming away before those steel-jacketed rounds hammered his chest and sent him flailing back. He was still reeling down the side of the GMC, holding on to both balance and weapon somehow, as two or three more rounds drilled him, the thought shooting through his mind the Kevlar might hold, but it was hardly holding back the fire knifing through his ribs, the air squeezed out of his lungs as if an invisible suction cup was fixed to his mouth and nose. Whatever the leviathan on wheels sailing past, it dawned on Benton those were Gatling guns and cannons blasting away from the top and down the portside, and sweeping a lightning barrage, stem-to-stern of the convoy.

He was falling, not sure who or what he was cursing, just as the roof of his GMC was sheared away by the deafening blasts of those mammoth guns. Glass and metal shards, what looked like dark misty clouds were taking to the air, in his face next, the shrapnel winging off his cheek and scalp as he dropped the final two or three feet. The little bit of wind he'd managed to suck back into his throat was punched out of a mouth that was on the verge of bellowing a scream of horror and rage.

Something told him lack of immediate oxygen and personal sentiments was the least of his problems.

The thunder of explosions, the rattle of weapons fire and the shouts of his men took on a surreal evanescent quality. His senses were so shredded by the ferocity of the assault, the sickening awareness men under his command were getting cut to ribbons that a sudden urge for self-preservation and the furious desire to strike back seized hold. He sensed then saw his would-be executioner, as he crabbed toward his assault rifle. He wasn't sure, but he actually thought the bastard was smiling as he strolled ahead, weapon coming up when a mangled strip of fiery wreckage bounced off the asphalt and twirled past him. The SOB hardly broke stride, coming on and drawing a bead with the assault rifle, still sporting that stupid but infernal grin. For the briefest and most agonizing instant yet, Clay Benton saw the faces of his wife and two children flash before his eyes, knew, even as his hands hauled in the M-16, it was all beyond hope.

For their sake, by God, he had to try. The very notion he would leave behind a grieving widow and fatherless children—and as he was murdered, no less, in the prime of their lives and their needs—was more than enough for him to kick it into angry high gear.

CHAPTER SEVEN

Mitch Kramer did not need stone tablets shrouded in fire and floating down from the sky to tell him the truth, or that dazzling arrow of conscience to point the way.

The worthless years, thanks be to God, were over.

Flaming truth be told, the past was so dead so suddenly it made the present so alive the ex-cop and now ex-Son of Revelation knew beyond any doubt he was responding to the call of his immediate future.

And his ultimate destiny.

The fork in the road now ended somewhere in front of him.

He was topping the next rise in what he found was the last series of humps across the grassland when he took in the ferocious attack that appeared all but one-sided in favor of Grant's reprobates, thanks to the black battleship on wheels. Braking to an abrupt halt, fifty or so yards out and west of the road with no name, Kramer was momentarily stunned by the murder and mayhem that looked to have nearly savaged the Special Army-Spook convoy, and nearly to a vehicle. A few of the rigs, however, were attempting to bolt in various degrees around the compass, but began slamming into each other in a macabre bumper-car derby as roofs, engine housings, bumpers and whole panels stem to stern were sheared away like the flimsiest of cheap tin under those long tempests of Gatling gun fire. Armed men in black were being shredded all over the road, limbs virtually dissected in front of his eyes. A few of the more hearty were returning fire, but, discretion being the better part of valor in this instance, most next began scrambling for cover as comrades were chopped down like so many bloody straw men. No, he wasn't privy to the finer details of the ambush, wondering briefly what he would have done anyway without—

He threw a look due north, wondering where was his guardian angel in the flesh and what he strongly suspected was nothing less than a super warrior. No sign of the big nameless one in black, but with the prairie rolling out like a sea frozen in mid-tempest Kramer was certain the man was somewhere out there, and moving in for the kill.

Time to do his part, but how?

He felt the weight of the HK subgun in his hands, the nylon bag hung over his shoulder and stuffed with what he'd discovered were a dozen extra clips and an equal number of lethal steel baseballs, the grenades marked by colored strip and according to their nature of ruin. As he heard then spotted the next line of explosions marching through more men in black hopping back into the few standing vehicles about midway down the line, seeking to drive on while other figures were mowed down by the chain saw threshing of Gatling gun and cannon fire, he gave a lengthy scan to all the hell and havoc being wreaked by the mammoth war bus.

He searched for some decent point of penetration, preferably from the blind side and far away from the blazing black juggernaut that held, slow and steady, on a due-north course while pounding out one great wave of blasts and man-eating lead after another. A vague awareness wanted to warn him that Grant was probably moments away from bringing on the cavalry to mop it up, assault the armored vehicle near the end of the line, hijack whatever the cargo. That would make it about thirty anticipated additional guns, but he had no idea who or how many were manning those monster platoon slayers inside that raging—and what appeared armored—leviathan, as machine-gun sprays from the Humvees sparked off and sailed on from the beast's hull like streaking space rock before what few shooters hammering back the return fire were cut and blasted to mangled shreds. Whatever the final SOR tally, Kramer's gut told him he would need every round, every deadly egg before it was over, and that he would not walk away from this unscathed, if at all.

So be it.

He ran east, pumping his legs for all he was worth, surprised at how light and nimble his old war bones felt, as he spotted a tall figure in a knee-length bearskin coat and black Stetson hat, now shuffling down the road to roughly his ten o'clock. The patented Wild West trapper costume told him that would be Dobson, a big-mouth know-it-all former member of the Aryan Brotherhood and who, rumor had it, had done some State time for rape and dabbling in Internet child porn. The reprobate had an assault rifle in hand, taking his sweet time, it looked, as he advanced on a man in black crawling for the back end of a GMC that was all but pulped and now sprouting flames around the engine housing. Neither man appeared aware or concerned that the gas tank was sure to blow any second.

With raw energy fueled by racing adrenaline, Kramer charged yet harder, angling for a point on Dobson's rear. He had never given much serious thought to the implications of killing another human being when he'd been a cop, since it was a given he was on the side of the law, buoyed by badge, backed—sometimes—by the judicial system, and booze had always provided the magic salve those two times he'd shot and killed an armed miscreant. Now, though, since his conversion, so to speak, and acting outside any law he was aware of…

Something told him in this instance he was meting out justice while saving life, not all that much different really when he'd been sworn to uphold the law.

Kramer made the slight adjustment, current distance gauged at roughly twenty yards, give or take. He skidded to a halt at the edge of the road and held back on the subgun's trigger. He started low, around the kidneys, allowed for the rising burst that chewed up bearskin as the line of 9 mm Parabellum rounds scorched its way up to a point between the shoulder blades. Impact spun Dobson, the SOR cowboy snarling out a curse, his assault rifle flaming toward the sky. Kramer finished him off with a short burst to the chest, sent the reprobate dancing back for the GMC a second before the gas tank ignited and Dobson was engulfed in the fireball. The ex-cop was barely aware of the flaming scarecrow launched into the air, the wreckage flying out in all directions, the man in black leaping to his feet but bowled down by the shock wave.

Fresh enemy blood had arrived.

Grant's cavalry, six SUVs strong, he saw, came racing over the low rise on the far side of the road, maybe a hundred yards out but bearing down, hard and fast. Figure four miscreants to a rig…

He could work with that.

There was rolling thunder in his ears, as two or three more explosions thundered to the north, pillars of fire and whirlwinds of debris, climbing for the sky. Stepping onto asphalt, he saw the murderous leviathan on wheels lumbering to swing around as the driver ground the clutch and jerked it out of reverse. The Gatling gunner on the roof, shielded in the cocoon of black armor, began sweeping another burst in the general direction of the wounded. How many left down there in the bowels of Hell, it was impossible to say, but Kramer caught the cries of pain and shouts of rage mingled with withering autofire that was hurled back at the war bus, for all the good it did.

Heading roughly his way from a southeast angle, the first of Grant's war wagons bounded onto the road, screeching rubber as tires clawed at asphalt and the engine revved like a pride of bloodthirsty lions that hadn't eaten in months.

Kramer lifted his submachine gun, gave the point SUV some lead. He hit the trigger and blew in the windshield on a pair of startled faces.

IT WAS WELL beyond any strategy that resembled methodical, cohesive, failsafe. That left skill, experience and determination. All of which Mack Bolan was never in short supply.

Originally, as soon as the big guns began decimating the convoy—two spinning Gatlings sandwiching what looked like some type of triple-barreled autocannon—the soldier had opted for a dubious end run, intent on skirting the rear of the convoy and making due haste to intercept the war bus.

That plan was shot to Hell, along with most of the Humvees and GMCs as he charged to within decent shooting range. M-16 up and tracking the hellzone, south to north, he was now sixty to seventy yards from the rampaging war bus as it wheeled around to give the starboard gunners free shooting dibs on any survivors.

There was no doubt in the warrior's mind the beast of murderous burden was thick with armor, probably titanium-coated to boot. Beyond autofire slicing off the war bus and with those rounds appearing little more than mosquito bites if he judged there was nary a dent, he bore witness to a launched TOW that went skidding off the top of the hull. It did, however, blow, but in a sort of sliding firewall that boiled far enough away from the rooftop gunner to leave him virtually unscathed inside his armored shell. The Gatling gun hardly missed a beat, as it roared back an eyeblink later, eating up some of the walking wounded in both eviscerating and dismembering bursts. Those rounds, spit out like endless streams of lightning bolts, had to be somewhere in the low double-digit millimeter range and armor-piercing to shred the troop transports in heartbeats flat like the warrior saw, judging the air around evaporating canvas, thick cyclone with sailing bodies, twirling weapons and blossoming red mist. To say he was outgunned, outmatched and boring into the eye of the storm…

The Stony Man warrior hit the road, veering off for the smoking veil of two GMCs for cover, the occupants down and bleeding out in beds of glass shards and twisted metal. As Bolan looked to the armored vehicle, dumped on its portside where the Gatling gunners had blown out the tires and the windscreen, it was a safe bet to figure the SOR hardforce wanted whatever the deadly cargo inside.

Northbound, then, but that was easier assumed than done, he next discovered.

Number one priority was to somehow cripple then board the war bus. Figure one pair of hands to each monster weapon, with gunnery mates standing by to reload—call it twelve on-board, plus driver, but the problems weren't only obvious, they were compounded in the next moment as to how he would perform such a miracle.

Bolan squeezed off a short burst at the rear tires, but, as feared, they were Kevlar-wrapped, the 5.56 mm rounds bouncing off like rubber bullets on rubber. The soldier was a step ahead, entertaining another idea and seizing cover behind the GMCs when two of the three Gatling gunners directed heavy metal thunder his way. To stay put was tantamount to suicide, Bolan knew, as a minefield of glass and metal shrapnel blew over his scalp, forcing him to eat asphalt.

Another plan flared to mind, as Bolan crabbed to the deep end of the GMC, scanning the killzone that led toward the overturned trophy. He had seen just enough of the gun holes to know he had but one shot to stem the tide. The A-list shooters had the big weapons framed in a cross that allowed for just enough vertical and horizontal movement where they could fire on with little fear of a stray round claiming a lucky kill. All he had to do...

The Executioner dumped a 40 mm buckshot round down the gullet of his M-203, locked, loaded, all set.

Maybe.

As the storm suddenly stopped tracking him, he was up and running for the next demolished GMC. On the fly, he noted the war bus was suddenly swinging sideways, jerking to an abrupt halt. Now it blocked the road, about dead even down the line of trashed wheels, but it was able to lend both starboard and portside gunners clear fields of fire, north and south.

Bolan saw why the sudden change in tactics.

One of the arriving SUVs, its windshield obliterated, was sailing off the road, upended in midair next as its tires were punctured by the long stream of blistering lead that raked its side. The unmanned rig hammered down, flipped, the jarring impact hurtling one hapless occupant into the air along with a shower of glass meteors. Before he could line up a shot, three SUVs were tearing past his position. He blew out a back window on the last rig, but they began bobbing and weaving as they slowed to use scattered wreckage for cover while racing on for the downed cargo, clipping and banging the metallic rhino charge through shredded bumpers, crunching over bodies and strewed doors. To further complicate an already chaotic hell, the length of the battlefield had become so littered with wreckage, walking mangled and outstretched bodies he couldn't accurately determine were living or dead, and with the drifting haze of black smoke from burning vehicles and the air thick with cordite enough to want to blot out the sun, the soldier could only compare it to a chessboard where a sore loser slammed his fist down and scattered the pieces haphazard.

In other words, the warrior was staring at a lethal maze that could hide combatants, both hostile and the few friendlies left to shoot it out. And even the armed stragglers of the convoy were a huge question mark, and who would most likely turn blazing weapons on any armed stranger, on the side of justice or not.

Bolan spied a squad of SOR rabble piling out of

their SUVs to the east, what would be the nose and port-side of the war bus.

The unholy racket of small arms fire and the buzz-saw din of spinning Gatlings torqued itself up to another ear-shattering crescendo as half of that pack of armed Sons of Revelation split, vanished around the starboard side of the juggernaut while the other human vipers, Bolan found, set out on foot.

And coming his way.

The Executioner drifted into a space between a Hum-vee and an overturned GMC, burning gas, blood and cordite in his nose. He lifted his assault rifle, lining them up as they charted a hard weave through sitting wrecks and slabs of jagged debris, the enemy now going for head shots on the few soldiers still in the game. Whatever was happening, out of sight on the other side of the murder machine, Bolan had a general suspicion, but he was in no position to lend the ex-cop a helping hand.

He had problems enough of his own right then, six, in fact, and that didn't include two Gatling guns and an autocannon primed to drop the hammer on him.

The Executioner squeezed the trigger on the M-203, and sent the warhead packed with razor-edged flesh-eaters streaking on for the nest of armed snakes on two legs.

CHAPTER EIGHT

Jeremiah Grant smiled. Right away, he could feel the expression lacked the necessary fervor and confidence it needed, and from an appointed leader sent by God to save sinful Man from the Apocalypse and eternal ruin, no less. The smile wanted to return when he found he was on the verge of congratulating himself for so skillfully manipulating men and events, but only so far.

That was the problem.

He wanted to feel good, in charge, crystal clear that he was dictating his own fate, steering all events, large and small, the way he deigned them to be. But there was a dark cloud hung over his head, an ill wind he sensed gathering off the stage of the mission he proclaimed as the Day of Reckoning.

There were any number of fearful mysteries and aggravating riddles that needed solving from the predawn events. Such as who had attacked the compound, and

just for starters. Then there was the matter of the High
Son, a former cop who was strangely missing now that
the Day of Reckoning had summoned all the faithful.
Then again, maybe the attack wasn't so strange, after
all, Grant considered, given the organization had recently been infiltrated by two Feds. Despite the fact he
might view their executions as a necessary evil, he could
be sure the United States government and its deputized
killers of the FBI wouldn't see it quite his way.

The lying murdering hypocrites never did. Waco, Ruby
Ridge, but to just name a few grievous outrages inflicted
on American citizens by the Sons of Cain who were taking the entire nation straight down the toilet, concerned
only in looking out for number one, their rich crony
friends, the various lobby groups they bent their knees for
in order to stay in office. What was a God-fearing, patriotic man on the side of righteousness and justice to do anyway about fighting, nay, slaying the evil that spewed out
of Washington, Wall Street, Hollywood? Grant thought.

Well, he decided that he was in the process of doing
it, fighting the good fight, that was, though he wasn't
sure how much he feared God. He couldn't see God,
after all, but he could sure see money.

Grant then decided to follow the advice he'd given
the troops before heading out. Divine justice would sort
out the mystery in due course, and God would slay their
enemies before them, wherever the new Babylonians
reared their heads. They were to a High and Low Son
to gird their loins, go forward, carry out their sworn and
holy duties as prescribed.

Amen.

As he surveyed the slaughter through his field glasses he had to admit he was more than pleased with initial progress. Of course, Attila had done most of the killing thus far, but his foot soldiers—the Low Sons— were in the process of mopping up what Army troops and spooks had escaped the first waves of what he thought of as nothing less than Apocalyptic thunder and lightning. He counted ten of his SOR faithful already disgorging their vehicles to descend on the armored car, way to the north.

Outstanding.

He took a deep breath, decided he could indulge another smile, this time with mustered confidence and courage that all was going well, albeit not quite according to plan.

Come what glory may, he had still come a long ways, indeed, down the path to his chosen paradise, he reflected, since those days of palming kickbacks from county meth dealers and running his own little prostitution ring out of several mobile homes on the outskirts of Boise. It had been close for a while there when his wife had discovered what he'd been up to when he claimed overtime had likewise been stealing his nights as well as days, only it wasn't the job that was grabbing all that nocturnal devotion. Since she was a known heavy boozer in about twenty different taverns and saloons around town, the fatal accident on a winding road north of Boise was more than plausible. Especially in light of the rumors that had become public knowledge—thanks to a leak by his deputy to the scribblers of the city paper—the woman's husband-sheriff had somehow managed to see her walk on two previous DWI charges, not even the proverbial slap on the wrists. Talk about the media getting squeezed for a good cause for a blessed changed, the fact no one bothered to check the brakes on her brand-new SUV wasn't his problem, either. Of course, human nature being what it was, general suspicion and slander after her untimely demise had eventually sent him packing in search of a bigger and more profitable dream.

Enter a few good Christian soldiers—or rather, ex-lawmen grousing over beers and whiskey about the sorry state of affairs in America—with a dream and some decent spare cash to spread the word. Soon their humble origins were branching out like ripened grapevines to recruit like-minded men with both principal and backbone buoyed by plenty of weapons at ready disposal. Originally, however, he recalled how it had been something of a cynical slap in the face to Christian values, and which he had always held in contempt, at least from a private point of view. But something itching in the back of his mind had prompted him to go forward, a voice telling him he might someday soon be laughing all the way to the bank, that he shouldn't be so ready to look down his nose at what he wanted to call the superstitious blather of fools who didn't know how to live life to its fullest. Many in these parts were searching for answers that would explain away the drudgery of their own miserable impoverished lives. The rest of

America was, in fact, appearing to be going straight to Hell. Using religion to prey on the fears of local militant rabble, down on their luck in all respects, had not only launched the Sons of Revelation, but opened doors where he would soon see the pure gold of his noble efforts.

"What do you think, Jeremy? Looks to me like the United States Army is down there, busy reenacting Little Big Horn."

"Only with the modern twist of Homeland Security playing the coward's role of Major Reno, hanging back instead of full retreat in this case while their Custer gets scalped."

Grant threw a look to both sides. Ben Jameson and Richard Tomlin, former Missoula cops, were smiling, chuckling, just plain enjoying the show. With what had happened earlier, they were a little too cocky for his liking, and even if they won this battle, the war was far from over. He was about to remind them as much when the autofire seemed to shoot to new levels of relentless anger.

Pockets of relative fierce resistance, Grant found, were breaking out from down yonder in the abyss, but with Attila stretched across the road it was difficult to accurately assess how his soldiers were faring, at least on the far north side. Attila's big guns went silent, at least for the moment, as the crew inside wisely opted to stay their hands while the foot soldiers moved in to clean it up, nail it down. There was, however, the unexplained violence that had seen one of the SUVs flying off the side of the road, moments ago, where it had crashed and was now burning, the face of Jake Petersen a twisted mask of pure and bleeding agony as he framed it clearly in the lens. The man's silent scream vanished next against both distance—three hundred yards plus to the parked Bronco alone—and when his warrior collapsed from either pain and shock or flat-out died from internal injuries inflicted during the wreck that had seen their vehicle turned into a cannonball for reasons he was still trying his damnedest to sort out. It looked like Petersen had been dragging along a broken leg, clearly indicated by the blood-flecked shards of bone jutting out where his shin had been snapped in two like a stale pretzel. The man wasn't moving, and Grant couldn't tell if his chest was rising and falling, or what.

But from the outset he had factored in casualties, KIA. The cleansing fiery truth be told, he was counting on the fighting force being shaved by a few heads, the more the better, when he considered the pot of gold that waited at the end of his rainbow.

Something was happening just beyond Attila, but with his troops suddenly swallowed up by a wafting cloud of smoke black as the devil's heart...

Silently, Grant cursed his hilltop scouting perch, as some gnawing dread he couldn't put a finger on its source kicked in and wanted to ruin his whiskey buzz, sour a mood he hungered to embrace as nothing short of dazzling triumph. The sideline had been selected where he could watch both the road leading in from the south while scanning the vast prairie for unforeseen problems, such as locals traipsing around with rifles and shotguns, in search of bagging an early morning elk for bragging rights at their favorite watering hole. Any decent determination of the battle's progress, though, was obscured by distance, his low altitude in relation to the road, and with all those teeming barriers of smoke, the winding maze of wreckage that hid various darting armed figures it was next to impossible to tell who was who, what was what. The trouble with dry runs and initial reconnaissance was that the pictured perfect outcome of events never held true to form, not when the real thing came screaming to bloody fruition.

All that business, he reckoned, about combat being a fluid situation. Right.

"They're late, Jeremy."

That was true, and perhaps that was the cause for some of his dammed-up anxiety. Wondering what could possibly be keeping the spooks—since they were the ones who had insisted on all hands maintaining a strict timetable and to the minute—Grant lowered the glasses, scanning the tree line that swaddled the foothills of the Swan Range. It was a beautiful, crisp morning, big blue sky with a few scudding clouds, the dew just beginning to evaporate off pristine rolling grasslands.

God's Country, they called it, but for the life of him he could never figure exactly what they meant by that. At present, it sure as hell was a bellowing misnomer for the carnage stretched out and heaping up, fast and furious, down the nameless spook's road.

Grant looked at his watch. He was about to respond when both men barked questions in near unison.

"What the hell?"

"Is that who I think it is?"

Grant spotted the trouble in question, hard to miss since those were his guys getting waxed no sooner than they disgorged from out of their SUVs on the south end. Panning due west, and—son of a bitch—he discovered what had happened to his AWOL ex-cop. He cursed the very day the man was born, the storm of rage building as he watched Kramer cut loose with a submachine gun and kick two more of his people off their feet. Blood was pumping from the chests of victims he determined were Stan Matthews and Jonathan Hill, two of his better shooters. Before now, he would have been more than happy to scratch them off the coming payroll.

However, this was no routine situation. Kramer didn't strike him as the crusading type, a lone wolf avenger marching out there to tackle odds that were so stacked against him, they were suicidal, to say the least. Or...

Kramer fell back into a gap between two downed GMCs, a sustained burst of weapons fire from the traitorous bastard driving seven or eight Low Sons to cover as they attempted to outflank the man who had shown his true colors.

Yellow.

Soon to be red, or so Grant hoped.

"We've got another problem besides our boy Kramer."

Grant choked down a stream of obscenities. Now what? He lowered the glasses, and glared past Jameson, in the nick of time to find the first of six unmarked State Police cruisers streak into view. The good news, as far as cops went, was that Attila's EMP shield was good for a thousand yards around the compass, would—check that—should prevent them from calling in yet more smoky backup, unless they already, in fact, had done just that. The bad news—at least for the immediate present—was that their own flying cavalry had yet to show, and without the spooks...

"Gentlemen," Grant said. "I suggest we monitor progress for only a few more moments, then we make all due haste for our jet. Something tells me the State of Montana is about to get very hot. Another General Custer I do not intend to become."

No sooner had the words left his mouth and Grant heard a chorus of hideous shrieks. He determined they erupted from the dark side of Attila, but the din alone of men in great agony, holding high and hard, froze his blood.

FOR SOME STRANGE REASON, Kramer wanted to put names to the faces, but they all began to have the same Anglo-Saxon ring. King and Milton, he believed, those were the first two SOR miscreants tagged by his burp-gun as they tried to roll straight his way, all rage, malice and arrogance, as though he was nothing more than some cockroach to be stepped on.

They picked the wrong Christian, wrong day.

Next came James and Henry—Frick and Frack in their matching Stetson hats, black leather vests and pants and flaming Aloha shirts—as Kramer stitched them with 9 mm Parabellum manglers, left to right and back. He held back on the trigger, sent them dancing away in what struck him as bloody Elvis gyrations. Partly shrouded in a swirl of shredded cloth and crimson bits and flecks, M-16s chattered out rounds, skyward sprays, impotent as dashed fighting spirits.

Two more, down and out, on their way to eternal judgment.

The fact they were doing their most vicious to kill him should have given Kramer instant recourse to turn up the angry boil another notch, or feel the first icy tendrils of certain death reaching out to claim him. But, as he backpedaled, spraying the HK down the flaming humps of GMCs and Humvees, Mitchell Kramer had the strangest sensation drop over him. He was neither gripped in killing heat nor afraid to die.

Yet he was both.

The first round he barely felt. It was little more than a bee sting, as he flinched, grunted, spinning halfway in the direction of a dozen or so corpses strewed down the side of one of the troop transports. He was winging back another short burst, one-handed, digging inside the bag for a grenade, then a burst of cold fear sliced through some of the adrenaline. Bullet number two had way more bite to it, tearing like a knife superheated over barbecue flames through his ribs, before he felt it punching an exit hole out the small of his back.

Snarling against the white-hot agony, Kramer fed
his submachine gun a fresh clip. He whirled in the direction of two SOR flunkies, hosing the area with a wall
of lead hornets, but which only sent them scurrying to
cover behind a pile of gnarled junk. A steel egg in hand,
he was stumbling, facing front, hacking on smoke and
stink, when he took another round to the back of the leg.
Screaming, he sent the grenade hurtling in a sideways
whipping motion. Limping ahead but sweeping a long
burst behind in blind spray and pray, what sounded like
no less than the wail of all the burning souls in Hell
nearly drowned out the thunderclap of the blast to his
deep rear. Something real ugly, he knew, was happening, and just beyond the troop carrier.

What was that?

A big tall figure, swaddled in black, floated into
Kramer's view. There was no mistaking those moves,
all steel, all ice.

All iron wrath.

A pro.

The big man's M-16 scorched a line, raking victims
out of sight, right to left. The screams were all but silenced a millisecond before a grenade chugged out of
the stranger's M-203. There was a muffled but loud
thud, followed by another chorus of shouts, punctuated
by a new round of shrieks. Kramer thought he heard another similar dull blast, then the massive engine on the
war bus was snarling to life. He sure wanted to lend a
helping killing hand to his guardian angel in the flesh,
but he had a full plate himself. The one man wrecking

crew seemed to have just vanished anyway—or was maybe swallowed up by smoke and surging on.

Do something!

This was it!

The supreme hour.

Kramer spied what appeared to be a half ring of demolished vehicles, just beyond the tail end of the transport, twisted garbage strewed all down the side of the road. If he could it make inside the impromptu circling of wagons, hang in there, with the big guy on his left wing...

He cracked home a fresh clip, to be on the sure side, cocked and locked. He hauled out another grenade, pulled the pin. Blood and sweat stinging into his eyes, he found himself bulling next inside the steel ring, the noxious fumes of any number of ripe odors swelling his senses, churning his stomach, bringing on the vomit. He kicked through a severed arm, slipping in a pool of muck before regaining his balance. Four, maybe five SOR goons were peeking around the front end of the troop carrier. He was letting the grenade fly, slumping to cover, low on his haunches, behind what appeared a Humvee knocked on its side.

The grenade detonated but Kramer wasn't sure if he'd scored bloody flesh, and since there were no shrill screams erupting from the direction of that boiling fire cloud...

He rose, wiping blood out of his eyes. There was no sign of the big guy, but with all the billows of smoke, with every yard, it seemed, in both directions choked with debris and standing hulls...

They were coming.

Somehow he'd missed two, no, make that three enemy heads as they swung themselves out around the other side of the troop carrier, and began flaying the general vicinity with autofire, leapfrogging, all the while, from metallic mound to mound.

He was searching the smoke, left to right, armed shadows darting this way and that, there then gone as they advanced through the dark curtains, using the field of rubbish, when another steel projectile seared through his upper chest.

He went down, groaning, gagging noises filtering through the chiming bells in his ears. Somehow, he willed himself to begin clambering to his feet.

Sacrifice.

It struck him suddenly that was one of five words—virtues—that were virtually extinct in modern American society. But there he was, ready to give up the ghost, if only to shave the odds for the big guy, perhaps clinging to hope and beyond the grave the deadly cargo would fall into the stranger's capable hands.

Humility.

Charity.

Turning the other cheek was long since out the window, as he drilled a shadow on the run and sent him flipping over a heap of debris. And now that he was stepping onto the threshold of eternity, he might as well scrap charity, as far, that was, as the SOR reprobates went.

That left patience and perseverance.

The world began to fade, swimming in front of his eyes in a darkening mist. But Kramer gathered himself, standing tall, holding fast, his HK smoking and roving for the coming wolves.

There was no time for one last Act of Contrition, but the next words, choked and garbled as they were by bloody froth and spittle and pain, seem to come out of his mouth, backed by a power he couldn't tell belonged to him or not.

"Oh, Dear Mother of God. Will you plead my unworthy case before your Crucified Son?"

Then they rushed from both sides, charged through the shadowy veil, weapons blazing.

CHAPTER NINE

Ten to twelve 9 mm Parabellum shockers from the MP-5 submachine gun, and the last three of the Army specialists sent to him from Fort Bragg's fledgling biological counterterrorist division were dead on their feet, and falling. Slick blood jagged down the starboard nose of the NSMI custom-built classified gunship nicknamed *Pterodactyl,* but there was little he could do now about sloppy appearances.

Allen Braxton had far bigger chores to see to than washing down any amount of black-armored finish. That was grunt work anyway, assuming he was so inclined to give the order to detail his warbird in the first place.

Striding for the winged pylon that housed six Hellfire missiles—a matching number of devastating hightech spears to port—and the third highest-ranking man in the Department of Homeland Security slung the still-smoking weapon. A look over his shoulder, angling for the open hatchway, the four-bladed main rotor now spinning to life as the two GE turboshaft engines whined to high pitch, and Braxton barked at his six-man demo crew to hustle up.

They were on the clock, which was ticking down fast, now that his spotter just informed him the state police were hitting the scene.

As planned, and on schedule.

Initial reports looked good, beyond the annihilation of the Army grunts and specialists and the baker's dozen spooks that were not part of his handpicked team. The cargo—code-named Golden Boy—had been dumped on its side by the SOR rabble, some of which were now moving in to fulfill their role.

Time to play catch-up, though being late for the party was factored in advance.

Five of his six shooters, he found, were moving so fast and gathering yet more steam, it was all Braxton could manage to fight down a smile beaming with pride. By God, they practically soared into the belly of *Pterodactyl* like they were carried on the wings of angels.

Nothing like obedience.

It was a damn fine virtue for any man, soldier or otherwise, to acquire and claim, once, that was, it was disciplined into his spirit, but he was old-school dinosaur, and nothing less than iron men need sign on for his ship of wood.

Away with all that ease and pleasure seeking and chasing of money just to maintain personal comfort zones. Away with all that excessive eating and drinking and piling on an extra five thousand calories before the bloated carcass of the average citizen flopped to sleep at night. Away with the cell phones, the e-mails, all the mindless distractions the average John or Jane Doe didn't have any use for other than to slander and gossip and blather out the idle chatter. Away with…

Braxton caught himself, realized he was getting whipped up into a frenzy but good, and before the real heat was even scorching their way. But, for damn sure, he and his people knew a lot about mortified flesh, sacrifice, duty, honor.

Obedience fashioned in the image of strength and courage.

As had the majority of the others in the Defenders of the National Security Military Intelligence they had pulled some stunts in Iraq—pre- and post-Gulf II—that would have really given the soft libertine civilian crybabies something to rail about.

Virtue.

He, like the others, had earned it, and the right to call the shots as they saw fit. Without them, there were at least five major American cities that would have erupted in anarchy and bloodshed, and would have quite possibly been X-ed off the map. One tactical nuke of Hiroshima-wallop, ten tons of plastic explosive and a matching amount of ammonium nitrate and two U-Hauls stuffed, floor-to-ceiling, with radiological material so toxic he had to imagine the very stench of Hell would have been easier to breathe, had been captured, thanks to their noble and hidden efforts.

Gergen barely broke stride as Braxton accepted the small black box.

Just about showtime, he thought, and bounded up into the fuselage. *Pterodactyl* was configured somewhat similar to the Apache, only larger, with a fuselage that had room to spare for ten troops, space enough designed to house gear, ammo crates, sat links for two full squads. The politicians back east, and who signed off on blank checks for black projects couldn't possibly know it, but they were indirectly responsible for what would prove...

Later, he told himself, all in due course.

"Go!" Braxton shouted at the two-man flight crew.

He depressed the smaller of the two buttons, activated the red light. They were lifting off, Braxton easing toward the doorway, when he gave the small compound a grinning farewell. Three Black Hawks were parked near the steel rectangular walls of what was nearly a duplicate of the Idaho complex. They were sanitizing as they went along, no question about it, but that was how the game was intended to play out from day one. Loose lips had ceased flapping for good just across the border, but that was only part of the program. And since this was his show, start to finish out here in militant country, with the Sunshine State...

Two hundred yards out and sailing, Braxton figured clearance enough, as the *Pterodactyl* soared, up and over the tree line, straightened out and began its short run to the south. He hit the larger button. A millisecond later, he wasn't disappointed in the least, as the compound and Black Hawks were lost inside a mammoth fireball he figured gave new meaning to Big Bang.

How Bolan originally missed it all was not beyond him. Between dodging bullets, waxing SOR scum and improvising the flimsiest of strategies on the hit and run, in short, trying and barely avoiding getting diced to shreds or blown out of his boots...

There were two main and very fat exhaust chutes running along the bottom of the killing behemoth. Countless spent casings were being spit from holes that likewise were engineered to pump out all the smoky fumes of cordite, with the same design on what was now the far—port—side. Conclusion number one was the Gatlings were spitting out a mix of armor-piercing and high-explosive incendiary rounds, judging the manner by which nearly every other vehicle in the convoy was now wrapped in the slick fire of white phosphorus, touched off on impact as those big projectiles tore through vehicles as if they were nothing more than wet paper. With tanks detonating, here and there, to spew yet more potentially lethal shrapnel, Bolan glimpsed armor-plated doors with gaping fist-size holes punched through them, fat reinforced glass sheets that had all but been obliterated draped over the front ends of numerous wrecks. Final conclusion was that between the murderous technology he was facing, the way in which the convoy had been demolished so quick and so thorough, and with what he strongly suspected was a cache of WMD waiting at the deep rear end...

It was a huge red flag, to state the glaring obvious, and it signaled the soldier this was a lot more sophisticated operation, beyond the scope and means of a bunch of armed riff-raff with huge chips on their shoulders. This was an inside job, but he had feared as much since bagging Kramer.

As he navigated through the crackling fangs of two more torched GMCs, the Executioner scanned the slaughter field—autofire and angry shouts ringing in his ears from some point to his rear and roughly five o'clock—then drew a bead on the war bus. After turning his band of SOR marauders into shredded slabs of prime rib, how well he'd scored with two quick follow-up payloads of buckshot was debatable. But there was blood streaming down beneath the T-slot where he'd knocked out the auto-cannon shooter. The Gatling gunner on the roof was also silenced, the shell around him sporting crimson evidence he was out of play. With what sounded like piercing screams of men writhing in some serious agony inside those rolling black walls, the soldier decided to compound their misery. He was lining up another buckshot round in the hopes shrapnel would cripple the big gun closest to him, as it blew its load up in a heated whirlwind of devastating steel bits, when he was forced to turn angry sights elsewhere.

Three SOR goons came running from the general direction where Bolan reckoned they had finished their business with what he suspected was a dead ex-cop, another hardforce of four in Stetson hats and fur and sheepskin bolting to help their comrades secure the cargo. With the bus rumbling away and gathering steam, its guns quiet for the moment, the Executioner began taking care of Kramer's unfinished business. One of the threesome yelped a warning to the others, their assault rifles up and swinging toward the threat, but the soldier nailed them with a sweeping wall of 5.56 mm tumblers that bowled them, down and out, a few wild enemy rounds streaking off for big blue sky.

The Stony Man warrior veered for cover behind the front end of the first troop carrier. There was no time to get a second wind, but the soldier stole a few moments to make a decision, assess standing numbers. At quick search, it looked as if he wouldn't have to worry about getting cut down by whomever the dead he had hoped to help. There were two, maybe three pitiful moans filtering through the hungry crackle of flames, and Bolan offered up silent hope the good guys held on somehow. He admitted his intention to find them breathing—later, he hoped—wasn't altogether altruistic. The soldier needed intel, names, facts and other details.

Bolan cursed.

The first two black cruisers, lights flashing, were churned to flying trash as the big war bus turned its guns back on. What he believed were four more Montana State Police vehicles came barreling over the rise next, and charging straight for what would be the next tempest of decimating hell.

MARK DROBBLER WAS sure he was going to puke. Nobody had mentioned anything about killing cops, but that only scratched the surface of his shock and horror. Beyond that, the total assault on his senses seemed like an endless beating by invisible hammers.

Through the three-by-two-foot porthole he saw two cruisers obliterated to flaming meteors. At less than thirty yards out and to his one o'clock and rolling, some of that debris came shooting in his direction. They were giant saw-tooth flying disks, slashing off the plated window with such force the wheel was nearly ripped out his hands.

It was more than he could take. Panic was fast setting in like drying concrete, the cloud of sickness roiling into brain. He eased off the gas, tapped the brake.

Now they were cop killers!

Drobbler gagged, as the hot bile lanced up his chest, squeezed into the back of his throat with its first greasy wave of worms. "Oh, God," he heard some voice cry out with sudden savage desperation from the deepest darkest cavern of his mind, "Save me!"

Despite the heavily padded mufflers over his ears, which doubled as a com link, the fans meant to pump out the noxious stink, all the unholy racket of cannons thundering off round after round, with the Gatling guns like a thousand chain saws ripped loose at once, and with fat floating bands of smoke seeping into his armored box his senses were beyond stretched to their nauseating limits.

The vomit gushed forth, spattering the wheel and instrument panel in a torrent that for him to simply view spilled another dam burst.

Whatever he was going to do, as he shouldered through the steel door and reeled onto the platform, he had nary a clue.

"What the hell are you doing? Get back behind that wheel!"

It took a full second, maybe more for the horror of what stretched in front of him to sink in. Whatever projectiles that had, moments ago, hit Attila, Drobbler choked on more bile as he tried to assess the gruesome results, peering, shocked, through cordite. Three bodies, stretched out on the floor, looked to be chewed and spit hamburger, facial skin sheared to the bone, blood streaming from where eyeballs had been torn out of the skull, and this when their eyes had been protected by goggles. There was another victim, thrashing and moaning all over the floorboard near the black box that pumped out the EMP screen, leaking blood from so many raw open wounds.

The so-called gunnery sergeant, Morton, was sweeping out of the drifting smoke, his eyes bugged with rage and terror behind the goggles, mouth working in a gathering frenzy as he screamed into his throat mike.

"I heard you."

"So, get back behind the wheel."

Drobbler read the threat, loud and clear, as Morton shifted the aim on his Colt Commando, a few inches from drawing a bead on his chest.

"You know the way to the evac site! So get on it!"

"Those are cops out there, Morton!"

"So?"

It suddenly occurred to Drobbler he'd left his own assault rifle by the seat, but Morton hadn't overlooked it, as he brushed past and claimed the weapon.

"If you don't wish to drive, Drobbler, I can…"

"Get out of my way," Drobbler snarled.

He shouldered past the maniac.

"You gonna drive us there, or do I have to baby-sit?"

"Go back to your post," Drobbler growled, and dropped into his seat. He hit the gas, and found he was just in time to watch another state police vehicle torn asunder by what he knew was a 40 mm HE projectile, while a tempest of 30 mm armor-piercing rounds ate up earth and asphalt around the remaining cruisers in a frenzied search for more law enforcement blood.

THE EXECUTIONER TURNED his M-16 on three more SOR killers, the trio caught out in the open, between the rear edge of an armored car and their own SUV, but providing Bolan with a static shooting gallery. Pounding out a dozen or so rounds from his assault rifle, he nailed them, left to right, a stitching evisceration that sent them flailing back, slamming off their vehicle as blood and gore splashed their ride with a sloppy paint job.

More shooters out of play, but the soldier suspected the grim task was about to become even more difficult, if not one colossal long shot by which to mop up the new arrivals and seize whatever the cargo.

It did.

He couldn't see the action on the other side of the armored car, but he knew what was taking place. From his questionable cover and firepoint behind a Humvee, blood and smoke cloying his nose and tearing his eyes, the black oversized version of the Apache looked to the warrior like no less than a flying battleship. He could see the rotors spinning beyond the armored rig, make out what sounded like orders being bellowed for the marauders to hustle up.

Return autofire began searching out the soldier, as three, then four SOR goons staged what he intended to be their last-ditch stand behind a Ford Explorer. Invisible rounds slicing the smoke above his head, Bolan went low to the edge of the Humvee, flung himself around the corner and chugged out a 40 mm HE round. The projectile turned the Explorer into a mangled hearse, the fireball engulfing the SOR foursome, launching them their separate ways.

Two more snarling SOR hardmen were rolling around the edge of the armored rig as the gunship lifted off, their assault rifles chattering. They were cannon fodder, being used by what the Executioner could well reason was a treasonous brood of intelligence vipers inside the big Apache knock-off to cover their quick flight out of there. Now that they had what they wanted...

Feeding a fresh magazine to his M-16, the soldier was forced to hit the deck as two HK submachine guns opened up from the hatchway, the shadowy forms of men in black opting to cover their own asses as they dropped a wave of 9 mm rounds over the soldier's position. They were sailing on, but still throwing back double withering walls that spanged metal, whined off

asphalt, inches from Bolan's face, but with the immediate threat rolling straight his way, the Executioner
concentrated on the greater of two grim dilemmas.
Leaping to his feet, the warrior darted to his left, away
from the tracking lines of autofire, and shot from the
hip. He felt the hot slipstream of two or three near
misses across the back of his neck, but the SOR duo was
in electrified jig-step next as the Executioner rang them
up with a zipping line of 5.56 mm tumblers across their
chests.

Two more were on their way to face judgment, but
the soldier heard he wasn't quite done with the murderous rabble.

Bolan vectored toward moaning that reached out
from the east side of the trio of SOR SUVs, scouring
the compass with assault rifle and hooded gaze, undecided whether that was the sound of physical torment,
or what the hell. The gunship was nap of the earth, he
found, southbound and holding on a dead run, straight
for two cruisers that had parked, or were immobilized,
he couldn't quite tell. The war bus, however, was topping the rise, vanishing down the far side. For now they
were leaving behind a savage legacy, but the Executioner had every intention of making the cannibals, both
on-board and otherwise, pay the ultimate price in the
here and now.

The Stony Man warrior found the source of grief.
At first, he thought the guy was injured, on his knees,
nursing some grievous wound. Bolan gave him a quick
once-over, found nothing but a few streaks of blood

running down his face from flying glass, then discovered all that bewailing was over none other than a few bullet holes drilled through his Stetson hat. As Bolan couldn't decide what made him angrier—all this senseless loss of life doled out by traitors on the homefront or this reprobate damn near weeping over some cherished worldly possession—the SOR creep became aware of Death marching toward him. Too late, he was sweeping in the assault rifle when the Executioner hit him with a rising burst up the side, flung him to earth, where he sprawled, flat out, across the source of his misery.

CHAPTER TEN

"And you're just telling me all this now why?"

Braxton spun away from Groggins before his spotter could sputter out some feeble excuse as to why he'd neglected to inform of a wild card who sounded like a one-man barbarian horde storming the gates. Supposedly this one big guy in black and weighted down in full combat harness and vest regalia had been kicking some major SOR ass, and right up until the very second they had Golden Boy retrieved, secured and flying on. Whoever—belay that—whatever he was, Braxton had caught a glimpse of their mystery shooter—or so he believed—when they lifted off, winging back the HK subgun fire at a dark armed figure that had hit the road, dropping out of sight.

Maybe he was alive, or maybe he'd tagged the wild card with a lucky round. Either way, he felt there should be pause for concern, but he had other weighty problems to contend with as he squeezed into the cockpit hatchway. There was a chance, as slim as it was, he considered, someone on the team had gotten cold feet, jumped to the other side of the tracks. Despite all the hue and cry that various intelligence and law-enforcement agencies had to exchange information, work with each other, nothing much had changed since 911. He knew. He worked for the fledgling Department of Homeland Security, which was the only new implement on the war on terror, as far as he knew. And since he was part of National Security Military Intelligence that operated on covert grounds, within and outside the DHS, there was very little that went on under the intelligence roof and across the alphabet soup board he wasn't privy to. However, the wild card could simply be some young Army hotshot who had stowed his own gear—against regulations, that was—and who actually believed he was some Hollywood incarnation of a one-man army. Still, be all that as it may, Braxton admitted he was a little unsettled with this last-minute encounter with a guy who, from what little he saw, knew how to shake and bake, supposedly responsible for racking up a double-digit body count. SOR scum or not, that still took a big brass pair. And the owner of just such a package of steel would be backed by three very important criteria. Experience, martial skill and officialdom, be it U.S. military or intelligence.

They were soaring, maybe thirty yards above the highway of death when Braxton spotted the two state troopers, their vehicles stalled or parked, in the rapidly depleting distance. It didn't matter, since they had to go. Smoke, he spotted, was curling from both mangled hoods, tires flattened out all around. One uniform was shouldering his way through the door, the other trooper looking to be digging for something along the dashboard.

"Take out those smokeys," he ordered his two-man flight crew, fighting to shake out of his thoughts the mystery shooter they were putting behind. They nodded, busy the next second lining the targets up in their HUDs, roughly one hundred yards out and closing. The 30 mm Chain Gun in the nose turret thundered and made quick work of man and machine. Braxton watched the storm of Armor Piercing Incendiary Rounds—API—shred the cruisers in a fiery gale of glass, metal and what he barely discerned as crimson mist detailing whatever was left of the two last state troopers. He searched the grassland, the road leading out to 83, but there was no sign of Attila.

Make that "his" Attila.

No sweat. Where there was a problem, he always had a ready solution.

Besides, he'd never planned to let the Department of Homeland Security get it back in one piece anyway.

"Okay, gentlemen, listen up," Braxton told his pilots. "Your next orders are as follows…"

WHEN NATIONAL SECURITY Military Intelligence Commander of United States Southern Borders for the Department of Homeland Security Thomas Overstreet heard the news, he looked at his watch, and hit the stop button on the side: 20:53:12 EST.

His heart did a short flutter next, as he saw the black-and-gold tarp draped over the last of the four black-as-coal beasts of burden. Gold Charter Tours smoothed out down the fronts and sides as the crews quickly fastened the straps to the coverings at both ends, underneath the chassis, then two eight-man teams with nylon bags in tow began boarding the first two behemoths. The ruse would not pass close inspection, say, if a state trooper pulled them over, he knew, but in that unlikely event…

"Sir? How do you propose to handle the situation?"

The satellite phone with secured frequency gripped tight to his ear, Overstreet strode toward the steel door, threw a finger at Chalmers to hit the button and bring it up. Big diesel engines growling to life, he kept Miami hanging for several stretched seconds, weighing the crisis on the other end. He told Miami to reset his watch to the new countdown, but freeze it. As the door rolled up, the "Chief" of Manexx PetroChem Security strode for the opening, adjusting his shades to the harsh glare of sunlight that danced off this stretch of the fifty-mile Ship Channel. He took his first whiff of the late-morning air, which always smelled to him like bathroom cleaner, running down logistics against what he considered a minor setback.

Two Sons of Revelations trash, it seemed, had been picked up for drunk and disorderly in a strip joint in Dade County. He turned to watch Godzilla and Kong rumble past before they swung to the left on their pri-

vate dock marked Pier 100, which was officially declared off-limits as it was property of the United States
government. It would be a few long minutes before
those wheelmen even got them out of the Pasadena-
Baytown Industrial Corridor, the petrochemical wasteland that went a long way to making Houston the new
boomtown of the twenty-first century. Once they hit the
interstate, the traffic of the largest city in Texas would
prove worse than the L.A. freeways. But if they stuck
to the timetable, and what with all potential traffic snarls
factored in—short of a fifty car pile-up and a tanker
trailer with toxic waste spilled all over the highway—
they would be in the Sunshine State just before midnight. As soon as Kong rolled out of sight down the pier,
Chalmers brought the door down.

"Sir? We cannot leave them…"

"I'm way ahead of you," Overstreet told Miami.

Anticipating trouble, he knew, and dealing with it,
were two different creatures, but both had to coexist,
complement the other, in truth, or neither was of any
use. The former required a near psychic ability, and that
rivaled Biblical prophets, whereas the latter needed no
more than the sufficient backbone and savvy of the seasoned professional. It was wise, but only up to a point,
to calculate and ponder all potential crisis points before
any operation was launched. This outing was no different—on the surface, at least—but the one plus, that fat
shining golden star when intelligence operatives went for
themselves was that they knew how to cover their tracks,
nail down all contingencies, improvise as they went

along. Beyond the handpicked teams of former U.S. servicemen and their own covert group, beyond the recruiting and infiltration of foreign enemies to the very government he had sworn an oath to protect and defend...

What was done was done, but he was still a long way off from sitting in the driver's seat himself.

Fortunately, Overstreet had the good foresight to deal with the present Miami crisis. Foresight, by and large, involved reading people. That in mind, he knew the SOR rabble were little more than backwoods morons, angry loners, down on their luck, stuck in life in all respects, with a few cops who had flopped off the force or just plain burned out. By all accounts and prior indications by way of his background checks, the usual demise and tainted shields were the result of incorrigible vices. With a few decent dollars in their pockets, it stood to reason a titty bar would have grabbed their attention as soon as they were allowed to leave their motel rooms to sightsee a big city infamous for its nonstop debauchery.

"Send two of your people. Use the full backing of your authority, but get them released on bail without delay. Inform the magistrate in question they are undercover narcotics agents—whatever it takes to get them free. I will assume you understand how to proceed beyond that?"

"Their employment is terminated."

"You would be correct," Overstreet agreed. "There is an alligator farm just a few miles down Tamiami, past..."

"I know where it is. And our own schedule, sir?"

"Check back in thirty minutes. Depending on your progress report, I will let you know something. Oh. I hope I needn't remind you to not disappoint me."

Overstreet severed the connection just as Miami began to copy the order. He took a few steps across the concrete floor then looked around the massive warehouse. What was this? he wondered. No call for nostalgia here, his teams were busy sanitizing the entire complex, but he couldn't help think about the labor of love he had been overseeing for the DHS, going on two years now. Laser machinery and computerized meters used to fine tune and calibrate weapons not even the U.S. Military had at its disposal were being lowered by crane into the giant steel tank, steam now rising from the surface as the sulfuric acid began to eat up the last of the loads. Satchels stuffed with laptops and shredded documents would go next, then the warehouse would be mined, top to bottom with incendiary explosives that would turn the entire building into a giant torch he figured they could see from one end to the other of the Ship Channel. That alone would create a citywide panic, as every fire and police department would be tied up racing onto a vast industrial preserve, so choked with any number of volatile chemicals, any of which were so toxic...

He stopped the smile from breaking over his lips just as it began to stretch the corners of his mouth. This was no time to start a victory dance.

He laid a lingering gaze on Black Rhino, then Mastodon. Now a brief stab of angst was almost called for, he decided. It was a damn shame, he thought, so much money, time and effort had gone into creating those high-tech war buses. There were blank checks from Congress, for starters, then those A-list weapons engineers from Lockheed Martin, Martin Marietta, and GE, with aerospace and computer geniuses shipped here from NASA to help design from the ground up what were meant to be the prototype urban combat vehicle. In the event martial law was declared, the war buses had enough firepower on hand to turn more than a few city blocks under siege in America into smoking heaps of rubble. And decorated, on top, with a five-figure body count, when he factored in the big guns onboard, the number of rounds. Beyond its capacity to deliver Hell on Earth there was surveillance and countersurveillance equipment, radar jamming complete with EMP suitcases...

Briefly it galled him when he considered whose hands America's future in urban guerrilla warfare was, more or less, falling into.

How had this all come to pass? Beyond a bad marriage, he wanted to reflect on that some, but there was last-minute business to shore up. Suffice it to say he was sick and tired. The first Gulf War had been an indicator the world was fast being pushed to the brink of Armageddon, given what he knew Arab factions were maybe six months away from having at their disposal. Try telling the American public at large, though, that Israel was still in the WMD crosshairs of at least three more rogue or militant Arab states, that it was simply not a question of "if," but "when" the Middle East went up in a nuclear glow, and as the Mid-east went...

Well, the longer he was around, the more hopeless he began to see his own station in life. Even though he was one of the most powerful intelligence operatives in the land, these days he saw himself as no more than some hapless servant standing off by himself on the *Titanic,* a coffee cup to bail the water while the rich and powerful slashed their elbows through all the little people to be the first ones into the lifeboats. Yes, oh, yes, he knew there were plenty of cynics always hovering about, snickering and jeering how he was simply envious for never earning—or grabbing—his slice of the juicy pie called the good life. Be that as it may—and it wasn't, not by a bloody long shot—given what he knew about the present and projected state of affairs, both national and global, he gave it about another ten years, maybe less, before the End of Days hit Humankind with a thundering right cross.

And what he knew about the coming Apocalypse, was, for the most part, this—it would be orchestrated by the rich and the powerful, seeking to save themselves at the expense of the mass of suffering humanity. Yes, oh, yes, he knew all too frightening and all too despicable well how they denied such a heartless cataclysmic scenario. They always did—he had seen it with his own eyes, heard it with his own ears—while they were planning their next corporate takeover, or which dictator, in power or deposed, would fatten their personal coffers so said tyrant could keep butchering and oppressing and selling weapons of mass destruction while their stock portfolios and numbered accounts reached to the skies.

Oh, but the insufferable madness.

Now it was his turn.

Now it was his time to shine, to bail, to fling back a middle finger salute.

And he knew precisely who "they" were.

Best of all, he had the keys to their kingdom, poised and ready to be seized. All of this, and yet another reason to go for number one, albeit ranked third on the priority list of the operation. The others on the team may refer to it as blackmail leverage, but as far as he was concerned being armed with the truth of the ages might well at some point save his bacon. Especially when he considered…

The crane dumped all pertinent intelligence gathered in those black bags. He looked away from the big vat, began striding for his office to wrap it up. Yes, indeed, he was looking forward to the future, but knew there were many miles yet to travel before he could start enjoying retirement.

Countdown to the future was temporarily on hold, but Overstreet had little doubt the doomsday clock would start ticking once again. And as for failure? It was most certainly and always a ready option, but if it looked that, by chance, the end had come, he was ready to pull the plug. Yes, sir, make no mistake.

It would begin with America.

And with the terrible power he would soon wield it would not be a stretch to wipe out more than six billion souls. If it looked he wasn't meant to live the way he envisioned, then he would take the entire planet along with him into oblivion.

Thomas Overstreet could emphatically state that he had never been accused of being a people-lover. But with the knowledge he had, how he knew the future of the world was being shaped and guided by the vile worms, the slimy maggots and the howling hyenas, he damn well figured he had earned the chip on his shoulder.

And he dared the first SOB who thought he had stones big enough to come along and knock it off.

CHAPTER ELEVEN

Mark Drobbler saw it, and couldn't hold down the brief fit of cackling. He knew gambling had been legalized all across the state, no longer confined to the Flathead, Crow and Blackfoot reservations. The mammoth neon sign, all three stories of it, confirmed Montana had come a long ways from gold to now casino fever. Whether it was a tear brought on by panic, anguish or pure insanity, he couldn't say, but it was rolling off his chin, eyes watering up but good and obscuring some the thirty-foot grinning Indian with raised tomahawk and flowing headdress. It was a twenty-four-hour joint, as he recalled, Crazy Horse Hotel and Casino flashing, loud and proud, maybe a quarter mile and rising fast beyond the porthole. Hotel was somewhat misleading, he thought, since most of the rooms were low staggered blocks done in pink and blue pastel, ranged out back of the main casino, giving the impression it was more of a trailer park.

Caesar's Palace it wasn't.

As he stuck to prior directions and swung hard off Highway 83 to a fresh round of cursing, he couldn't tear his gaze, for some reason, off the gleaming stadium-shaped complex. It was brand-spanking-new, and he'd only ever been inside the casino once, but recalled how it was so huge he figured it could probably squeeze in the whole population of Montana. What he really remembered were all the young waitresses in their little cowgirl outfits and boots, those All-U-Can-Eat buffets for less than ten bucks a pop, the glittering sports bars around the compass with all the latest lines and sports books tied in to Vegas and Reno, often drawing a few big spenders and pro athletes from back east as far as New York. Oh, but they were hopping inside, he could well imagine, all the keno, bingo, poker and slots, tourists and locals...

He found himself wishing—no, saw himself inside the Crazy Horse, a stiff drink in hand, trolling the gaming pits, cowgirl on each arm. Actually, he wanted to be anywhere but where he was.

He wanted to be saved from this madness, yanked from what he knew was for all of them minutes, if not less, from being plunged into the bowels of Hell.

Now that one of them was screaming about an attack helicopter coming in from the north...

He hit Little Big Man Avenue at about 50 mph. The only street, wide and freshly paved, it bisected two rows of glass-and-stone shops and eateries. It was all becoming a blur, as he tried but failed to deafen his ears to the shouts of men in great pain and rage, Morton and his pack of killers cursing everything under the sun, it sounded. He pushed a button on the panel, hackles rising on the back of his neck as he suspected all the fuss was about something real serious. The steel plate lowered, as he found trembling hands were suddenly wrestling with the wheel, and he had to concentrate to keep the rig online and rumbling in the direction of Little Big Man airfield.

He was turning to have a look over the rooftops and the wooded hills beyond, then heard the thunder of the rooftop Gatling. A fresh wave of panic and nausea was rising, as Drobbler wondered why they were shooting at what he gathered had to be their spook gunship when he spotted the winged behemoth.

Drobbler bellowed out a curse as the missile streaked away from the starboard pylon, locked on and hurtled straight for them.

In a blind panic, he stomped the gas, threw the wheel hard to the right, the thought occurring to him that was a stupid move.

Their screams were swallowed up by the blast, just as his eyes filled with bared white teeth. Whatever the missile, it seemed to lift the war bus, even as he would have sworn the seismic shock waves were confined to the roof. The whole rig was propelled forward as if shot out of a howitzer.

And Drobbler joined the chorus of shouts and vicious swearing, felt his eyeballs bugged to their limits. The rig shuddered like some gored and heaving beast

before the wheel wrenched out of his hands, then Attila was shooting on like the wounded rhino. A split second later, he plowed through the grinning Indian, an
avalanche of glass descending, steel support pipes
thundering off the window then screeching their metallic havoc down the hull and roof. It sounded to Drobbler like an entire mountain was crashing off the rig, as
he glimpsed any number of figures blurring out of his
way. A heartbeat later he bulldozed through the lobby
doors, spewing out another glass and metal volcano but
with meteors of concrete rubble now shot out from
walled facade above. Yet more human pinballs darted
every which way across the foyer, then he was blasting
on through the first banks of slot machines, and screaming out for God to save him.

EVIL CREATED WHAT Bolan liked to call the ripple effect.
Whether or not Man was born inherently good was
open to debate, and it was a question the soldier knew
was best left to a power far greater than he to give the
final answer. But, over the course of his War Everlasting, evil, was, in fact, what he fought, day after day,
campaign after campaign. Sometimes, it seemed, the
good fight was barely enough just to stem the ever-
growing tide of madness and savagery, the dark forces
barely kept in check from spreading their poison where
it would slay the innocent, ruin futures, crush hope and,
sadly, infect any number of those who straddled the
fence and became easy prey to greed, lust, anger.
Whether evil was a sleeping or roaring lion on the prowl

searching for victims, once it struck it had an insidious power to multiply its ravages with very little effort. For some reason, the late Mitch Kramer wanted to flare to mind, what with the ex-cop's apparent quest for redemption and salvation, as Bolan's memory traveled back through the years, and he searched for his own answers to the ages old question of evil.

The more grievous and obvious transgressions— murder, rape and robbery—were clear as to their cause and effect. Generally speaking, crimes of malice, though, involved more than one victim, since the psychological trauma and emotional scarring reached out to shatter more hearts and lives than the one murdered, raped or stolen from. Next came the vices, and Bolan could be pretty sure no man below the divine rank of saints and angels was exempt from this realm of succumbing to the flesh. These were the subtle but no less insidious and havoc-wreaking transgressions, which, at first, usually seemed harmless enough, pleasure indulged and such, until...

And thus his beginning of his War Everlasting, what seemed a thousand lifetimes ago, where he was a young Green Beret, coming home to bury his murdered family. Evil, that was due, in no small part, to his father's outstanding gambling debts to the local Mafia, where the father had put the daughter—Bolan's sister—into the hands of the flesh-peddlers to work off the stain of which he had created in the first place, until his father had snapped—

Bolan was jolted back into the present as the war bus

exploded deeper into the casino, vanishing altogether when he straightened out to give the chase its final leg. Having commandeered the weeping cowboy's SUV, the soldier had done a quick mental review of the immediate towns, airfields and so forth. Logic dictated a far graver agenda waited in the wings, and with the murders of intelligence ops and state troopers on their hands, the warrior figured the surviving enemy force would flee, the hyenas gone into hiding now that the lion was awake and angry. The flying battleship, he glimpsed, was already sailing on, in the general direction of Little Big Man airfield. Whoever they were, they were responsible for assisting the war bus on its rampaging course into the casino, after a direct hit had blown the Gatling gunner off the roof.

Which had indirectly helped the soldier cut the gap without having to worry about getting blown off the road. That he had made it this far with little more than superficial wounds, the worst of which would require stitching, various nicks, gouges and scrapes from passing lead and flying shrapnel, with face and neck scorched raw from fire and eyes singed from smoke.

Too soon to count any blessings. The Executioner turned grim deathsights on the pandemonium in front of him. He eased off the gas, dropping the needle to 20 mph, as wheels crunched over glass and metal and he banged through hanging shards and strips. The way ahead was clear of noncombatants as the war bus began slowing but bulled on through slots, tables, roulette wheels, players, stragglers and pit bosses and what looked like brown-shirted security men scattering pell-mell all over the floor, shouting and flailing about in a well-understood panic. The behemoth demolished a clone of the smiling Indian statue gone to memory out front, but once again bringing down headdress and tomahawk, the whole works in a flying wave of glass and twisted metal. Tempests of debris swirled the air in its wake before the runaway bus slashed off a massive glass pillar, tore through a section of upraised cocktail tables, then flipped down on its portside on a thud that was off the Richter Scale as the soldier felt the seismic waves ripple through his bones.

The Executioner hit the brakes, took up his M-16, barged out the door to a din of terror, as the stampede began in earnest in several directions. He found himself situated in the flotsam of slot machines, some of which were shooting out sparks, with paper and glass storms swirling in all directions, coins still showering to the carpet. He had to move quick, he knew, the bogus Justice Department credentials ready to flash, but he wasn't counting on the security force to pause long enough to hear the voice of authority.

Advancing on the war bus, he scanned the immediate perimeter, found heads shuddering into view, here and there, with patrons, for the most part, charging en masse for the exits. Somewhere outside all the shouts and screams he made out the rapidly closing sirens.

Bolan was fifteen or so yards out, when the first two SOR goons poked heads and assault rifles through the crumpled door, slithered up and over the edge like the murderous snakes they were. No sooner had their feet touched down on polished marble, the Executioner blew them away with a rattling burst of autofire.

THE FIRST THING Drobbler tasted was his own vomit and the blood streaming down into his mouth from any number of gashes across his forehead and eyes as he clawed his way back into reality. The first thing he heard was what sounded like a howitzer, just beyond the smashed-in door that seemed a mile above and away in his slanted sweat-and-blood-hazy world. It sounded like the thunder of doom, that trumpet blast of Judgment Day calling the living and the dead that Grant was always going on about.

Drobbler caught an armed figure jumping off the side of his armored shell, grabbing the edge of the bottom step where the doorway had been turned into a mangled skylight of sorts. The raccoon-skin hat told him that would be Jimmy Boogler, scrambling his skinny butt to haul it out of there.

Which brought Drobbler to full fearful reality.

The rig had been dumped on its side, and the others were bailing, not so much as bothering to check whether he was still breathing.

That awful pealing thunder rang out again, followed by shouts and curses and short stutters of weapons fire that seemed to go silent, one by one. His people, he was sure, shooting it out with someone who sounded likewise armed and dangerous but most likely more than pissed and with a head full of vengeful steam. Casino security? Or was it a small and now very enraged army of state police? Both? And were they backed up by county cops? The FBI maybe, flying onto the scene, when he considered recent events?

He wasn't sure how much he cared to find out, but he couldn't stay here, burrowed, riding it out like some frightened rat backed into a corner, waiting for doom to find him, cowering and pleading for mercy it was a safe bet he wouldn't see in this life or the next.

Dilemma, no question about it. The alternative didn't look much better, either, since it sounded as if he would be walking straight out into the Alamo, if he judged the racket of weapons fire, the cursing and screaming and hideous grunts of pain that struck him like the noise of the walking damned getting checked off Planet Earth and thrown back to Hell. It sounded like one gun, a big weapon, at that, but...

One guy? Come on now.

How long had he been out of it? Could he even trust his senses?

He found his assault rifle resting against the side of his head, grabbed and checked it, groaning against waves of white-hot agony in the process. Full clip, then he locked and loaded. But for what? Suddenly, after bringing down half the casino then crashing and burning, he wondered how much worse it could possibly get. Or, the very fact he was still breathing, despite feeling as if he'd been pummeled with tire irons by some angry loan sharks—was this, though, a sign he was meant to make it? He recalled...

Grasping the edge of the armor-plated doorway, he heaved himself up, swung around in a sort of climbing-roll, then flopped on his back. His ragged breathing seemed flung back in his face as he recognized voices of his comrades somewhere out there on the casino floor. One familiar voice was cursing—or calling to someone else.

That damn cannon exploded again, silenced the voice he believed belonged to Boogler. And left him wondering just how many shooters they were facing. Did he ditch the weapon? Go out with his hands up? After all, it was the others who had blown away those troopers. He was just their wheelman, a dupe, a pawn, never knew the first thing about any raid on a military convoy carrying a biological weapon. What's that, sir? They were United States Army Biological Weapons Specialists? That would be news to me. Feel free, sir, to run a paraffin test, never fired the first shot in anger.

Sure, that might work, the innocent lamb routine, led into something he discovered too late was way over his head, but they threatened to kill him if he didn't drive, truth be told, they kept a gun to his head the whole time he was behind the wheel. At least it sounded plausible, and being that he was a former employee of the United States government it wasn't a stretch to coat his story with another layer of truth mixed with half-truths. That, of course, was assuming he didn't get cut down before he could start squawking his innocence.

He flinched at the sound of another wave of rolling thunder.

So much for a second wind.

Drobbler reached up and grabbed the edge of the bottom of the doorway, groaning as he heaved himself up, setting a boot down on a step, getting his balance. There was shouting, more sounds of panic, but fading. Other than that, the shooting had stopped. He didn't like it, almost dropped back to his shell.

He looked over the edge, staring out at the floor of what looked to be one of the sports bars. Tables were smashed, mirrors on pillars either cracked or shattered to expose naked mahogany.

Then, as he hauled himself up, swung a leg over the edge, he saw the bodies, and froze. They were strewed all over the floor like broken mannequins, but two or three still twitching out in spreading pools of crimson. Those were his guys, no question, as he noted a few familiar faces contorted in death masks, eyes bugged out into oblivion. There were big bloody holes punched between the shoulder blades, exit wounds from what he was sure was produced by that howitzer he'd heard. Suddenly a hand shot up from below. Too late, he realized his assault rifle was hanging down, giving the big guy below all the leverage he needed. The startled cry of terror went with him as he was yanked off the edge, falling hard and fast. He was no sooner flat on his back, sucking wind, than he found himself staring up into a pair of blue eyes that looked carved from glacier ice.

It was the stainless-steel handheld howitzer he discovered aimed, rock-steady and right between his eyes that forced out his next words. "Can we talk about this?"

CHAPTER TWELVE

"I tell you what. The next time I hear some pampered, self-indulgent, spoiled Hollywood sack of shit raving to the camera while he sits in a South Beach nightclub how South Florida is Paradise on Earth, I'm going to track his sorry ass down and tell him to pack up the wife or the squeeze of the week or both and live for about month or two in Overtown or Opa-Locka or Little Havana. I mean, locked down there, on foot, having to take the bus and just to go the liquor store. No fancy six-figure wheels, no platinum credit cards, no agents who do everything for them. I mean, nothing but having to survive on nothing but whatever they've really got inside, but which is probably nothing to begin with. What do you think about that, Paul? In case you didn't know, those are three of the worst and poorest sections of Miami. Do you need me to embellish that with some social background as to the neighborhoods?"

Radfield stifled the groan. Every few seconds with the guy dragged into an hour or more of Purgatory. Bad enough when the op was silent, no, it was beyond maddening and an outrage he was even here to begin with, Radfield thought, a thousand miles from home, four futures hanging in the balance over what he did or didn't do. Between fear, depression and anger that ebbed and flowed with murderous rage, it was one wave of racking then gnawing black emotion after the other, until he began to wonder how much more he could take before...

Toughen up. Dig a little deeper. It had been the endless day already, and now...

He had flown out of the private Manexx airfield outside Houston, midafternoon in the company jet, accompanied by a trio of goons in shades and black suits and packing heat. Where they'd landed—somewhere east of Miami when he judged all the swampland detailing Glades Country—he wasn't positive. The former Special Forces captain wasn't that familiar with the city beyond its outer suburbs to begin with—not necessarily a plus, since he was head of security–but he knew he had been driven in a limo to a towering new condominium complex, edged up against Biscayne Bay. What he knew, for a fact, was that the lean buzz-cut muscle in black sports shirt and matching pants and wingtips, with the .45 Para-Ordnance semiauto pistol worn openly in shoulder holster wasn't only an opinionated, arrogant SOB, but he was a colossal pain in the ass. At least one, maybe two choice sarcastic replies flared to mind as he glanced over his shoulder at the black op who wanted to be called Mr. Brick, but Radfield figured the whole point to the creep's diatribe was to see him sweat.

Sweat this, he thought as he felt his fist clench tight.

Radfield had grueling cyberwork to do anyway, knew there was no point in stewing over circumstances that were, for the moment, beyond his control. The grim trouble was, the longer he worked on cracking the three access codes they'd given him, not to mention implementing a new series of codes that would bypass the firewalls, allow them free and ready access to the entire building…

The condo's air conditioning kept the living room at icebox temperature, but Radfield felt a bead of sweat break out on his upper lip. He had a nagging suspicion what he was being asked—belay that—ordered to do. Fear wanted to edge toward panic, but he tried not to think about whatever their scheme, if only in the hope of seeing his family again, unharmed, alive. The truth was, the less he actually knew, the greater his chances of being returned to his wife and children in one piece.

Then again…

The safe-condo setup pretty much told Radfield he was mired in a fly-by-night black operation of some type, to be sanitized with little or no fuss when the curtain dropped on their act. The lone leather recliner was perched in the middle of the living room, square in front of the television, and other than the small table on which sat the laptop with its modems and cables, there was no furniture. They had done something to the lighting, so that most of the room was bathed in dark shadows, or maybe the bulbs were painted and meant to cast silhouettes in different directions, something like an occult light show, a séance but in freeze frame. The balcony curtains were drawn, night by now, but Brick hung on to his sunglasses, as if that alone would keep him from being recognized or remembered.

Damn it! Between the guy's running commentary and channel-surfing, the way he sipped his beer and sucked on his cigarette like an alcoholic just released from detox, with all his grunting and groaning noises, the lie he was forced to tell his wife earlier, he was so boxed into a corner he began to suspect he would be gator bait when his task was completed.

Radfield nearly put his fist through the laptop's monitor, but somehow contained himself.

He took a moment to gather his composure, staring at the screen as the software raced through the numbers. The Trans-World Bank of Miami used the standard 128-bit encryption code. Cracking in wasn't the problem, since he had helped install what was called the A Link, which was pretty much the nerve center that allowed entry into all the other electronics and computer hardware. It was the series of codes he was being asked to break and rearrange to suit whatever his captors' purposes that raised the red flag. Eventually, it would be discovered by some cyberwizard at the T-WBM what had happened, which set off another round of alarms in his head. His fingerprints would be all over this piece of cybernetic vandalism.

Instinct warned him that was only the beginning of his woes regarding his chore. The more he thought about the Trans-World Bank, what little he knew about it, any number of dark questions wanted to leap to mind. It was officially listed as, yes, the Trans-World Bank of Miami, but it had been erected right in the heart of downtown, rising, twenty stories over Brickell Avenue, and almost overnight. Rumors were that it was built—like so much of the glitzier prime real estate down here—by drug money.

Which begged a question he was almost afraid to even think. Most of the problem areas that he was to re-code involved doors, elevators, rewiring the works so that an automatic timer kicked in from the bank's central computer, locking every way in, or out, escape specific designated red zones. There was more, and he shuddered just to think about those implications. With the blueprints of the building on the other half of his split screen, the area they were most interested in was the basement, or what his watchdog kept referring to as the vault. The question dangled in the back of his thoughts, but he couldn't ignore it any longer.

Were the lives of his wife and children on the line over a lousy bank heist?

"You know what really bugs me, Paul?"

"Oh, for the love of… What! What really bugs you?"

"Easy there, Captain. I was going to say, the rich and famous, you ever wonder why they always want to make a big production whenever they give to some charity, like this clown here, supposed to be a big action hero, but he's always having these little hissy fits when he goes out in public, getting himself arrested then doing Letterman and Leno and making some further big stink with phony apologies and such. But back to my original thought—why is it they always trot out some flunky mouthpiece to announce the exact dollar figure when they give to some charity? Huh? Like the rest of us peasants are supposed to be awed over what great and wonderful people they are. Compared to what they really make, all their big generosity doesn't even amount to breadcrumbs. What do you think about that, Paul?"

"I think you ought to shut your filthy pie-hole and let me get some work done."

Under the circumstances, Radfield couldn't quite believe he'd said it, edgy, with some threat of violence behind it, but he was glad, nonetheless.

Mr. Brick wasn't. He went utterly still, Radfield wondering if the man had maybe expired on the spot from a few tough words, but that sounded too fantastic and too much to hope for. Radfield began to find the silence unsettling, as he stared at the sunglasses, the face a portrait of stone.

"Shut my filthy pie-hole?"

He said it, soft and quiet, sounding like his feelings were hurt, the lips barely moving. He flung the words back yet again, rising, slow, smooth. And Radfield tensed. He knew a psycho when he saw one.

As the black op strolled off for the kitchen, pausing, repeating the words, sounding as if he was torn somewhere between angry disbelief and grudging admiration, Radfield tried to focus his attention on the monitor. The sound of the refrigerator door opening and closing cracked through the pulsing heartbeats in his ears. For some reason he all of a sudden noticed the digital clock in the upper right hand corner. It read 12:45:23, and was counting backward.

Counting down. T-Minus.

He flinched a little as the op reappeared, muttering back his words for the fourth or fifth time. Radfield tensed, as the SOB smiled and set a bottle of Heineken beer beside the laptop.

"I'll pass. I'm working, remember."

"Humor me."

The eyes may be hidden, but Radfield could see just enough to know the man was contemplating murder. Radfield took a sip of beer. He was thinking along the same lines, but reason warned him that even if he did kill this bastard there were others somewhere in the general vicinity of the city, waiting to know something, one way or the other.

"You ever wonder why the newborn always come into the world, squalling and wailing? Huh?"

His heart was in his ears, a jackhammer, but Radfield forced his best neutral expression and voice. "I don't know, but it sounds like you're going to tell me."

"It's like it's some programmed instinct, like it's God already playing some joke on us, telling us it's all downhill from there. It's like the newborn already knows it's coming out into some awful place, where they really don't want to be, and would prefer, if they could, to crawl right back into the womb, where it's all safe and warm. It's like we know from the second we're born and sound off that first terrible round of bawling something's just not right and that's only going to get more wrong. We know before we even know that there is nothing but pain and misery and hardship and crushed hopes and annihilated dreams, and for any number of years we have nary a clue as to how long all this horror and suffering, but which we know we're going to end up checking out the same way we came in. Naked. Bawling. Terrified. Worse—worse, I daresay, if you are the religious sort, there's the distinct possibility of eternal damnation waiting at the end of all of this joyless march through a valley of tears. What do you think about that, Paul?"

"I think you're a sick man."

The op paused then bobbed his head. "Good for you, that's good, Paul. Remember that."

Radfield felt his heart skip a beat, his arms and legs tensing to spring in one fast lunge for the weapon, as he wrestled with the decision to go for it, take his chances. His captor made the decision for him, turned and silently walked back to his chair and television. But he had lingered just long and close enough, that Radfield's every instinct screamed at him that the man had read his mind, was, in all likelihood, disappointed he hadn't made his move.

Soon, he promised himself, and went back to crunching numbers.

One way or another, the ex-Special Forces captain was near one hundred percent certain his hand would be forced.

If it was the other way around…

And if his present tormentor or anybody else lurking about had a foolish notion that just because he was no longer active duty, that age had set in, that suburban life had watered down the fire of the warrior spirit…

Well, he had no problem proving to them that would be their last error in judgment. Oh, no, they weren't aware of it, not yet.

But they had already committed their first and fatal mistake by threatening the lives of his family.

EVERY CITY THE WORLD OVER had its own unique flavor and style, no question, based in roughly equal parts history, location, modes of commerce, landmarks, government or religious institutions. Whether a city appeared a tropical paradise edged against the ocean, nestled in mountain foothills or sprawled along the industrialized banks of some muddy toxic river, the soldier knew they all shared one common denominator, a cold fact of life that was both inescapable and immutable, and which rendered it all, more or less, a daily struggle for survival of the fittest, the richest, the meanest hearts.

The human factor.

For the Executioner's purposes, though, make that the inhuman factor, and which, on the giving end of things, was his stock-in-trade.

As the soldier stood, harnessed in the doorway of the Black Hawk gunship, an MP-5 subgun slung around his shoulder, he gave the lit-up heart of downtown Miami and its upraised Metromover a first and for the moment final surveillance. By day he knew it all looked pleasant and inviting enough, with Biscayne Bay choked with pleasure boats, the five causeways leading to Miami Beach on the other side where the trendy New Age jetsetters and snowbird tourists flocked to consume the good life. All that may be just fine and dandy to put some sparkle on the sunshine label, but what the travel people most often neglected to mention was that by night downtown Miami was virtually deserted, except, of course, for the criminals and every other kind of predator the city powers did their damnedest to make sure the rest of America believe didn't existed. Take down the palm trees, strip away the beaches, nail the doors shut on all the swank clubs, bulldoze all the condos and high-rises and Miami, as far as he was concerned, was just another big, sprawling urban jungle, where there was gaping, glaring division between the rich and the poor, and where quite often the haves down here were more notorious criminals than the have-nots.

The Stony Man flight crew kept the chopper—on loan from Homestead AFB, thanks to the clout that Hal Brognola wielded—on a steady course, heading north. He wasn't sure what he was looking for, if anything specific, and that only served to further compound Bolan's mounting dark suspicions. Despite the fact that a former high-ranking DOD Storm Tracker had spilled his guts, the hard truth, as it turned out, came up short.

Bolan threw a look over his shoulder. Drobbler was cuffed and sitting against the bulkhead, looking sulky, when the soldier figured the SOR High Son should be grateful just to be breathing. If there was, in fact, some major terror operation about to be sprung on South Florida—and his prisoner had alluded to as much, though he was shy on particulars—then Miami faced the same numerous hazards, hurdles and obstacles every city the nation over had to deal with when it came to defending itself against a well-orchestrated attack by a heavily armed enemy force come to wreak havoc and pile up a body count, the bigger the better. It was humanly impossible to secure every road, waterway, airport, both public and private. In short, it was beyond any amount of manpower to batten down every police precinct, courthouse, government or financial abode. There were train and bus terminals, there was the Port of Miami, there were shopping malls, restaurants, hotels, wherever large and unsuspecting crowds gathered...

In other words, the soldier knew the enemy held the advantage, but only up to a certain point. The problem was, the enemy had the luxury of picking the time, place and manner in which to strike.

The obvious solution, then, was to find and get to the enemy before they struck. To do that, Bolan needed more intelligence, and it looked as if any real gains in that arena would come the hard way.

The soldier turned back to night-gazing the empty city by the water, the gleaming skyscrapers that had been built on top of swampland. For some reason his eye was drawn to the rising black glass-faced tower along Brickell Avenue—Trans-World Bank Miami. Given the few facts the cyberteam at the Farm had so far pieced together from Kramer's marching orders, there were suspicions mounting that the T-WBM was so far beneath board, submerged in a cesspool…

They didn't know exactly what went on behind those walls, other than what appeared a whole lot of offshore transactions, but between Brognola's contacts and the connections of the Farm's mission controller, Barbara Price, to her former employer, the NSA, the buzz was that some blank checks had been cut back in Washington to build the twenty-story building in about the time it took a hurricane to blow through South Florida. And there were hints on the Farm's end the building was some major intelligence warehousing-transshipment staging-finance ground for covert operations, and by which every one of those tags was aptly albeit most suspiciously applied. Which begged two questions in Bolan's mind. What really went on there? And what were they hiding? Some red flag wanted to hoist itself up in his mind's eye, the longer he looked at the Trans-World Bank Miami. There were loose pieces all over the board, wanting to come together, but…

Not enough information.

As the soldier spotted flashing lights of cruisers several hundred feet below, parked or racing around Brickell Avenue and beyond, the last eight to ten hours took on something akin to missing time. Under any other circumstances, Bolan would have considered his quick evacuation from Montana nothing this side of a miracle. But the power Brognola wielded—not to mention he was backed by the Oval Office—had freed Special Agent Cooper from the angry grasp of roughly three full squads of local troopers and cops. What had been close to miraculous was his quick and brutal demolishing of the SOR crud back in the Crazy Horse casino, that he hadn't actually been forced into a confrontation with security guards and the law that had stormed the place just as he'd snapped the cuffs on Drobbler and flashed his credentials.

But just when the flames of one crisis were put out, another and more insidious critical mass had drawn the soldier into its vortex. The spook gunship was nowhere to be found, even after the Farm had combed the countryside with every piece of satellite imagery at their disposal. That led to crisis two, which was the vanishing of what Drobbler had referred to as the Armageddon Plague.

It suddenly occurred to him that without the late ex-cop stumbling into his play—was it simply two paths of destiny colliding?—the Stony Man warrior might not have gotten it this far, and where he was headed next was a matter of debate. Nor would a few lives—eight at last count—of what had turned out to be a special U.S. Army Division involved in the security of the nation's so-called counter-biological weapons program been saved.

As they began soaring north by northwest, past the Airport Expressway and over Hialeah Racetrack, Bolan began to feel the hand of the doomsday clock. Given what little was known about the Armageddon Plague, the fact that it was somewhere out there in the hands of American intelligence operatives with an unknown agenda, the soldier had hashed it over with Brognola who, in turn, had run it past the President on how to proceed. The Man, to his credit, was keeping his cool, but all available resources were being marshaled and briefed at that hour, meaning God only knew where it all went from there. Every law-enforcement agency in Broward and Dade counties was on standby, but only the top tier of the FBI, the Justice Department and the military in Florida knew there was the potential for a terrorist attack.

The Man was emphatic, though. No panic buttons were to be pushed. And Bolan had his role defined.

As a deniable expendable, the Executioner was cut loose, though he had his own team of Justice Department Terrorist Task Force agents at his beck and call. Bottom line, however, the order from the White House was do whatever it took to track down the missing plague and take out any and all threats to national security, be they Sons of Revelation rabble, foreign terrorists, or members of what he'd heard was a new black ops division inside Homeland Security called the National Security Military Intelligence. If it went bad somehow, meaning the plague was loosed…

If that happened, the soldier knew it would take nothing short of divine intervention to save the land. And since no one knew—or was revealing—the exact nature of the plague...

Bolan glanced at one of his four war bags. He had no intention of lumbering about in a HAZMAT suit, but more often than not in his world what he wanted and what he got were two different creatures.

There was some good news, however, and the warrior focused on that next.

It might seem, he thought, he held a hand full of nothing at the moment, but he had Drobbler.

Bolan moved for the sullen man to begin wiring him for sound.

CHAPTER THIRTEEN

It felt wrong, like he was being baited into a trap, but he had to know.

Sleep was impossible anyway, and with the urge coming on to relieve himself Paul Radfield noticed that the television set was silent out in the living room. His mind had been so tormented with worry, his nerves so frayed over what he suspected was up and coming in the morning that he considered it a forgivable oversight he had missed the strange and sudden quiet beyond his door. There was traffic noise filtering up from the boulevard, drifting through the open balcony door where he noticed the curtain was fluttering against a stiff ocean breeze. He felt his heart gather a few anxious beats as he stepped out in the living room, the excuse he was going to the fridge for a cold beer to calm his nerves on the tip of his tongue when—

The spook was nowhere to be found, but Radfield

knew that left the balcony, and no man could move around that quietly, no light that dim that wouldn't cast even the first flickering shadow. As far as he knew, it was a one-bedroom dwelling, but...

He was tempted to call the guy's stupid handle, but as he hovered near the curtain for a few moments he began to sense the man was gone, that he was all alone. Which could mean something, or nothing. The something part was that he was free to go, now that they had what they wanted. The nothing part...

He knew better. It wasn't that simple.

Looking over his shoulder, sweeping the room with a gaze that strained eyeballs to the limit, he brushed aside the curtain, poked his face out a foot or so, scanning the balcony.

No Brick.

Now what? Did he stroll right out the front door? Suddenly the traffic noise carried a melodious and soothing beat, the dark sky hung over the distant hotels of Miami Beach, all of it looking so close, the sweet sound and sights of freedom...

"I'd be careful if I were you, Paul."

Radfield spun, heart in his throat. He cursed as he found the damn guy no more than five feet behind him, standing there, lighting a smoke, looking back through those infernal sunglasses.

"We're nine floors up for a reason, Paul."

The guy was grinning, enjoying the startled anger, puffing away and wreathing his face with smoke like some fire-breathing dragon cooling down.

"We weren't planning on making a dive into the pool for freedom, were we?"

Radfield trembled, felt the impulse to charge the op, but noted the legs were splayed a little, as if he was ready, itching to go for his gun and start blasting.

"You ought to try and get some sleep, Paul. Tomorrow morning will be here before you know it."

"And when it's done? You're just going to send me on my way, back to my family, like whatever you're going to do never happened?" Radfield grunted. "Don't bother. You'd lie to me anyway."

"Show a little faith, Paul. Have a little courage. What did I tell you earlier?"

"That you were going to leave such a truth-seeker as myself the mother lode of intelligence that would shatter the very foundations of the United States military-industrial-pharmaceutical complex."

"Yes, I mentioned that you would have in your possession the truth of the ages, Paul. To do with as you please in the event you are ever approached by a situation you find uncomfortable for you and your family."

"Uh-huh. The blackmail leverage in case Uncle Sam wants to dump me in Leavenworth for the rest of my life."

"You sound dubious."

"Do I now? Let's see. You're going to hand me intelligence that is so classified that not even the President of the United States or any President after Truman knows of its existence. Everything the shadow government within the working government knows but doesn't want we, the little people, to know. UFOs, that they have irrefutable evidence of their existence, with bodies to boot in cryogenic deep-freeze out west. That NASA is presently on the verge of creating a time-space continuum with an alien fuel that could allow man to travel into deep space at light speed and beyond. Then there's the Extinction Level Event they know is on the way from deep space, a rock the size of Rhode Island they believe will wipe out one-third of the planet before the New Ice Age is brought on by this cataclysm. That biological and chemical weapons have been tested on the poor and disenfranchised in this country, and that there are maybe five million infected walking time bombs across the nation waiting to drop dead but not before they've spread the contagion. That the Pentagon and the DOD have a covert plan to seize Saudi, Iraqi and Iranian oil fields by using Arab militants armed with tactical nukes. That the CIA is helping to run the drug cartels in South America, Afghanistan and the Golden Triangle, and that they are building a doomsday warchest for an elite group of politicians and Pentagon brass who will rule the world after World War III, which they are presently engineering. That we have laser weapons that are boring holes in the ozone but only over certain regions of the planet, the nonessentials, I believed you called them, who will be irradiated in a select genocide program. Did I miss anything?"

"How about who killed JFK?"

"I thought you told me that wasn't in the package?"

"It isn't. That mystery was already solved and taken care of."

"Do tell? So Oliver Stone was right?"

"You don't want all these truths, Paul, I can—"

"I didn't necessarily say that. What I want…"

"Yes, yes, to be returned to your family."

"So, we understand each other. Then why not let me go now?"

"Once the job is done."

"You have the codes all rewired to your specifications."

"Not until the job is done."

Radfield took a step toward the man.

"One more step, Paul, and I will drop you."

"You're going to kill me anyway."

"Maybe, maybe not. But if I kill you now you'll never know whether the wife and kiddies made it."

Radfield nodded. "I tell you what. If it looks like you're going to kill me—and I was a soldier who can read that kind of moment and I don't care how much of a stone-cold psycho professional you may think you are—I'll do my damnedest to take a few pounds of flesh off you on my way out of this world."

"That's fair enough, Paul." He blew smoke, and smiled. "Now. If you don't mind, could you please return to your room so I can watch Letterman in relative peace and quiet?"

Radfield held the hidden stare.

"You want to know what this is all about, don't you?"

"I'd rather not, if it means I live to see my family live."

The op blew out a long funnel of smoke, pondering

something in a heavy pause. "Under the circumstances, once it's done anyway, there's nothing you could tell."

"This is you trying to bait me to ask."

"It won't affect your status one iota."

"Just my status?"

"Your family will make it, Paul, if you cooperate up and until this is finished."

"Okay. So what's it all about?"

"Would you believe it's probably just as you suspected?"

Radfield felt his stomach roll over then nodded. "The vault. How much is down there?"

"It begins with a 'b.'"

Radfield managed to hide his surprise. "A billion dollars."

"All of it in cash."

"Drug money."

"No, it's Washington's money, Paul. Specifically the projected black ops budget for the next five years in our country's global war on terror."

"If they're meant to be used to track criminals, my guess is those bills are marked."

"We have a way to unmark and clean them."

"But, of course, you have it all figured out."

"If you'd like, when it's finished, as a bonus I can send you home with a duffel bag or two."

"I'll pass."

"Right. A man with a conscience."

"I wouldn't know how to live any other way."

"I understand. But we all have to find a way to be

able to look in the mirror and hold eye contact with ourselves, Paul."

Radfield shook his head, snorted. "A thief, and a traitor, is that what you see in the mirror?"

"Hardly. I see a man who got smart and jumped aboard the Gravy Train before it passed him by and he spent the rest of his life doing the government's wet work and taking all the risk and maybe catching a bullet himself one night while the fat cats in Washington deny he ever existed when he turns up dead, and they keep on soaking up the good life while planning to take over the world at the expense of suffering and horror that no man can possibly begin to fathom."

"If you really believed that you'd do something about it."

"Like what?" The op chuckled, smoked. "Fight back?"

Then it dawned on Radfield. He felt his eyes go wide.

"That's right, Paul. Despite all your suspicions I want you dead, I actually intend to see you keep on breathing."

"To tell all of America the truth you will be giving me. What if I don't?"

"You will."

"What if I just bury it?"

"You won't. Eventually, you will be forced to reveal it, all of it. Why's that, you ask?"

Radfield felt sick to his stomach. "Because…"

"Because at some point in the future, there will be a

knock on your front door. There will be some official-looking men with official-sounding titles from some unofficial spook agency. And to see you and your family stay alive, you will have, in your very possession, the keys to what is no less than divine knowledge of the United States of America. What it's done in the past, and what it's planning for the future of the entire world. You will play your trump card, or you will threaten to. They will come back, again and again, until you reveal it all. Whether you go on some talking head show or straight to the United States Senate, how it gets done doesn't matter, as long as it gets done."

"Why?"

"Why? Haven't you figured it out?"

"Consider me in the dark."

"I'm part of that shadow government, Paul. I just happen to be buried so deep and so off the official books...well, let's just say I intend to keep it that way."

"In other words you hope I'll buy you and whoever else is part of this some time while you vanish off the face of the planet, spread the billions around, until they're safe and spendable. You're hoping if you obscure the whole bloody picture enough with a mess of rumors and speculation—and probably loosely based on fact, I'll admit—about shadow government conspiracies and planned genocide against its own citizens then all eyes, public, law enforcement and intelligence, will be turned off of you and your people. This whole truth of the ages is nothing but a giant smoke screen you hope I will erect for you while you stroll off into the sunset. Public outrage crying for scalps all over Washington, Senate investigations and so forth, get the whole nation bollixed up and in a blind rage for maybe years to come."

"Now you know…all you need to know."

"You're some piece of real nasty evil work, you know that?" Radfield stated.

"Why, thank you, Paul. But as far as your admiration goes, it would be better served to thank the very men in Washington who created me in the first place."

"And they would be?"

"If I told you that, Paul, I would, without any doubt or hesitation, have to kill you."

IT WAS BEYOND UNNERVING, but Jeremiah Grant decided it was wise, for the time being, to keep his cool. That was a stretch, just the same, when he began to factor in everything that was making him sweat, itch, scratch and bottle up what he figured was enough anger, irritation and paranoia to field an army of militants all by its lonesome. The mosquitoes were, by and large, the least of his concerns, but out here in the Everglades they were ravenous, big as small birds, he reckoned, and despite the fact the doors appeared locked tight, somehow the damn things were getting in, strafing his face and neck, feeding on blood that was boiling and fast the longer he kept steaming over all that had gone wrong, the questions that were left unanswered and the riddles that kept piling up. And whoever were the five men in black that had met them at the LaBraza Airfield ten miles west of Miami who kept telling him the same thing every time he posed the first question.

Relax.

Easy for them to say, he thought, smug bastards always following up with a curt they'd let him know something, but now he was reading his men—what was left of them—and clearly saw the worry in their eyes.

They were waiting for the other shoe to drop. Where there was worry, then fear and panic, he knew, were never far behind.

At the moment, they were waiting for Drobbler to make his appearance, and what about that? There were any number of questions Grant wanted to fire off at his High Son, but he had agreed with Drobbler that an unsecured cell phone wasn't the smartest way to play catch-up, though he intimated there was some kind of problem, unspecified as it was. Because of the drug culture and the flourishing epidemics of crime and illegal immigrants, Grant knew South Florida was awash in law enforcement, and they were armed with every state-of-the-art surveillance and countersurveillance gadget, the best Uncle Sam's money could purchase, so he was forced to wait and sweat it out some more. In yet another unsettling way the silence and the waiting was plain common sense, and if the law down here was even half as well-equipped in spook gear as the Homeland Security black ops...

Which begged another train of anxious thought. Why didn't the spooks want to get this show on the road? They were poring over maps, computer printouts, what looked like city blocks in grid with areas detailed in red. Some of it went into the shredder, but after quick perusal, about half of the paperwork remained on the table while the rest of it, along with some CDs and maps, was transported into the adjoining room.

There were four computers stretched along a table against the far wall, all of them with blank screens, Grant observed, but with CDs laid out in plain sight. Somehow, the whole setup smacked of unprofessional, or something else he couldn't quite put his finger on. Given what he knew about the operation, well, the area deep in Glades country was remote enough, but there was only one sentry posted outside. On top of that there didn't appear the first camera—or none that he could spot with the naked eye—or much concern at all for security. It was as if they didn't care who strolled up to the building, which was little more than some big wooden shack. Not only that, but for some strange reason, they left the engine on the two GMCs running, as if they were poised to make a quick exit. That there were two of those big SUVs implied there were other spooks in the vicinity, but where? And why hadn't they bothered to show themselves, unless they were hunkered in the sawgrass and surrounding woods, guarding this dreary fort. The foursome in front of him toted those ubiquitous MP-5s, wore the same grim expressions he had long since gotten used to, but something about their posture, their stony silence, was beginning to make him want to scream. Thank God, his men were armed with assault rifles down the line, but Grant found he was all of a sudden wishing he had brought more to the meet than his Glock 25.

Grant decided to join Tomlin and Jameson in a Cuban cigar from the box the spooks had put on the long wooden table. He reacted adversely for a second to the idea of trying anything that wasn't stamped and approved by the good old U.S. of A., but he was, after all, in Florida. And from what he'd heard and seen so far Florida was a foreign country that just happened to be planted on the Continental States. There was, however, a bottle of Jim Beam put out for the troops, and Grant helped himself to a refill.

To think only a short twenty-four hours ago he was something of a television celebrity, but he'd known all along going national with his group was out of the question. Oh, well, stardom he could do without, and the God angle had only been meant for the short haul anyway, though some kind of divine intervention, he believed, and felt the smile tug at the corner of his mouth, had seen fit to steer him toward a pot of gold that he had only ever fantasized about. It went without saying to any of those in the loop that it would be wise to quit America, but Grant already had a few choice spots down in the Caribbean staked out. And down there green was the only color they—and he—was interested in.

Glancing down the table and peering through the hanging clouds of cigarette smoke, the vision of anticipated wealth faded as he bitterly groused how he was down to sixteen men, including himself. Until he grilled Drobbler he wouldn't be able to accurately assess losses—or gains, when he considered the payday waiting at the end of the line. Two of his troops shipped on ahead were mysteriously absent, and when he'd put the question to the spooks about their AWOL status he was told to not worry about it.

Not worry!

All this to tie a great big knot in his guts, and so far there was no word on the actual mission, its status, logistics, the nuts and bolts of an operation he strongly suspected required not only a few thorough briefings and an iron-clad plan, but at least one dry run so they could get the feel of the layout. If something had changed, if there was a problem on the spooks' end…

Too late now, they were in for the full ride. Looking back to the very beginning, it had been his understanding they were meant to be employed in equal parts as drivers, spotters, scouts, muscle, and for what was to be an inside job against a bank in downtown Miami that stashed away what was a black ops budget for the country's war on terror, all of it in ready cash. There was some 9/11 aspect to the operation, but there again, he was not privy to details, though he figured it had something to do with the Armageddon Plague. Hindsight, he had always believed, was for sore losers, but when he considered what his men had helped to steal from the U.S. military, and with the blood albeit indirectly on his hands from servicemen and law-enforcement officers…

Grant killed his drink, poured another. A mosquito buzzed in on the sweat breaking down his forehead, and before he knew it he smashed the insect against his face. That drew a funny look from one of the spooks, the stone face looking set to break out in the first sign of life since he'd first laid eyes on the man. He couldn't read the expression, somewhere between amusement and contempt, he thought, then the smug granite face went back to the paperwork.

Now that they were supposedly ready to move details still remained vague, other than recalling his original orders they would be told what to do on a sort of roving need-to-know. And what the hell was that anyway? The money, of course, was what sealed it for all of them, though only a select few knew the exact figure they would receive. Which was why Grant was getting antsy to know the finer aspects, so he could farm out the more perilous assignments. He hadn't come this far, with so much cash riding on the line, to get gunned down in the street, or worse, which would be arrest.

Grant was putting a light to the end of his cigar when Tomlin leaned in. "How much longer…"

"Gentlemen."

Grant snapped startled eyes toward the biggest spook hunched over the paperwork.

"I am Thomas Overstreet of the National Security Military Intelligence of the Homeland Security's Southern Borders. I regret the inconvenience and the delay, but I would kindly ask you for a little more patience and that you remain silent."

Grant just looked at the guy who didn't bother to glance up from his papers. The impertinent bastard! Keep them hanging on the edge of their seats, treating them like they were less than flunkies, or foreigners that just fell off the turnip truck with empty hands and hungry bellies. "That's it?"

"For now, yes, that would be it. Once your man arrives we will begin."

Grant shook his head at his men as a few of them scowled, fidgeted, looked set to push the matter. The SOR leader looked at the curtained window then filled another shot, deciding he needed to stretch his legs. He was rising when he found Overstreet glaring at him.

"Remain seated."

Grant nearly exploded, but something was beginning to feel even more terribly wrong. Since it took a con man to know one, he heard his bs detector blipping on. He was on the verge of laying some verbal wood to Mr. Overstreet when the spook grunted into the throat mike of his com link, "Yeah."

There was some more grunting, Grant silently cursing the man for his poker face when the door suddenly flew open and in came Drobbler. Two spooks were manhandling him into a corner, one of them thrusting his subgun into his face while his partner began frisking Drobbler as if he were a common criminal. Drobber was sputtering protest when his handler began patting down his thighs, going north for his package. Beyond the look of understandable shame, Grant read terror in the man's eyes as a hand vanished straight down his pants. Drobbler made a sound between a squeal and yelp just as the offending paw seemed to twist and yank at some area around his manhood, then he came out with a black box about the size of a pager, displaying it like some trophy.

Grant's eyes widened at the sight of the strips of tape, a split second before he glimpsed all six MP-5s swinging in his direction.

CHAPTER FOURTEEN

The airboat swept through the sawgrass but rapidly lost speed. Timed with its cut engine, the big fan inside the steel-mesh cage stopped spinning altogether about thirty yards or so from the muddy banks of mangrove and cypress forest, now carried its black-clad shadow to shore on the final leg of a fading glide. Being right on schedule was a matter for grim debate, and since the beginning of this campaign Mack Bolan had learned a little something more about nasty surprises. Like trouble, they came in bunches, and when least expected.

Something flashed in the periphery of the Executioner's night-vision goggles as he roved the gnarled vegetation and brush with his sound-suppressed MP-5. It was splashing down, about eight or nine feet of fat scaly hide, roughly ten yards to his nine o'clock. The beast submerged beneath the black waters as it began slicing an easy swift course away from the soldier's impromptu beachhead.

Bolan gave the banks and tree line a final scan, left to right, spotted the narrow winding trail detailed by DEA surveillance photos "borrowed" by the cyberteam at Stony Man Farm. He hopped out of the DEA airboat loaner, subgun leading his charge into the ghostly green hue of prehistoric marsh and woods. According to Brognola's own sources, the so-far-unnamed-and-unknown U.S. intelligence agency had staked out this patch of real estate, just far enough beyond 1.5 million acres of national park boundaries—or about twenty percent of Everglades wilderness—they could declare it Private Property Of The United States Government. Who they were, Bolan didn't want to venture even a remote guess, but they were dirty, and that was all that counted in his world.

The play was set, and as the soldier melted into the deeper shadows he gave it a quick assessment, judged his chances of both bagging another high-ranking Son of Revelation or a black op gone bad as little better than slim to none.

No sweat. He would take the cannibals as they came, for better or worse. The former meant he nabbed a singing pigeon while the latter...

Death.

Simple.

That didn't mean, of course, he wouldn't give it one hundred percent of heavy metal thunder and bloody brushstrokes, even against the stacked odds, the flimsy hope of bagging a man-eater. Fully restocked with grenades and spare clips, his com link was a state-of-the-art masterpiece. It tied him into his blacksuited flyboys, the Justice strike force in holding pattern in their Black Hawks while allowing him to listen in on the cover story Drobbler would feed his fellow human snakes. According to a DEA source that had previously swept the area as a potential red flag zone for drug smugglers, the trail wasn't hot-wired to turn Bolan into an amputee or worse, but he used the EM scanner to paint any lasers, other sensors as he forged deeper down the trail. So far, the DEA looked good to its word.

The Executioner had what he needed, as far as steely determination, audacity and hardware went. As usual, however, there was good news and bad news.

Good news was that Drobber was already expected albeit late to make what the former DOD Storm Tracker claimed was the final brief. The bad news was that whoever the intelligence operatives who had seized the Armageddon Plague were keeping all SOR hands in the dark until their plan was at the eleventh hour of being launched off the pad.

That, Bolan assumed, would be right then and there.

As far as strategy went, it was real simple, but a roll of the dice nonetheless. March Drobber into the meet, wired for sound, then...

It didn't take a pair of X-ray eyes to see through the shabby compound walls in the distance to know his pigeon was plucked. Drobbler's squawk and a few unidentified voices wanting to know what the hell was going on hit Bolan's ears a moment before there was the sound of rustling, followed by a gasp and then an audible crunch that spiked the soldier's eardrums and told him it was over before it even began.

Bolan hit a knee behind a patch of thorny hanging vines and brier that looked as if it could skin a man alive by just brushing up against it. Shedding his night-vision goggles and adjusting his sight to the darker shadows by allowing his gaze to trail from the outer limits of the halogen lights hung from the big shack, he took into account no sentries, the size of the motor pool, noting both GMCs were running their engines, the open front door where more light and angry voices spilled forth. Between Drobbler's numbers and the vehicles on hand, the soldier had the standing enemy force at somewhere between ten to twenty shooters, twenty-five tops. Bolan keyed his com link. "Striker to Mothership."

"Mothership here, Striker."

"Bring it on."

"Roger that, Striker. Bring it on, it is."

"YOU AND YOUR PEOPLE are under arrest, Grant. All of you get your hands up in the air now."

It was all Drobbler could do to stay on his feet. The room was spinning, the bile back and rising in his throat, and there was plenty of pain to spare from where it felt as if half his sac had been ripped away where the mini-mike had been taped. As he caught a picture of Grant appearing set to faint away in his misty carousel, he was beginning to think the last of any nine lives had already been used up back in the Crazy Horse casino. And what seemed another lifetime ago and before Special Agent

Matt Cooper had shipped him off in a Chevy Caprice with marching orders he had come here with all due trembling and fear, suspecting they were...

The big cold bastard might as well have shot him back in Montana, since Drobbler wasn't that far gone on panic, terror and paranoia to read all the body language, judge the mounting rage and fear for what it was.

Human time bombs, and ticking down fast.

"What the hell are you talking about—arrested?" Grant roared. "You forget it was you people who came to us in the first damn place? It was you people who hijacked that shipment of plague? It was you people put this whole package together?"

This was bad, and getting worse, Drobbler thought as he saw the men in black spreading out on both sides of the SOR contingent, weapons trained down the table, ready to catch them in a crossfire.

"Hands up or we start blasting!"

As far as hands went, Drobbler was noticing the MP-5s were wielded in black-gloved mitts when the white beams hit the roof, doorway and curtained window on the far side of the room, the rotor tempest announcing the presence of a helicopter directly above, a second before a metallic voice boomed from a loudspeaker, "You, inside! This is the United States Department of Justice. Throw down your weapons and come out with your hands up!"

The panic could have been a living force, as Drobbler saw them all turned to living statues until the biggest spook growled, "Mr. Breem! Shag your ass out there and tell those idiots we're Homeland Security! Explain to them we've got a bunch of terrorists..."

"You have five seconds to come out!"

"On second thought, Mr. Breem, stand fast and lend a hand."

Drobbler saw it coming, and from both sides. He was a heartbeat behind Grant in nose-diving for the floor, but the rest of his SOR brethren opted to fight, chair legs scraping, assault rifles flying up and spraying a few lightning bursts. Three or four of his comrades were cut down in their seats as six MP-5s unloaded, sweeping the table, end to end.

Drobbler was down and eating floor, when something that looked like a small pineapple went bouncing past his face. The cacophony of weapons fire and screams and curses were lost to his own bellowed cry of shock and horror as he scrambled to his feet, vaguely amazed at how agile he felt, how swift he was suddenly moving. He was charging for the far wall, hoping to God he had enough time and clearance, cursing the day he'd ever laid eyes on Grant, when the grenade blew.

THE FLASH-BANG DROPPED a sense-crunching, eye-popping right cross on the slaughter show underway, but it only bought Bolan about two or three seconds before one of the more professional shooters started winging wild spray and pray in his direction. As the 9 mm firestorm ate up wood in a rising burst, the Black Hawk with his guys pulling the searchlights off the shack as they flew off to hold the prearranged firepoint to the side of the main dirt track that led to and from the spook compound, Bolan mentally digested the view he'd just gotten.

Ten to twelve gunmen still standing, or falling in various postures of agony as they absorbed lead that was flying all over a room he reckoned was about forty-by-forty feet. With smoky palls and swirling trash obscuring the killzone, Bolan couldn't tell which side held the upper hand, but knew he couldn't afford to waste one more second.

The MP-5's locust swarm above his com link abruptly ended. Judging by all the sharp grunts and screams of pain, the soldier's temporary standoff was over, and it was now or never to fully announce his presence.

He went low, sidling across an open doorway, delivering a precision burst of subgun fire from the hip that chopped one man in black off at the knees, dropped him in a tight spiral, lower legs all but crimson ruins and jagged shards of bone. The Executioner then stitched what could be none other than some SOR rabble as that line of 9 mm rounds tore through the bottom half of his sheepskin coat, about kidney high, flinging him, blazing Colt Commando and Stetson hat, into another militant buddy who was being gutted, crotch to sternum with an invisible lead scalpel now hurled from the other side of the room. A body slammed off the wall, to Bolan's left, with enough force to split wood and shower down some mossy grit and grime. That, along with the clamor of weapons fire sounding every bit as loud and relentless as the initial burst, warned the soldier any hopes he came there with of bagging someone higher-up than Drobbler were dimming fast.

Since it was all going to hell, the Executioner whipped the MP-5 around the doorjamb. He held back on the trigger and rang up two more SOR hyenas, kicking them in a windmill of tangled arms and crossed assault rifles into the far wall.

MARK DROBBLER BEHELD one of several sudden and stark revelations, much to his mounting horror and despair.

The quick-fix remedies in life always turned out to be exactly what a man usually suspected but denied they might be. But when he realized the truth it was generally way too late in the game to do anything about it. For most of poor miserable humanity—like his filthy carcass, he decided—it too often seemed to come when the gong of the supreme hour sounded, and the Angel of Death appeared out of the dark. And when least expected, at what seemed the worst of all possible times and scenarios.

When, yes, the gold of one's cherished illusion dulled to reveal the dross of its hideous reality—what was no less than a pact with the Devil—then the truth came biting a man, a scorpion's stinger spiked into his rear, all the pain and poison fairly screaming at him that, hello, there were no short cuts, no earthly elixirs, no smooth glide and soft landing onto Easy Street. Charades and their con men—Mr. Grant—always met a bad fate.

Why he was suddenly struck by these reflections, he could only conclude was due to the terrifying fact he dreaded his own imminent end, and simply because his own life was a twisted and slimy maze of serious transgressions—corruption and vice just to name the B list—for which he had done next to nothing to account and atone for. To make it worse, even more unbearable, was the sudden grotesque light of doom cast over the supreme hour that he had been misled, duped, used, and now to be discarded like so much garbage cast into the incinerator. And when, in the beginning, he knew in his heart that for all of Jeremiah Grant's ravings and ramblings about God, the End of Days, the Last Judgment, it was all about one thing.

Money.

And Grant.

And more than likely, both were inseparable.

From the beginning, for all of Grant's talk about the Almighty and Divine Justice, he had never heard one voice raised in prayer, never saw one tear shed in contrition, never once caught so much as a fleeting glimpse of the first face cast down in sorrow and remorse.

Oh, but the screaming madness, the lamentable horror, the paralyzing truth, the agonizing lateness of it all!

Now destiny—ultimate destiny!—was, he knew, being fulfilled. That the nature of the hypocrite, the course charted by the reprobate who seized everything life had to offer and at the expense of all and everyone was a sick and stark, an iron but slimy testament to its character and that led to untimely but certain death. And because, Drobbler believed, he—Grant and the others—either couldn't wait, pay dues to the Creator by way of repentance and self-denial, or figured they needn't bother since the first wicked one of them would never see eternal reward anyway.

With bugged eyes he took in the carnage that was fast piling up all over the floor, his hands scrabbling forward to haul in the discarded Colt Commando assault rifle that was still smoking near the twitching paw of Earl Roberts. The former Missoula cop was choking on blood, head lolling like it was spiked on a broken stick, and Drobbler would have sworn the guy was staring him right in the eye, accusing or beseeching him for help, maybe both. Then he rasped out the final croak, the death rattle lost to all the unholy clamor of weapons fire, guys screaming and cursing out the ghost. As Drobbler grabbed up the assault rifle, he briefly congratulated himself for having the good sense to cover his head, squeezing his eyes shut while in the process of clamping his elbows tight over his ears. Thus the mere act of self-preservation had kept him from having his senses cleaved to shreds by the flash-bang grenade, allowing him to hold on, move forward with sight and sound in relative working order.

He saw two or three black-clad killers were taking a terrible shellacking on the far side as whoever the unseen wraith was busy blazing away from the open door, the long, stubby snout of the sound suppressor sweep-

ing them like they were bad animals in a carnival shooting gallery.

Unless Drobbler missed his guess, that would be the
big bastard with the blue graveyard eyes and voice to
match.

Time to fly.

As luck had it, one or two of his fallen comrades had
the foresight to hurl the table up, providing a nice little
barricade between himself, standing shooters and the
window, dead ahead and—

Grant was a blur as he hurtled himself through the
window, his fat rear taking the curtain with the ungainly
acrobatics, glass shards and splinters raining to the
floor, shredded fabric fluttering in the slipstream.

Drobbler lurched forward, hunched low, the body of
one of his slain comrades draped over the table in the corner of his eye like so much bloody refuse. The spooks
were holding on, he had to give them credit for guts and
a silent mental hope that they would dig in long enough
for him to pull off a desperate vanishing act. Their black
raid suit were getting cut to red ruins, but they were returning fire at the lone avenger, weapons spraying the wall
and ceiling as they began jigging out the final dance steps.
A few rounds tattooed the wall above Drobbler, eliciting
a startled cry. He was too close to freedom now, cursing
the fact he might get mowed down as the darkness to freedom veiled but beckoned on the other side of the window.

It was reflex and panic more than malice, but he
flung back a covering burst in the direction of the front
door before he left his feet and dived out into the night.

CHAPTER FIFTEEN

Thomas Overstreet fought back the sickening wave of despair, but he was still standing, still in the mix and going strong.

What else was he going to do? he thought.

There had been some gross mental lapses, granted, such as lax security, cameras and sensors and so forth. It was a reality check that had struck, too late. Chalk it up to arrogance, he figured, the fact they were tied in via cyberspace and paid HUMINT to the DEA, FBI and the intelligence of every military branch down here that was worth spitting on, the standing orders—vague as they were, but with the seal of authority from the DHS—they were to be left alone to do whatever it was they were doing.

Which was, in reality, sticking it to Uncle Sam.

The game here was dead, and if that was a G-man hurling around flash-bangs and chopping down shooters on both sides of the upturned table, then somebody at the Justice Department had been granted way more carte blanche and open interpretation of the *Patriot Act* than even the Defenders had claimed.

Overstreet burst into the adjoining room, feeding a fresh clip to his MP-5. Worst case, there was Plan B, and it was already laid out in the form of maps, CDs, all of it crafted for just such a contingency as he now found himself facing.

A few weapons were still tearing up the air, Speever finally giving up the ghost, he figured, as the man's hideous screams stopped, the bleeding out from legs that were all but diced to ruins run its course.

Overstreet inhaled a deep breath, paused at the side door. A look back at the slaughterhouse, another body pitching to the floor, he made out the sounds of two men engaged in a loud argument, but put them out of his mind.

He had his own world to save.

Starting now.

He kicked open the door, searched the black heart of the marshland.

Clear, or so it looked, and he ventured forth.

GREED AND AMBITION were fickle. When those so inclined to hoist their banners—which meant they were going for themselves, the world be damned—there was a sort of gathering storm that lent them their own violent energy, and which fed on itself, unable to stop, never sated.

Enough was never enough.

Bolan had to imagine it was comparable to a small fire being struck for the sake of keeping warm, then a little more wood was thrown on, but when the flames weren't hot and high enough, dump on some volatile fuel to kick in the desired effect.

More.

One thing about the greedy and the ambitious—they loved life and loved it large when all went their way. They laughed, they indulged, even grew chummy with those they secretly detested in their hearts, as long as they were on top, the sky's the limit, the world all theirs. On the dark flip side of all that illusory joy, when it didn't go their way, when the rug was getting yanked out from under them...

Bolan couldn't say, one way or the other, the bottom line on the feeding frenzy before him, but he could venture a safe guess it was about money. And when the greedy and ambitious saw their dreams and hopes going up in smoke, treachery and malice were right behind to lend a helping hand to seal their doom. What they did was bring out the beasts of rage and despair. The savage couldn't get what he wanted, so he either cannibalized himself or those around him or both. And no amount of hell to be paid could satisfy this sort of hopeless madness.

Unless it was stopped with the kind of permanent measures the Executioner employed.

For Bolan's purposes, their own wrath and despair merely served his cause, by way, at least, of strengthening his chances of walking out the other side.

Which was why he hung back an extra few seconds to allow the predators to feed on each other.

There was also the matter of Grant and Drobbler looking to run and hide.

They were on the far south side, according to his pilot's quick update, and they were embroiled in a bitter argument, Grant waving his pistol around in his High Son's face, the big man deciding how to proceed or how to best cut his losses.

That left the Stony Man warrior a few moments to deal with the last of the black ops problems.

Bolan hit the edge of the north wall at the same instant he saw the tall man in a raid suit rolling out of the door to the compound, midway down. "Drop your weapon!"

"I'm with Homeland Security, whoever the hell you are!" the armed shadow bellowed as he dropped back into the doorway. "You drop your piece and show your murdering ass right this second!"

"No deal, no more talking! Give it up or I start blasting!"

The response was a long burst of subgun fire that sent Bolan back on his haunches, the 9 mm projectiles sailing past his face, chomping up the edges. A long war cry rent the air as the storm of lead blasted out another chunk of wood. In all the excitement, Bolan thought, it had to have escaped Mr. Homeland Security that the Justice Department had already announced its clear and legal presence, and that they were supposed to be working on the same side, against a common enemy. Bolan knew better coming in, but he'd wanted to give the so-called good guys the benefit of the doubt, allow them the chance to confirm his suspicions beyond the pale of any specter of question.

So be it.

The soldier gave the guy twisted credit for wanting to go out the hard way. He was coming on fast, prepared to die on his feet, no less than a gored bull willing to take whatever secrets to the grave with him.

The Executioner saw no other way but to oblige the death wish. He primed a frag grenade at the same instant he saw the beefy figure that was Grant rushing for the motor pool. Opting for the greater of two threats, Bolan whipped the steel egg around the corner, the subgun going silent. He glimpsed the black op running to beat the kill radius, the Stony Man warrior pulling back from the edge a second before the grenade blew.

"Grant!"

The SOR leader nearly tripped and fell over his feet as he braked, wheeled and swung the assault rifle toward the general direction of the shout. Bolan hit him with four to five rounds up the midsection, then pivoted and turned the MP-5 on the armed figure rising from the dirty wisps of smoke and raining dirt, hacking and cursing.

"You dirty son of a..."

Whoever the black op, whatever his ambitions, the Executioner killed him with a short burst to the chest, sent him flying back on a howl of rage, the last of several wild rounds absorbed by the infinite blackness of the silent night above.

"Calm down."

"I am calm. I'm just passing on the problem. Thought you should know."

Allen Braxton checked his watch. 05:33:47.

"Hello?"

Braxton left his Miami front man hanging for a few moments, as he weighed the problem, but realized it was really no problem at all.

It just had the appearance of crisis.

From the start, any number of contingencies involving the team, the head shed and the foreign help were factored in. Despite the best and what appeared the most ironclad planning, it was impossible to cover every base. Human nature and its endless litany of weaknesses and frailties were always a consideration, but enough money was riding on this where even if one backbone was inclined to bend there was always the threat of being fired beyond the cash. And this was no boardroom charade, Braxton thought. He was dealing with men, warriors, not a bunch of starry-eyed kids and some pampered priss they believed held the keys to some magic kingdom of their futures.

But, even out here in the real world, where it all boiled down to guts in the face of life-and-death decisions, final reward, always measured against immediate reprisal or any glitch, outshone the risks. And all of them knew that once they let the genie out of this bottle there was no turning back.

No matter what.

Less than six hours before the show started, Braxton knew they had reached the final fork in the road.

Sat phone pressed to his ear, Braxton strode out of the massive hangar. The last bit of grunt work was underway behind him, as the Gulfstream was packed with the merchandise, the state-of-the-art communications and tracking center bolted down to the cabin floor. The C-130 being the primary beast of burden, the Hercules and the main workhorses—three Black Hawks and the two Chinooks—were getting a final pre-flight rundown, topped out with fuel. He was giving the dark wall of cypress beyond the chain-link fencing a hard scan when Lawhorn cleared his throat. He let his man in Miami stew a few more seconds, taking in the night beyond the private airfield. One tower, one hangar and two runways, there were a few twin-engine Cessnas and executive choppers parked to the north, all for appearances' sake. Not in plain view, housed on platforms beneath the north and south tarmacs, were the machine gun and the antiaircraft batteries with SAMs, all of which were tied into a sophisticated computer bank inside the hangar. Officially, Homewash Charter Flights was listed as the up-and-coming executive's personal flight school. It had been something of a royal pain, turning away the swaggering, bejeweled Latinos who often came rolling up to the office in their stretch limos and briefcases stuffed with hundreds...

Lawhorn was clearing his throat again, but more insistent this time.

"It's confirmed, then. Black Cell is down?"

"I thought I told you as much. To a man, sir, eighty-sixed. Including Mr. T."

Braxton checked the smile. That was good news, but he wasn't about to let Lawhorn know how he really felt. With Overstreet and the Glades crew out of the picture, there was really no cause for alarm, and his cut had just been fattened. Further, there was confirmation that Overstreet Operation Steering Wheel was out of the gate. With the transponders fixed to each war bus, Braxton's Miami team was able to monitor their progress on the road from this end. The other two juggernauts were sitting, sticking to the timetable, and with this piece of sudden news Braxton began to wonder if that might not prove a problem. They were dealing with fanatics, after all, volatile to a fault. Yes, they all appeared willing to proceed as planned, eager to accept their role as martyrs if that meant killing scores of infidels. Yes, they were trained overseas, families to be left behind paid a handsome sum of cash that would see them live comfortably through the next generation. Yes, there was commitment, resolve, and confirmation of such by the team overseas, but...

"Do we proceed on schedule, sir?"

"I don't see why not, Mr. B. Are you forgetting who we are?"

"Not in the least."

"Are you forgetting that our cannon fodder was meant to meet just the kind of fate you are describing?"

"Not at all. But..."

"Yes?"

"From what I gather the strike was official."

Braxton had wondered about that, too. "I understand your concerns."

"We can't watch our imports every second."

Braxton lit a cigarette. "Meaning one of them may have been grabbed?"

"Or we have a leak somewhere down the line."

"I don't think so, Mr. B, but it's something to bear in mind."

"Watch our backs."

"It goes without saying. If it was going to go south on us, I am of the mind it would have happened before now. What about our boy? How's he holding up?"

"Shaky, but he'll keep. He's the praying kind."

"Indeed, a God-fearing, family man. That's why he was chosen. Now, you did tell me that everything is all set on your end?"

"Yes, sir. All we need to do is follow up."

"Then, what's to worry? Unless a dire emergency crops up, the next time we talk should be bright and early when we make our withdrawal."

"You're the man. I'll be seeing you, bright and early."

He was the man, indeed, Braxton thought, as Lawhorn's parting words rang in his ears. From where he stood, though, that would either make him a hero, not to mention the biggest thief on the planet and the most wanted criminal or…

He let the pessimistic thought die before it took formidable shape. Positive thinking was required from here on, to the finish line. Besides, if there was any sacrificial lamb to be offered up, he had something beyond Paul Radfield's head to put on the world chopping block.

In a few short hours, he would be armed with enough money to buy and sell any number of small nations run by criminal regimes, petty thugs living the big life and looking to hold on to it at all costs and who were more than willing to grant him refuge.

Beyond that, he would have all the leverage he needed to hold back any wolves from Washington who might come howling at his door.

He would be armed with no less than the divine truth of the ages, and it would be more than ample enough blackmail, enough clout.

The way he saw it, the powers-that-be in the nation's capital would only be too happy to see him take the money and disappear. No, they would practically beg him to keep his mouth shut. They would whimper behind their desks. They would wet themselves every time the phone rang. They would hide under their beds at night.

Oh, how sweet it would be!

The power. Oh, yes, that's what he would soon wield, able to strip off their masks of invulnerability, wipe the ingratiating and smug smiles off their lips at any time, reveal them for the slobbering wolves and the feeding worms and the slimy maggots they were. The knowledge. Oh, yes, that was a trump card so devastating it could topple the entire infrastructure of the United States government, and where he could see them, if he so desired, bend their collective knee before him, tear-streaked faces and quivering lips pressed to the ground and begging he spare their reputations, their money, their lives.

Oh, the beatific triumph! Oh, the untouchable soaring joy!

Why, the very fleeting notion of it all made him smile, and chuckle. He was no conquering hero, not yet, but he could feel the glow of invincibility burning from deep within, making him feel lighter than air as he turned and headed back into the hangar to shore up last-minute details.

"NATIONAL SECURITY Military Intelligence."

"Never heard of them."

"No reason you should have, Striker."

"Clue me."

Bolan kept one eye on the Special Justice Department Forensics Team, as he heard Hal Brognola pause, the big Fed pulling his own thoughts together, no doubt wondering what they had, and how to proceed. If, that was, the White House didn't give Bolan the hook.

It was a controlled frenzy of methodical grim work beyond where the soldier stood with his sat link, as he had to wonder himself just how much further he could push the mission on his own. There was no prisoner to be had, so Bolan had given the orders to start to finger-print and to photograph every face, sweep the compound, top to bottom, the perimeter for a quarter mile around the compass, down to the last blade of grass. It was a mess in the main room, the six-man team, he found, in their black nylon Justice Department jackets and white gloves doing their best to navigate through all the blood, bodies and spent casings, dragging out the high-tech gear and getting it all settled wherever there was a dry square foot to be found.

Bolan turned his attention to the sheaf of computer printouts on the small table in front of him, the contents of what CDs were found undamaged being e-mailed to both Brognola's computer at his suburban D.C. home and the Farm.

"I called in a few markers, as did Barb, but it doesn't look good as far as getting anything written in stone. At least, that is, on my end. I've heard them called the Defenders, but my sources referred to them more as the Invisibles."

"The Invisibles. Black ops."

"Worse."

"How could it be worse?"

"I should have said 'super' black ops. Carte blanche but from where and who nobody knows and Homeland Security just denied right in my ear they existed. My sources tell a story about shadow gunslingers and how they apparently have free and ready access to every black project and every weapons manufacturing contractor you could name, or so goes the scuttlebutt. Word is they've stopped about eight, maybe nine major terrorist attacks, but the way it's shaping up it looks like they groomed a few solid contacts overseas for whatever their end game. There are no concrete IDs on these unsung heroes, at least nothing that would mean anything, and whatever history the Farm's backtracked from Barb's sources is so blurred and blacked out just figuring out what branch of service they started with was a major magic act. In other words, when I said 'invisible,' you can damn near take that in the literal sense. You know the type."

Indeed, Bolan did. They—being the status political-intelligence-military quo—denied before man and God such entities of death, destruction and subterfuge existed, and that sometimes all this mayhem was perpetrated against its own citizens, or recently arrived foreigners who fitted a certain profile. That it was all just the fantastic fabrications of some journalist with too much idle time, too much ego, too much imagination and in search of his fifteen minutes.

The Executioner knew better.

Black ops were living ghosts in the machinery of the system, and armed and dangerous ones at that, with numerous aliases, bogus social security numbers, if they were even phony card-carrying members, which none of the covert dead so far had turned out to be. They could do anything, be anywhere, with every state-of-the-art surveillance and countersurveillance wonder toys at their ready disposal. They had access to men, matériel, intelligence and bases of operations not even the elite forces of the United States could access without executive orders. They could build then sanitize on the fly mobile command posts, ditto for weapons factories.

Which meant there would be no visible trace or tracking down of the black helicopter, already indicated by Brognola. Which meant the juggernaut that had murdered more than thirty U.S. Army bio-specialists, intelligence operatives and state policemen would never be traced to its origins of creator and warehousing. According to Brognola, a small army of men in black had already descended on the survivors, quarantined both killing zones in Montana, absconding, most likely, with any and all evidence that would point to this or that agency beyond any doubt.

But, not unlike Stony Man Farm, the soldier knew from experience that invisible intelligence agencies existed, so far out there in limbo that not even the Congress and the Senate had an inkling of who they were, what they did. Sometimes they were green-lighted by the Pentagon, DOD, the CIA or the NSA and through some loosely affiliated back channel to the White House or the Joint Chiefs or Central Command. But more often than not they did whatever they pleased, to whomever they wished, all wrapped up in the Stars and Stripes while they executed any number of sordid agendas that often went way beyond anything approved by the Founding Fathers.

All dismay and cynicism aside, Bolan knew he often straddled the same fence. But his fight was clear, with an arrow-straight aim to defend national security against America's homegrown and foreign enemies. That meant no stops in between to coddle drug cartels, schmooze arms dealers, play the lesser-of-two-evil tyrants or nation regimes against the other to fatten numbered bank accounts, or decide for themselves what the truth was in their own eyes. And the sickening truth in Bolan's eyes was that it hurt like hell when he was hunting down men who were sworn to guard the store of freedom and liberty but had tossed in the towel to go for number one.

"The guys you waxed, Striker, are more than likely part of this covert arm of Homeland Security, but we could have some freelancers from other agencies involved, not to mention the theft of a bioweapon we still know nothing about and that's vanished into thin air, destined for God only knows where or what end."

"Any good news?"

"Now that you ask, there is the whisper of a common thread among the Invisibles. They were recruited, on the sly, is my understanding, from Special Ops out of both Afghanistan and Iraq."

"Without, I take it, official authorization."

"You take it right."

Which led Bolan to give the big Fed a quick but thorough rundown of what he had on hand.

"So, what are we thinking?" Brognola asked. "Those areas you see, all marked in big bright red around Charleston, Norfolk and Baltimore are high value targets?"

"With the ports all but clearly red-flagged."

"Too clearly, if I'm reading the skeptical tone right."

"Nothing wrong with your ears," Bolan said, and paused.

"I'm going to have to give what you have to the President."

"Understood."

"But?"

"It's all too neat a package."

"I hear you. They did everything but tie a red-white-and-blue ribbon around it with a happy face bow on top. You're thinking the SOR scum were strictly patsies?"

"These unsung heroes, as you called them, wanted to pass the buck."

"Pin the blame on a bunch of militant jackasses, you mean, have all of officialdom scratching themselves while they went on to do whatever it is they're going to do."

"Which, more or less, answers the big question."

"And that would be?"

"It's about money, a lot of money."

"I know that tone, Striker. It tells me you have a good idea where you're going hunting next. And that you're just getting warmed up for some bloody magnum opus."

"Like I said, Hal, there's nothing wrong with your ears."

CHAPTER SIXTEEN

"Cheer up, Paul. Take it from a bona fide tough guy, a
warrior, a lion among hyenas, a David among Goliaths,
a Samson among Delilahs. I know life can suck, especially when you're holding the dung end of the stick.
When a man's the sheep, he doesn't know if he's being
led to the slaughter or back into the fold by a good
shepherd. Hey, I like that, good shepherd. That reminds
me, Paul, you're a man of faith, all you need to do, cling
to your religion, offer up a prayer or two on the way in
and down. Pray all goes well. Pray for money. Pray for
a safe and molestation-free evacuation. Think of your
wife and kiddies. Me? All of that God jazz, nothing but
white man's voodoo. Especially your religion, Paul.
Hey, but whatever gives you hope, Paul, cling hard,
hold fast, dig deep. You're in the home stretch, Captain,
suck it up, think positive thoughts. On the way to the
golden altar, the ticket to paradise, the keys to the king-

dom, all of which is right smack-dab past those beautiful black one-way doors."

Thus more of the world according to Brick the Prick, Radfield thought.

And Radfield heard what he hoped would be the last silent groan, the final grinding pangs of fiery anguish burning like smoldering coals from deep within his soul. Black briefcase in hand and holding his end of the deal, he was two or three feet to the man's right wing. They were strolling like a couple of executives, just another day at the office, marching across the small white-marbled plaza, sure and swift, though Radfield felt anything but certain.

In fact, the world around him took on an angry but surreal haze. Every man and woman was understandably unaware, indifferent to his plight, which made them, strangely enough, inhuman somehow, or obstacles to only loathe as they charged on into the normal routine of their harried day. Pigeons, he saw, were feeding, crapping all over the place where someone had thought it cute or whatever to dump a bunch of breadcrumbs and gnarled doughnuts. Some knucklehead had a boom box or a radio cranked up to jumbo-jet decibels, like everyone else was supposed to start dancing to the godawful thump-thump noise from hell. Horns blasted, up and down the avenue, where a few drivers proclaimed to the rest of downtown Miami they were a little more important than the next guy.

They were zipping everywhere, pinballs in suits and high heels, cell phones glued to their faces. Oblivious, apathetic, self-involved to the extreme, the more he looked at them all, the less human they became, more beast than man. But Radfield was too nervous, too keyed up, with fear edging fast toward terror, to really much care about any of the usual clamor and border-line sociopathological workings of the city, though for some godforsaken reason the sum total of racket and what was normal life all around him grated deep on already frayed nerves.

Until it was all he could manage to hold back a scream in pure primal outrage. Paul Radfield, Medal of Honor winner, pure war hero, the man of the hour but who felt himself absolutely one hundred per cent before man and God the loneliest, most miserable, wretched, unworthy, untrustworthy, despicable son of a bitch on the face of whole planet.

As for the infernal spook SOB, he glimpsed him grinning up at the blacked-out windows of twenty stories of gleaming monolith where all his hopes and dreams lay waiting, the rotten bastard who held four lives in his hands cool, calm, basking in anticipation of glory and greatness and pleasure. Little question Mr. B was occupied with his own world of fantasy, the large nylon bag in left hand bulged with what Radfield could easily guess were tools of his trade. Maybe…

Radfield killed the thought as soon as it wanted to take shape. Two more men in black were on his six, twenty yards and keeping pace. Where there were two, he could be certain there were more lurking, ready to pounce, wouldn't be surprised if there were snipers positioned on rooftops up and down Brickell.

He would be gunned down like a dog in the street. Or would he? Say he managed to slam an elbow through that smug face and drop the guy on his back, go charging off, melting into the crowd, crying for cops, hurling desperate accusations back at his pursuers...

Stow it.

Unfortunately, the damn guy was right. He was living on little more than hope.

What was even worse, he didn't know what to expect once they were inside. How would this billion-dollar heist go down? Clean—or bloody? There was security all over the building, a full squad and then some and packing Browning pistols. Or were they inside stooges? Given the net that had dropped over him, any rehashing of his previous background checks on security teams here didn't mean squat. Beyond floating and yet more potential enemies, the building itself was a few million square feet, a twenty-story maze of suites and offices, eateries and spas. Many of the office suites were fronts, he suspected, various plaques stating they were import and export nailed to polished mahogany doors, but beyond which were empty rooms and cubicles. But some of the floors housed legitimate businesses. There was a dentist, a few doctors, some computer outfit but that always looked as if little more than a skeleton crew of cyber geeks was on-hand, pretty much drinking sodas, playing games, shooting the bull the one time he'd wandered in to install laser sensors. Then there was a restaurant and health spa on the fifteenth floor, with full staff. Or maybe, since the enemy controlled everything else, they had somehow cleared the building of what would be deemed nonessential personnel. It would be easy enough, placing the calls to bosses, employees given the day off, probably with pay, with goons standing by at the lobby doors to send those who didn't get the word for whatever reason packing.

And what did a billion dollars in cash look like, anyway? Was it in crates, stacked on pallets, packed in a steel container or two? And how the hell did they plan on...

The roof. That was where the helipad was located, which was why they wanted the freight elevators recoded. In fact, the whole two top floors were a vacant sprawl, an empty warehouse—or so it was laid out according to blueprints—and that allowed choppers to park, stay hidden once they descended through the electronically parted tarmac. For that particular scenario to take place, Radfield knew the black op was coming there with plenty of muscle, the kind of clout that moved mountains within the intelligence-special ops arena.

As if he hadn't already expected as much, but now that the clock had ticked down to what was no less than the supreme hour...

As the sweat broke from his forehead, Radfield checked the early morning bustle up and down the avenue. The Metromover, virtually a ghost train even by day, would be due east, gliding over and just inside Bayfront Park. Port of Miami was due south and east, with MIA...

Now what he was thinking? Was he planning some bolt to freedom following on the heels of a desperate and perhaps suicidal escape attempt?

Radfield noted the black op enjoying the view of the skirts and suits scurrying to and from, grinning with, no doubt, visions of gold, savoring knowledge of his dark secret, probably condescending, contemptuous of all these working-class stiffs, this lion among the hyenas. Flagler Street was just ahead, he noted, past the Gusman Center for the Performing Arts. Flagler was the largest jewelry hub in the country, something like 280 jewellers, or so Mr. Brick had related. The Miami-Dade County Courthouse and the bunker-shaped Government Center were farther down...

What in God's name was he doing to himself? Why bother to enjoy a bright, hot sunny morning, as though he was something other than what he was?

A human chess piece.

And maneuvered into place to become one of the biggest traitors in the history of the United States.

Worse, he would be branded a thief, a co-conspirator.

As they closed on the massive black doors that led to the front desk and lobby, the black op hit speed dial on his cell and announced they were there.

It was time.

It was actually happening.

The doors opened and two men in black appeared, holding them wide.

No way out.

Radfield felt sick to his stomach, saw the infernal bastard smiling into the side of his face.

"Let's shake and back, Paul. The Trans-World Bank's open for business."

IT ALL LOOKED and felt so wrong that Bolan knew he was right.

As the soldier worked on the foam cup of coffee and wended a casual path through the work force, he watched through his aviator shades the two men vanish through the front doors, into the lobby. Same doors, same two grim faces in black business suits that had turned away the trio of G-men under his command with gruff words they were Homeland Security, and that his people needed more official authorization to enter the building than those Justice Department badges they were packing.

All confidence. All arrogance.

All stink of the cannibal.

Coincidence? Plain old rudeness on the part of rent-a-cops and who took what little authority they were granted with overbearing zeal? All of it meant to look exactly like what it appeared?

Not when the soldier weighed everything he knew about the Trans-World Bank of Miami and what he didn't, then tacked on the events of the past twenty-four hours. Despite all the state-of-the-art hardware and HU-MINT resources at their command, the denizens of the Farm had turned up a goose egg as they tried to hack their way into local government mainframes that would detail the interior of the building, likewise zero on whoever the original construction contractors. It was as if the Trans-World Bank of Miami existed in a physical limbo.

As for the on-site human factor, there were two men—military-bearing as he judged attitude and strides measured with purpose—and so far they were the only arrivals allowed inside, Bolan having counted thirty heads turned away beyond his guys. And he could read body language with the best of them, judge it for what it was, especially when it came to tension, raw nerves. Follow the sweat down the face of the one with the briefcase, the pinched expression that detailed worry, even paranoia, watch two more men in black business suits with noticeable bulges beneath their coats, checking the avenue, up and down, but with the kind of cool professionalism the soldier knew was an act, before they were let in, expected…

It remained to be seen whether or not more than two hours of watching and waiting for the doors to open to the T-WBM were about to pay off.

Bolan reached the black van, threw open the side door. He felt the eyes of his three-man team watching him as he shed the windbreaker, shrugged into his combat vest, buckled on the harness.

"Paul Radfield. Head of Security at Manexx Petro-Chem, central office out of Houston. Here's the rest of his résumé…"

Bolan slipped into a thin nylon overcoat. It would draw a few curious eyes, considering the sweltering

heat already baking downtown into a glittering con-
crete-and-glass sea of diamond, but it was roomy
enough to cover the small armory on his person, get him
to the front doors. Beyond that...

The soldier glanced at Special Agent Dominion. The
Justice team was working the computer console of the
communication bank. Minicams fixed to the antennas
had been busy snapping faces, and Bolan gave them a
mental salute for fast work. He listened to Radfield's
background. Wife. Kids. Military jacket. The man was
Special Forces, tour of duty being Gulf One, a lot of
classified stuff. Dominion had no cyber read on the
other guy, but Bolan had seen enough to know the kind
of company Radfield was keeping.

Or, the soldier suspected, being forced to keep.

The President was armed with what Bolan had
learned, as far as the obvious went. But...

There may or may not be something happening up
the Eastern Seaboard, with major ports slated for a
major terror touch. The Everglades hit and recovery of
supposed intelligence was too scripted, detailing
through encryption easily enough broken that the Sons
of Revelation had planned the heist of the so-called Armageddon Plague, as far back as a year, with cryptic remarks in half-joking tones about the murders of the
FBI agents. Everything, in Bolan's mind, but Grant's
picture and written confession was planted at the
slaughterhouse. Whether it was wise or not for Washington to quietly scramble the authorities in a low-level
threat warning without fully alerting the public...

Not his call, but it was his problem.

Miami was his call, but, for the moment, Brognola was keeping that bit of news to himself.

The Stony Man warrior was going in blind, but the more he thought about it all, the more certain he was it was about the money.

There was only one way to find out.

Finesse wasn't an option. Finesse was for the other guy. Finesse was for Monday-morning quarterbacks and sidelined talking heads and White House press secretaries.

And with his gut now practically screaming at him that the three cities up north were decoys, meant to deflect all official eyes from what he suspected was the main play here…

The Executioner buttoned up the coat, told his team to sit tight and wait to hear from him. He hefted the big fat black nylon bag and hopped out onto the sidewalk. Good old-fashioned war-honed precombat jitters were kicking in, sirens going off in the soldier's head as he rolled across the plaza.

The two goons weren't going to allow him to enter, all polite and amiable. If he was wrong…

Well, he was maybe betting Brognola's career and his life that his instincts were as solid as ever.

Bolan was a dozen paces and closing when he opened the coat. If there were cameras mounted above the doors, they were hidden. If there were eyes watching, then his first move would create a definite ruckus and bring the jackals running.

So far, though, he was following what was no less than a trail of carnage, where one mystery piled on top of the other. A manmade plague was out there, maybe even somewhere in South Florida, or, worse, set to be dumped on the international auction block. Then there were snakes on the home team, and who seemed to have power to do what they wanted whenever they wanted, and that was just this side of the President. Last but hardly least of all, there was some growing concern, unspoken and unconfirmed, about terror imports being steered inside America by these Invisibles.

It was time to get some answers, one way or another.

Starting now.

When in doubt, going straight to the enemy's front door with kicking foot poised to thunder down any barricade was more often than not the best, the only option.

And that particular anticipated door, dead ahead of Bolan, opened. The face of stone perched on top of gladiator physique was poking its way into open space when the Executioner thrust the Beretta's sound-suppressed muzzle square between those Blues Brothers shaded eyes.

IT WAS THE BEST KIND of rush Donald Lawhorn could imagine.

It was showtime, and he was grabbing the spotlight.

Sitting around waiting for it all to happen these past months was tedious, to say the least, and a man could only kill so much time with whores, booze, blow and cable-surfing. The edge dulled, skills could go rusty with too much R and R, the warrior lost focus of himself, the endgame, the goal line blurred to the point where doubt could set in, and he felt it all slipping away, beyond his control.

A warrior needed to be in charge. Of himself, of the environment, of those around him.

Lawhorn gave his watch a check, stifled the curse. 00:20:22. Ahead of schedule, and under different circumstances that would be a plus. But with the new codes, set for specific countdown to lockdown, to full launch...

Why grumble?

Take it like a lion.

Marching onward, he gave Radfield a quick look, figured the man would do his part, as he hauled out the MP-5 with its double duct-taped magazines. No sound suppressor, but he wanted this noisy, and messy.

The Board of Directors, he knew, was gathered behind those small car-length wide mahogany doors to what was called the Gold Room for the planned weekly brainstorming session. Meaning they wanted to know how those new embezzled funds and how much was being funneled through the offshore accounts were shaping up and who was tapping whose secretary and how fat were the stock portfolios growing. The vile worms included the president of Trans-World Bank, the VP, a VVP and six CEOs, all of whom managed to pay themselves a seven-figure annual salary but for the

life of him, Lawhorn couldn't see where they did much
more than bed their secretaries, hang out in strip clubs,
tool around in their Jags and Mercedes…

He smiled to himself. He had rehearsed this moment
in front of the bathroom mirror the previous night, both
dressed and naked, shades and sans shades, adjusting
tone and expression with each of two dozen or so takes,
as he envisioned their shock, their utter castrated horror. Hell, he couldn't wait to deliver the line.

It would be a priceless moment. The only downside
he could see was that it wouldn't be caught on film for
his future viewing pleasure.

Lawhorn came even more alive as he suddenly realized two of the bank's corporate lawyers would be on
hand.

Big shots.

But what they really were was living dung in the
flesh, and he couldn't wait to walk all over them, grind
them down to the lowly slimy little worms they were.
Oh, how he could feel the joy, the sweet bliss of anticipation, the blood getting hotter with each advancing
step, rushing, no less to the point where he wondered
if he might grow half a chubby.

At the east edge of the teak-and-mirrored second-
floor corridor, he found Jansen and Cutter rolling his
way, big and nasty stainless-steel SPAS-12 autoshotguns rising up from duffels they let fall to the carpet.
One thing about a shotgun, Lawhorn reflected, pausing
at the door as Cutter punched in the access code on the
keypad. They weren't worth a fart in the wind when it

came to distance, but they got everyone's instant and un-divided attention.

"Mr. Jansen, if you would please. Mr. Cutter, if you would do the honors."

Lawhorn lost the smile as Jansen took Radfield by the arm and Cutter grabbed the gold handle, thrust down and flung the door wide. It felt as if he was being carried on the wings of angels, as Lawhorn rolled into the sprawling, glittering abode of worthless men who were the epitome of money for nothing.

He had it all read and down pat, three strides in and vectoring toward the long knight's table. Ronald Tracht III, immaculate in his white suit, was scowling at his gold diamond-studded Rolex watch, but Lawhorn let the gasps and startled cries announce his late arrival. The CEO flunkies were on the far side of the table, five ducks in a row, pretty much as expected, with the lone holdout over by the wet bar building himself an early morning eye-opener. The lawyers were craning fleshy well-fed faces of indulgence his way, the bleary eyes of hard drinkers going wide. With the whiff of whiskey in the air, Lawhorn briefly thought he had a real sweet view of Miami Beach, all glistening and rising for the blue early morning sky over the Atlantic, as he lifted his MP-5.

"Gentlemen," Lawhorn announced as they began sputtering and whimpering and shimmying out of their seats, "You're fired."

CHAPTER SEVENTEEN

There was a downside to bulling the action.

Sometimes the bull got gored.

It was a hard and near-fatal lesson that dropped on Bolan out of nowhere, an anvil of reality. Before he knew it, the Beretta was swept up and away, and he found he was stuck in instant dire straits, ready to lose it all and before he was even four feet inside the lobby, the door behind barely snicking shut. A lonesome 9 mm Parabellum round went chugging away, tearing apart some prehistoric palm fronds hung from the mirrored ceiling, as the soldier caught a flash of Goon Two charging out from behind an upraised black marble horseshoe that had to be the main security post. His immediate problem was not only lightning fast, but the open-heel pile-driver to the soldier's chest had the strength of pure charging rhino behind it. Bolan took the cannonball right to the sternum, wind belching out lungs that felt as if they were being squeezed like an accordion. He would have sworn that was a grin breaking over the guy's face, but he was in way too much pain, sailing back as if he'd just stepped on ten pounds of C-4. The soft body armor beneath his blacksuit didn't do much to cushion the punishing blow, but he knew that was about to become the least of his pain and problems. Another round of starbursts exploded in his eyes as his head hammered into what felt like concrete but what another wave of white-hot pain told him was reinforced and probably bulletproof glass.

Somehow, the warrior found the Beretta still in hand, up and tracking on pure instinct for self-preservation. Somehow the fractured maze in his eyes pieced itself together quick and long enough for him to see the 9 mm Browning pistol clearing the gladiator's coat. There was a nanosecond where Bolan thought he glimpsed surprise or confusion on the goon's face that he was still even conscious, then the Executioner shot him between the eyes.

"PUT THE WHISKEY down. Whiskey is for tough guys, real men."

The moment was pure magic, Lawhorn thinking he couldn't have scripted it better if he tried. The seventh kill—the last lawyer—was just toppling from his seat, when Lawhorn shifted the smoking MP-5 toward the standing CEO. The guy was shaking so bad, the cubes were rattling, drink sloshing over the edges. "And you, son, don't look like any Brick Lawhorn to me."

"You're insane!"

Lawhorn smiled at Ronald Tracht III, the president of Trans-World Bank. Why did they always say that anyway?

The former "banker" for high-ranking officials of the Department of Defense, he saw, was a spattered red mess, from coiffed gray head on down the front, soaked with blood and gristly flecks of flesh and tattered silk. Those blue eyes were bugged and looked set to pop, the lips quivering, Lawhorn decided, like some chicken squawking as it got chased around the pen by its executioner. The deep tan had lost its luster. Understandable, since he'd just seen one of his vice-presidents and the lawyer closest to him both get decapitated by blasts from Cutter's SPAS shotgun and caught a face full of brains and chunks of skull in the process. The Miami Beach skyline had also been altered. The image struck Lawhorn as a macabre painting of a crimson sunset over the city, what with all the running streaks of blood and gobs of gray brain refuse, little smears and driblets sort of stuck but trickling out over divots and cracks like a spider shot full of morphine and didn't know which way to spin out the web.

Cool.

"The key," Lawhorn said.

"Wh-what? What key?"

Lawhorn gave the man a full second to think about it. Some of the fear was melting away, replaced by greed, Mr. Tracht III looking to stall, bluff, lie his way through mortal danger. Not even the president of the

Trans-World Bank was allowed into the vault, Lawhorn knew. If it was opened, a signal was immediately sent to the DHS and the CIA and who kept a watchdog crew on permanent standby in Miami. Tracht III knew what was down there, since he had signed a black contract in the beginning, and under the watchful eye of one of Lawhorn's associates. Without a presidential directive sent via the director of Homeland Security or the director of the CIA, the key itself was to never leave the man's lockbox in the computerized access-coded top drawer of his desk.

"The key."

"I don't know—"

"Mr. Cutter," Lawhorn said.

The shotgun blast drowned the startled cries. The autographed picture frame of the sitting President of the United States hung on the wall just beside the doors was obliterated. The majestic smiling visage gone, a steel panel with a lone key slot was exposed.

"The key."

"I can't..."

"Mr. Jansen," Lawhorn said, and nodded at the CEO. "Trump that one."

The scream was just ripping from his mouth when the CEO took the SPAS blast square in the chest and went flying away on a mist of blood and whiskey.

"Now you're down to these two eunuch pukes," Lawhorn growled. "Once they're dead, it's just you, Ronald. The key."

"It's in my office."

"I know as much, you old fool. But it's real convenient for all of us you're just down the hall," Lawhorn snarled, watching Radfield move to the panel, the battery-powered screwdriver in hand as he went to work removing the steel faceplate to rewire the circuitry, thus neutralizing the trip switch that would alert Washington the heist of the ages was under way.

Radfield hesitated, looked set to protest, but a nudge to the spine from Jansen's SPAS got him moving.

"If I try to open that lockbox without official clearance…"

"Already covered. And I'm about as official as they come. Let's get moving, Ronald! Time is money!"

THE GLASS STARRED behind Bolan but didn't shatter as Gorilla Number Two strolled forward, blasting away with the 9 mm Browning pistol as if he had all the time in the world. The guy was too calm, too sure, and with his buddy laid out with his brains leaking all over polished black marble…

Reinforcements were more than likely en route to bolster all his cool arrogance.

Small comfort he was right about the doors being bulletproof, which left him briefly wondering if they were also soundproof. The soldier was a split second ahead of the tracking line and would have been nailed if not for the quartet of palm trees that began absorbing hits, wood slivers threshed over the back of his skull. The Executioner thrust the Beretta between two trunks, squeezed off three quick rounds but saw that only served to chase the shooter to cover behind the sofas and chairs of a lounge section. Then Bolan saw the cavalry charge into the lobby.

They came on, blazing away with MP-5s and mini-Uzis, five or six shooters, two of them a little on the shaggy side and donning Don Ho shirts. Local thugs? Mercenaries? Left over SOR rabble?

Mentally, Bolan gauged the lay of battleground, nine to three, best he could as the 9 mm tempest began wreaking havoc on the lush transplanted scenery. He snagged a fragmentation grenade off his webbing, armed it. Thirty yards roughly between his barrier and the security platform, a wide corridor leading past the front desk, probably the elevator banks…

If he didn't hit a homer with the first steel egg, he could at least give them some shrapnel and bloody wounds to chew on. He judged the bulk of the shooting somewhere to his eleven o'clock, figured they were the cover team while a few hardmen tried to outflank him. Bolan flung himself toward the edge of the palm, hurtled out the grenade in a sideways whipping motion, then plucked another steel baseball and armed it as the first round of panicked cries and desperate yelps sliced through the weapons fire.

IT WAS A FEELING Lawhorn wasn't used to. It was something to be handed out to the other guy and keep on shoving down his throat. It was something to wield, the ultimate power to cripple or cower a man useless with doubt and submission until he served his purpose.

Fear.

The combat veterans say it motivated, he knew, and perhaps that was true. But the few times he'd felt it in his life it usually brought out the blackest of rage. Experience proved true to form, as he propelled Tracht III away as soon as he marched back into the Gold Room, sent the disheveled lump missiling toward the table where he crashed into the edge, bounced off on a loud guttural belch and flopped to the carpet. Lawhorn actually had to look at the tac radio in his hand to make sure the voice he heard from the control room in the basement was real.

"Sir?"

It was too incredible to believe, but one big bastard decked out in commando regalia was now lobbing grenades around the lobby. Four, no, five were down and bleeding out, according to Runtner, the invader cutting loose with an M-16/M-203 combo and scything through the howling wounded like rats in a barrel. Lawhorn didn't need a blow-by-blow to know they had a serious problem. Through a red haze, he saw Radfield fiddling with the modem attachment from his laptop, frowning as if he was puzzled, connecting it a little too slow for his liking to the circuitry module of the exposed keypad on the lockbox. He barked at the man to hustle up as Tracht III groaned and groped his way up the bloody back end of a wingback to stand, the VPs to his left quaking so hard the leather appeared to actually ripple down the backsides.

"What's our perimeter look like?"

"Clear. No signs anyone heard the problem."

"And our A-list channels?"

"Nothing out of the ordinary, sir. The usual traffic."

Thanks in no small part, Lawhorn knew, to construction specs that were state-of-the-art, the battle raging in the lobby was wrapped tight in its own soundless vault. Top to bottom, the building was built to hold up against the worst hurricanes Ma Nature could hurl, up to and surpassing category five. It was also soundproof, bulletproof and unless someone had IR scope capability there was no way to see past the windows. All legitimate working personnel—maybe all of two hundred—were given this day off on orders from their respective employers as of last night. A few of the workforce who couldn't accept this charity for whatever reasons or didn't get the word and had shown up at the lobby doors had been turned away, no exceptions. As for the sudden arrival of some badass shooter with clear malice of heart, the only thing he could reason out was that Feds or aboveboard ops from DHS or the CIA had smoked them out. Hell, after all, he and the others *were* security; what they said might as well be written in stone. They knew every inch, every nook and cranny, nut, bolt and piece of wiring, with a few of the others having a major role in the building's original design—and with this very moment in mind from the beginning.

Only now…

All indications were only one shooter was on the premises—that they knew of. Given the mess, though, out in the Everglades…

"Go into lockdown, throw up the EM shield, and keep yourself tuned in to the need-to-know frequencies."

"But, sir—"

"Do it. I'll worry about our choppers as soon as we're in."

"Aye, aye, sir."

"We're on the way. Keep your doors on manual lock, and do not, I repeat, do not send any more shooters unless I tell you to."

Lawhorn cut him off as he copied the order.

"What about them?"

Lawhorn glanced at Cutter who was pointing his SPAS at the VPs, one of them making a croaking noise like he was going to vomit or faint away. "What about them?"

"We might need hostages."

Lawhorn saw the green light flash on the laptop as Radfield bypassed the signal trigger and he heard the lock unlatch. Jansen opened the case, plucked the gold key, shouldering Radfield aside as he rushed for the wall.

"Too much baggage to carry."

Without ceremony, Jansen swung aside a formal portrait of the Tracht family, which revealed a plain rectangular panel box. He flung open the faceplate and inserted the key in the single slot. A red light on the panel turned green. When he got the go-ahead, Jansen depressed a yellow button, which would summon the elevator to the vault.

They were bawling in unison, the VPs rising, as if to make a break for it, Tracht III screaming and folding at the knees when Lawhorn held back on the subgun's trigger and chopped the VPs down with a left to right burst, sent them spinning, chewing silk to red ruins. They were falling, draped over the table when Lawhorn saw the carpet bubble before him.

"Please, for the love of—"

"Shut your pie-hole," Lawhorn snarled, throwing Radfield a grin before he reached down, fisted a handful of gray hair and yanked Tracht III to his feet as the carpet parted in a square where it had been sliced. He watched as the gold box rose. Red streaks slimed up the car as it kissed the underneath of the table and lifted it seven feet in the air.

Lawhorn smiled. The long table was balanced perfectly atop the elevator. They may be going down, but that elevator was their ticket to Heaven.

Payday.

Lawhorn dragged Tracht III by the hair as Radfield stepped up and began punching in the access code. He was angry, more than a little concerned about the trouble in the lobby, but the old goat bleating out his pain and terror seemed to lighten the dark mood.

THE EXECUTIONER FLAMED the line of autofire over the last two standing, knocked them off their feet with the 5.56 mm wrecking ball. Two fragmentation grenades had pretty much nailed it down here, but the soldier knew he had only ventured the first step onto the hellfire trail. That no more shooters had charged into the lobby meant one of two things to Bolan. They were either too involved grabbing loot or they couldn't spare the manpower. Maybe both. He slammed home a fresh magazine.

He plucked the tac radio off his belt, but when he punched in, the static was loud and clear through the chiming in his ears. He threw a look back over his shoulder, noted the thinning herd of the workforce scurrying on down the avenue, clearly oblivious to what was no less than all-out combat. One-way glass. Soundproof, to boot. The enemy had control of the building, an EM screen thrown up to prevent any incoming or outgoing calls. He could safely assume the building had been cleared out for just such this occasion.

He was in lockdown.

On his own, with the Justice backup sitting in limbo.

Good enough.

Turning grim attention to the corridor that led to the elevator bank, he watched, listened. Sure, nonetheless, he was still being watched, he gritted his teeth against a wave of fire that tore through his lungs as he touched the two rounds that were impaled in body armor.

"You're not going to make it."

The guy gagged on bloody froth, glaring with eyes that were fast glazing. "You think…you rotten bastard…you know how much money you robbed me of? I had plans… I had dreams…"

"I'm not interested in your sob story. How many?"

The guy laughed, croaked. "Forty…"

"Before or after?"

"After…"

"Where's the money?"

"The vault…down below…"

The guy was giving it up too easy, but Bolan read the defiance in the voice. He'd heard it before. He was one gun against the odds, good luck. The cannibal beneath him was checking out, dying with his annihilated dreams. If he couldn't have what he wanted, why not deny the others?

"How do I get there?"

"Gold Room…first floor…"

And the savage went on his way before the Executioner could ask another question.

Bolan breathed in the stench of death. He gave the plaza one last look. There was no point in trying the doors, certain the building, top to bottom, was sealed, inside and out. How this had all come to pass, what was a major heist in the early-morning hours of the heart of downtown Miami by black ops of Homeland Security…

The soldier felt cold anger driving deep to the marrow of his bones, then discarded the useless emotion. There were times, like this, when it hurt, when he hated being right.

The Executioner took in a deep breath, checked his rear and flanks.

Clear, and all set, but for what?

Bolan hefted the war bag higher on his shoulder. He lifted the M-16/M-203 combo and swept out of the last of smoky tendrils. The elevators were out of the question. The service stairwell, then, and from there…

It all remained to be seen, but the Executioner had the blood of savages in his nose, the fires of justice stoked in his belly, and a heart pounding with lethal intent.

CHAPTER EIGHTEEN

They were understandably speechless, frozen just inside the revolving black doors, and Lawhorn felt compelled to indulge his men a few moments of shared and much-deserved awed silence. Why not? he figured. Consider all the planning, the greasing and the payoffs, the noose hung over the right heads, here and there, and twisted, some more than others. All the anxious months, surveillance and counter, chasing and dodging shadows, slapping sense, or worse, into some spineless whiner, wondering even up to then if someone somewhere had gotten cold feet and gone running with a guilty patriotic conscience to the Headshed.

In short fashion, all the blood, sweat and tears.

But there it was.

Behold and enjoy.

Yes, they had been told what to expect, the numbers of pallets, each one close to seven feet tall, fat enough to fill the average bed of a pickup truck, then the steel container that was destined for removal by the scaled-down, custom-built tractor-trailer with government plates. Yes, the vault had been lain out during two previous briefings from the original purloined blueprints, and every man had a specific assignment. And since they were on the clock, Lawhorn wasn't about to allow any of them more than a few seconds to try to absorb the sight of one billion dollars in cash.

Since there was something to be said about seeing to believe, it took a wave of his hand and a barked, "Chop, chop, gentlemen," to get the hired help moving. Then they charged out, thirty strong. They may be special ops shooters, or black covert shadows from various intelligence agencies for the most part, with some mercenary rabble thrown in the mix but who came with the proper credentials and a solid warrior heart. Right then they were mighty damn expensive human mules. They fanned out, split up to their assigned row, each man lugging his allotted six body bags to his prescribed pallets. Standard drywall cutters carefully sliced away thick plastic, hydraulic power snips snapping through thick double-wired bands, rubber padding around the edges tumbling to black-painted concrete. They went to work in a silent controlled frenzy, banded stacks by the hundred thousand swept into the body bags, bulging nylon in seconds flat.

They were beautiful to behold, this fine-tuned machinery, these professionals who didn't waste one move, one second.

Lawhorn almost forgot about Radfield and Tracht III. He turned and grinned at the two men. Where the former Special Forces captain looked grim and worried, the bank president's jaw was hung, lips wet, eyes popping.

"What's that, you ask? How could this be happening?" Lawhorn laughed. "That, gentlemen, is this nation's slush fund for the War on Terror. That, gentlemen, is some of your hard-earned tax dollars at work. That, gentlemen, is my retirement fund. Mr. Tracht the Third, what you don't know is that in two weeks some of this cash you were going to be ordered directly from the Department and the CIA to begin funneling overseas. The funds were destined to get moved, or rather, vanish temporarily through various interest-bearing accounts, where it was fated to double within a year. Unfortunately, sir, plans have a way of getting changed. Mr. Radfield, I believe you still have work to do." Lawhorn gestured with his MP-5 toward the trio of freight elevators against the deep east wall.

Radfield hesitated, then trudged off.

"Cheer up, Paul. You can play with the big computer like I promised, just as soon as you get those freight cars up and moving. What's that, you say, Mr. Tracht the Third? How am I going to get away with this? Why, if I told you that, sir, I'd have to kill you. Suffice it to say once our cleaners get it all nice and washed and they take their thirty-three cents on a dollar—the thieving sons of bitches—it's a done deal."

"And me?"

Lawhorn was about to answer that he wasn't sure yet, when he found Jansen stepping up to him. There was a dark expression on Jansen's face, the man not saying a word for what felt like an hour. "You look like you just swallowed the world's biggest turd."

Jansen's lips parted.

"What is it!?"

"Sir…in all the excitement, I guess…I left the key behind."

DURZHEB THOULZRIC CONSIDERED the moment. He felt stuck and maybe sinking in frozen time, his spirit shredded and floating somewhere between sorrow and hope, regret and great expectations. Whatever the truth, it was too late to do anything other than stay the course, both figurative and literal.

Still, the Chechen rebel had allowed certain distractions to slip into his thoughts during the thousand or so mile journey, which only served to agitate. Even though it was actually happening, he found he could not even begin to count the number of close calls when all looked lost, possible detection by enemy forces beyond the principals—and who were, in fact, their sworn enemies but had become their grand paymasters—and where they were scuttled from camp to camp, Iran to Syria. Follow up with months of nerve-racking technical training then there was a brief layover in Spain before they were flown to America, to be settled into various Arab communities up and down the Eastern Seaboard. But, no sooner had they landed than they were then filtered, in twos and threes, into established safehouses in South Florida and East Texas. All contact was established with written instructions via regular or overnight mail, along with the necessary cashier checks for living and traveling expenses. Post office boxes in various cities had been helpful in guiding each of them to their next destination, thus arming them in writing with their next round of standing temporary orders. His hands fisting the big steering wheel tight, he had to smile at that much, using, that was, the American postal system to bring the big event to its culmination here in South Beach.

As he checked his watch and saw the timing was near in perfect sync with their instructions, he looked back into the past yet again, and for what he suspected would be the last time. In the beginning, he had worried that it was all too good to be a true, a setup, he and his fellow brothers-in-jihad being led into ambush—until they all discovered the infidels in the black hoods were true to their word. And that large sums of cash had been couriered to their respective families, enough so that their villages, in fact, could live in comfort for years to come, and the brothers they had left behind could purchase all the small and hopefully large arms they wanted. Of course, it had been the Iranian who had sworn before all of them and God that the infidels could be trusted to fulfill their part in safely smuggling them into America, that ultimate jihad was their destiny, if they so wished.

And now…

The Iranian most certainly looked to have been blessed, chosen, in truth, by God to both select the right warriors and steer them all to what was no less than divine retribution against the Great Satan.

Close to eighteen hours since rolling out of Houston, and there had been plenty of time to reflect, pray for guidance and protection, and to discover if the dream was just that. Sticking to the posted 70 to 75 mph for the duration, the interstates clear of traffic jams or even moderately paced vehicle flow, and there was no point in monitoring the digital screens any longer, as he guided the behemoth off the MacArthur Causeway, slowing to fall in with the traffic on 5th Street.

Lummus Park was just ahead, their starting point.

Their statement.

Still, though they had arrived, safe and unmolested, he had to marvel at how easy and uninterrupted the journey had been. Between their police scanners, radar jamming and their short- and long-range tie-in to local weather and travel channels…

The shame of it all was that they were going to die here, and that so much expensive state-of-the-art equipment and weapons would only see them rack up just so many dead and maimed. There were plenty of hotels, eateries here in what they called the Art Deco District, and with the sprawling length of beach…

If all went according to plan, they were hoping to settle the body count in at around a thousand to two thousand, hopefully more. Beyond the dead, there was, of course, the terror and panic they would wreak on American society, and the knowledge of how their mission would quite possibly unravel the fabric of this corrupt nation of fatted calves and mindless pleasure-seekers, may well see him smiling from beyond the grave.

There was some sort of all-day international music festival already under way on Lummus, as the FedEx package had stated during the last rounds of orders. Which meant the park and the beach would be choked with bodies, the infidel hordes basking in the sun, the music, the good times.

The weapons, he knew, were the key to success. Five Gatling guns total, each one capable of pounding out 4,000 rounds of 20 mm ammunition per minute. The loads were mixed HE, armor-piercing and incendiary antipersonnel. With the Miami Beach Police headquarters six blocks north, sure to be scrambled as soon as the first rounds exploded into the crowds…

He smiled again.

The infidel law didn't stand a chance.

Thoulzric checked the troops behind him in the special sideview glass mounted on the edge of his armor-plated door. The two 30 mm autocannons, one to port, one to starboard, were getting a final inspection by anxious hands as the boxes were snapped into place.

He wanted to offer up one final prayer, but he felt the excitement and the fire rise from deep within as he swung onto Ocean Drive and began slowly rolling north. He couldn't even begin to count the bodies.

There were legions, in fact, too many infidels to even venture a rough body count.

As expected, they were laughing, drinking, eating, playing their games in thick pockets along with the vast stretch of white sand. The music was thundering, a cacophony of different sounds and rhythms, and Thoulzric had to smile one last time, envision the carnage as he took in the sight of the teeming crowds on both sides of Ocean Drive.

The clock struck.

He saw one of his brothers-in-jihad reach up and snap the main cord, the nylon drape falling away from the war bus, allowing the platform with Gherhazi to rise through the parting roof, his hands wrapped and ready on the big stainless-steel weapon.

Thoulzric almost forgot to slip on the special ear pads with com link. He was settling the protective-communication headset on just as the first salvos erupted.

IT WAS EITHER a mistake done in the heat of the moment or the key had been left behind on purpose. Mistakes did happen, rare for the professional, but considering what the enemy was chasing, the Executioner was fairly certain they had their talons opened and ready to swoop down on the big prize. Bolan had brief pause to wonder if he hadn't just committed what might prove a fatal error by dumping off the war bag behind the base of a palm tree standing on the edge of the stairwell platform leading up to the first floor. Shedding the added weight had been his prime consideration, the overcoat now gone to give him free and ready access to spare clips and grenades. The M-16/M-203 combo was hung over his shoulder, just in case.

Bolan gave the Gold Room a quick inspection, and spotted the family portrait, which had been swung aside. He swiftly crossed the room, spied the key that had been left in the slot and gave it a turn. A red light turned green, and the soldier figured the yellow button had something to do with it. He pressed the button. No sooner had he done that than he heard movement out in the corridor, judged the noise of men charging hard coming from both east and west. The M-16/M-203 combo was perfect when it came to open range fighting, but for close-quarters combat he had the MP-5 in hand. For a second too long the sunlight that speared into the slaughterhouse warbled as sudden dizziness descended. Whether or not he was on the verge of falling victim to a concussion at the worst of times…

It took another heartbeat or two to suck in and let go a deep breath, clear the cobwebs, and by then he was sure his eyes were failing him as he spotted the floor rising beneath the table. It looked like a gold rectangular box, doors already parting.

He plucked a fragmentation grenade from his vest as he spied two armed figures, bearing down from the west, thirty feet and closing, hugging the wall closest to him, grim advance reflected in the walled mirror across the hall. The Executioner armed the steel baseball, pitched it through the doorway just as the elevator car hit the table and he caught an eyeful of rising buzz cut heads, MP-5s extended over the edge of the floor and cutting loose with a blistering line of 9 mm lead. The wall above and behind tattooed with thudding divots, the soldier opted for a sudden Plan B.

Run, gun and draw them to him. Easier said than done, since they had his flanks and rear sealed.

They were shouting in panic to his left, bolting from the sounds of it from bouncing death, as the Executioner beat the tracking line of weapons fire on his six out the door. He had another frag bomb armed and flying east, as he caught two more shooters in the corner of his eye, the other half of the pincers blazing away with Uzis but staying their hands at the sight of the sailing egg that forced them to cut and run.

As the first blast roared, Bolan hit the double black doors across the hall with a raking burst of subgun fire, hoping to hell and gone they weren't shatter-proof.

Lupe Import-Export vanished in a tumble of glass shards.

The Executioner ran a few yards, hosing the boiling cloud with a quick one-handed burst, then crouched, hands shielding his face. He was bulling through the jagged teeth, his shoulder catching a fang that tore hard and deep, just as the second thunderclap chimed in and he felt the wind driven from his lungs where two steel missiles drilled between his shoulder blades and propelled him on his way.

JOHN BRENDON knew the truth.

The United States of America was one cataclysm away from anarchy. Whether it was a tactical nuke set off in downtown Manhattan or D.C., a few dirty bombs lighting up some shopping malls, restaurants or movie theaters, or if the land was hit with a wave of dynamite or plastic explosive-vested martyrs who started blowing themselves up on crowded sidewalks, hotel lobbies, train and bus stations, Americans, by and large, would come unhinged.

Patience and sacrifice, he thought, goodwill and charity were in short supply these days in the American spirit. Truth be told, there seemed to be a darkness spreading over the land, a senseless anger, a malice and greed that seemed to be feeding on itself more every day. It seemed that Every Man felt entitled to the big life no matter what, and, further, he wasn't accountable for his actions no matter how heinous. Morality and Truth were in the eye of the beholder.

Though they had to publicly tone down the rhetoric in the interests of political correctness, the intelligence and military powers-that-be knew as much, and had several martial law plans ready to spring when American cities eventually collapsed into lawless and disorder meltdown, none of which called for gentle persuasion and a simple imploring for peace and quiet. Brendon knew all about it, since he had been on hand for these post-Apocalypse briefings, and had personally reviewed the contingency safety valves to keep America from circling the bowl.

Here's how it went, as he recalled it.

The brass and their war-gaming Doomsday minions envisioned wholesale panic, sweeping coast-to-coast, border-to-border, lighting the torch for anarchy. There would be riots and looting, traffic jams on every interstate and main artery, no end in sight to these parking lots all over America's roadways, and this just for night-mare openers. Walled enclaves of the rich and famous and even the relatively secure middle class would come under mass assault by frenzied mobs who envied and despised them and who knew they could never aspire to the American Dream, but who saw their golden op-portunity to vent all their rage and frustration, plunder what they could. Shopping malls and local businesses, especially pharmacies and liquor stores, they claimed, would come under siege right out of the gate. Armed vigilante groups would hole up or take to the streets in their various privileged communities, defending their life and property with a bloodthirsty zeal as cops and Feds were overwhelmed, outgunned, outmatched by the sheer force of numbers and ferocity of the lunatic legions. Class division would become a bloody clash to the death where Army soldiers, Special Forces com-mandos and the National Guard would hit the streets in tanks and helicopter gunships and mow down any and all the disobedient and disenfranchised if they didn't cease and desist, submit and return to their shabby rat-holes of poverty and despair. Murder and mayhem would be the order of the day. Only the might that was right would restore it all to sanity.

Brendon flinched as the first fireball erupted. It was a blazing mushroom cloud that rose maybe six to eight hundred feet or more, smack in the middle over the Macarthur Causeway, blotting out his spectacular view of those massive triple-deckered cruise ships berthed beyond in the Port of Miami. Before he could suck breath over the initial shocking sight, the firestorm whirled out into a screaming tunnel of pure white-hot inferno that swept over the traffic jam to the west, consuming untold numbers of vehicles and pedestrians who'd gotten out to gawk and gripe, some of the oncoming eastbound traffic vanishing on their end of the dragon's spray.

One down.

Eighteen stories up, hugging the retainer wall, he panned on with his field glasses, taking in the bird's-eye view, south to north up Biscayne Bay.

Ditto for the Venetian Causeway, the Julia Tuttle and the John F. Kennedy.

The gong for the big event had resounded.

The fireworks went off, damn near to the second.

It had been simple enough, he thought, made infinitely too easy since there was no security, no checkpoints on any of the causeways, nothing but long lines of cars, he thought, with unsuspecting passengers ready to be incinerated in those rolling or parked hearses.

Enter four three-man teams right before the supreme moment. The two leading vehicles created a little fender-bender, sluiced and braked all over the causeways, then drivers hopped out and started a little shouting match for show, blocking all lanes best they could in the process. Trailing six-wheelers, stamped with the label of their private moving company—Safety Lines—and packed with two thousand pounds of prewired radio-remote C-4 would slow, wait a few minutes while the traffic stacked up then those wheelmen martyrs...

Boom!

None of it was enough to bring those causeways tumbling down, he knew, but there was enough concrete, mangled shells of vehicles and flying stick figures for him to be reasonably certain Miami Beach was a few short moments from going into pure panic mode.

That breakdown of American society they talked and war-gamed about in the E-Ring.

Far below him he found they were partying and schmoozing up a hurricane. It was a convention of condo sales reps and prospective customers, a well-heeled herd of upper-crust local snobbery. Three to four hundred strong, they were poolside, diving into the buffet of lobster and prime rib, swilling champagne, chattering away, glittering and shaking to another beautiful Miami morning of bright sunshine—or so they foolishly believed.

The rolling thunder was just reaching their ears, blue sky over the Bay bedazzled into a giant flashing starburst, causing a few heads to turn bayward, when Brendon lowered the glasses and watched the two large nylon bags sailing over the wall. At one hundred pounds apiece, gravity went to work quick and Brendon was barely able to catch another breath and let go when the first bag slammed through the cabana on the south end. Impact sensors appeared to be in working order, as he watched the thatched roofing explode in billow of smoke and fire, the blast hurling all manner of debris clear across the pool.

The stampede was just getting warmed up, bodies

sailing, spiraling to splash down in the aqua waters, the first churning cloud sweeping over maybe half of them when bag number two plowed through the bar's sawgrass canopy and erupted at the north end. They were screaming now, as the clouds thickened and meshed over them in palls he figured would have done the factory-toxic blanket over the Gary, Indiana, skyline proud. Bodies went reeling all over the deck, shrieking mannequin things thrashing their way out of the green haze, a few of them, he watched with another scan through his field glasses, clawing at throats and eyes, tongues protruding and flicking around like gassed snakes.

Brendon smiled. Teary eyes and lack of oxygen was about to become the least of their woes. It took a few seconds, but the Adamsite laced with a special compound used to clear out the bowels of racing horses before they hit the track kicked in with a sudden fury.

Brendon was grabbing up his MP-5 and turning away from the sights and sounds of the horror below when he heard the first few loud chugs from across the roof. Striding for the stairwell housing they'd locked from the outside with the cutting edge magnetic keypad latch, three 85 mm shells were already arcing for the glittering skyline of downtown Miami, due south and west. He took a moment of what was no less than pride and astonishment, as McBride and Douglass and their three-man tech-and-demo crew veered from the high-tech fire zone at the west edge, to check the hardware. It was so state-of-the-art maybe ten men outside the architects—and all seven of said armorers were no longer among the living—knew of their existence. The plates were bolted down to the white-graveled roof, plenty enough hold to maintain the works against being torn from what was near negligent recoil from the stainless-steel heavy mortars. With their range up to 6000 meters, with one hundred shells ready to fly from each belt, Brendon knew there was enough firepower set to rain down that Miami from Opa-Locka Airport to Little Havana would get hammered.

Welcome, he thought, to the new world of high-tech warfare.

No. Welcome to his cut of a billion dollars.

Cables, he saw, gathering speed as the next trio of projectiles were pumped out, ran from three laptops and were attached to the small battery-powered electronics box on each tube. The belt feeds were battery-operated and were tied in to the programmed computer software that fed the correct trajectory for each round, depending on the target, range, elevation and such. No more than three seconds elapsed between each launch, as the tubes whirred to the computer's tracking system, and kept on chugging.

Brendon chuckled, as his men opened the door, MP-5s thrust around the corners to check for any alarmed security flunkies. The designers of the software had likewise met a sudden and untimely end when those programs were written to spec, and Brendon had to wonder if they might have felt the same way Einstein had when he'd helped to build the bomb.

Who cared, he decided. He was old-school warrior,

but he had to admit, as an HE round plowed into the glassy facade of high-rise near the Design District, there was something to be said about this new age of battle-field gizmos.

He pulled up at the stairwell door, turned as Douglass palmed the black box. The screams and shouts and distant thunderclaps rent the air, and Brendon smiled as the final touches to what was no less than genius flared to life. It was invisible, but Douglass took the EM read on his unit, gave him the thumbs-up. The web of sensors, string-thin and painted white to blend in with the roof, would send a signal to all twenty silvery boxes that at a passing glance would look like air vents. In reality, they were shaped charges of plastic explosive, wrapped in silver lining to further pass fleeting inspection. Should one SWAT commando boot hit the roof, he'd been informed the blast alone would be enough to take out everything down to the next floor below.

Outstanding.

Then there was the rainbow of wiring inside the door that would hold back any Metro-Dade bomb squad elite, and it would take them five minutes or so alone by their best judgment just to figure out if there were sensors, pressure plates ready to set off the ten-pound block that had more digital readouts and decoy panels than he could imagine ran down the length of one bank of NASA control panels. While they sweated and cursed and fumbled to disarm that block of C-4, Brendon could well imagine their horror and frustration as they listened to the steady chug of more airborne death flying away for the city.

Douglass swept the gloom below with his MP-5 then shut the door behind him and armed it with yet another block of C-4. They were by no means in the home stretch, payday in hand, but as he heard those rounds keep on chugging, John Brendon had to believe the brass ring was theirs for the grabbing.

Speaking of brass, he tipped a mental salute to the big boys in the E-Ring for clueing him in, thus allowing him to create and implement his own unique brand of counterterror plans.

Thanks for the memories, he thought, and sailed down the steps, eager to be on his way to lay eyes on a billion-dollar payoff, courtesy of the very United States government he still officially worked for.

CHAPTER NINETEEN

The Executioner flung himself over the first bank of workstations, using his head and shoulders like a battering ram as he plowed through the wallboard. Experience had long since warned him that no matter how well a plan was scripted and run back and forth through the mind, reality always had its own ideas. The intention, or so he briefly envisioned, had been to draw them into what appeared empty office space save for some decorative furniture and workstations, then roll back a grenade or two as they hunched beyond the doors, figuring out their next move.

It didn't happen.

In fact, the savage beast called reality scribbled down its own script and handed it to him on a roaring blaze of weapons fire.

Bolan was tumbling down and eating carpet when the first stuttering waves of MP-5 subgun fire hit the

room and started tracking his blood-soaked and pun-
ished frame. As the tempest of plaster and trashed computer terminals flew overhead, the Stony Man warrior
armed a frag grenade. He counted off two ticks and
tossed it over and through the raining flotsam, mentally
gauging his present position to the layout he'd left behind, taking a face full of glass and wood in the process.
They were coming hard, berserkers and demons in
human skin, weapons stammering so fast they were
chewing up his cover in great threshing waves from
what could have been three different firepoints.

A sonic boom rent the air next, and what looked like
half the standing partition on his rear was obliterated.
There was no mistaking the sound and fury of an autoshotgun, as another four feet of wallboard vanished.
One way or another, the Executioner knew it would be
over, seconds flat.

He was up and bolting for a series of empty work cubicles, trying his damnedest to hear something through
the chiming in his ears, flinging subgun fire over his
shoulder, waiting...

Bolan pressed his hands to his ears as best he could,
for all the good it would do. A beehive of angry lead
hornets scorched the air, singed his scalp as he dived behind a few wingbacks parked against a long table, a split
second ahead of thundering blast.

Had they come in, lobbing grenades, or bull-rushed
with more than three or four shooters, had they taken a
few extra seconds before charging in with heads filled
with angry steam, thinking they had him outgunned

and outclassed, sterling odds in their favor, the warrior might have been defeated.

Perhaps, Bolan thought, they were saving the heavy artillery for cops or SWAT who might somehow get wind of the heist, or they had come in with only small arms from the jump, thinking it would be a quick and easy skate to the vault, total control of the premises, any unforeseen opposition little more than flies to be swatted. They hadn't planned on one man, albeit armed to the teeth, to come here, stepping all over their dreams, Godzilla on the rampage through the Trans-World Bank Miami.

The M-16/M-203 combo was off his shoulder as he saw a body sailing from the roiling smoke, the crimson and shredded rag doll launched out of sight behind another row of workstations.

The office suite looked to gobble up some decent space, as far as he could tell, roomy enough to hold two or three dozen with plenty of elbow space to spare, what looked like cubicles running, east to west.

The autoshotgun roared from twenty feet away, resounding out from across a stretch of couches and coffee tables. Bolan ducked as the wave of double-aught buck cleaved off a chunk of doorjamb above his head. The soldier reached on instinct, pure adrenaline, the 40 mm round streaking off before he realized he'd tapped the trigger. He was toppling back into empty office space when the HE round blew.

The Executioner rose up, rolled out, M-16 leading the way. One step beyond the doorway, he heard a hideous groan, saw a mangled crimson stick figure shuddering through the smoke, the stainless-steel howitzer swinging his way. Bolan blew him off his feet with a 3-round burst of autofire, the SPAS blasting a hole in the ceiling that brought down enough plaster and light fixtures to bury the guy.

Slowly, his eyes scanning the ruins and swirling dust, Bolan crunched a path toward the door. He counted four bodies, or what was left of them, before he crouched near the opening and listened. He held his ground, the ringing in his ears easing off just enough thirty or so seconds later for him to hear dead silence out in the corridor.

What waited, if anything, with the next few steps...

Nothing ventured, he figured.

The Executioner dumped a 40 mm buckshot round down the M-203, then squeezed through the glass. A long search in both directions revealed two more savages littering the hall to the west.

It was hardly getting better all the time, but he was shaving the odds, and doing it the hard way.

Each yard gained, each body tallied with nothing but blood, sweat and pain.

The vault, he was reasonably certain, would be the toughest part.

Nothing gained, not yet.

The Executioner turned, reentered the Gold Room and headed for the elevator.

ALLEN BRAXTON BELIEVED he couldn't have diagrammed it, connecting all the target dots, any better than what he saw.

Miami was hot, burning.

For the stand-up acts and grim purpose of the Invisibles, the mere sight of what he had engineered was well worth the price of admission. He demanded no less than perfection from his team on down the line through the hired hands, but this was better than even he had hoped for. Between steely professional nerves, seasoned skill and the pride of lions, couple all that with rabid Islamic determination and hatred, and so far the mission looked a surefire winner.

At first roving and eye-popping scan, it was near impossible to take in all the mayhem, count the explosions still peppering the length of Flagler, Brickell, Biscayne, and what with all the fires blazing out of control, bringing on the fire and police and EMT brigades, they were all but sealed, stuck, screwed. Then the swarming mobs, the stampedes in full roaring earnest and crushing the weak, the slow, the paralyzed, terror-stricken, the frenzy of snarled traffic turned into rending pockets of marathon bumper-car smash-ups. Panning on, he needed to get a feel for how the play was developing, deciding to get his money's worth out of his buzzard's-eye view. He wasn't quite ready to smile and dance on the clouds, but it looked to be shaping up his way, in a hurry.

Waiting on status reports from his communications team about Tampa, Houston and Dallas-Fort Worth, the Invisibles' Leader filled the port hatch, holding on to a canvas strap. Their lead Chinook was bearing down on the T-WBM from the south, cruising at about two thousand feet, slowing to somewhere around fifty, sixty knots as they veered to the northwest over Rickenbacker Causeway, leading the Black Hawks, the second CH-47 picking up the rear of his billion-dollar parade.

As for the causeways, chaos reigned, bottlenecks, Baghdad imported to the land of the free and the home of the brave. Creating a local fly-by-night moving company was nothing less than a stroke of genius, he decided.

"Air Clearance Security Code is Alpha-Zero-One-Niner-Omega-Two-Six-Six. We are five birds strong, three Black Hawks and two Chinooks. Copy that, Homestead."

As the big troop transport began losing altitude, Braxton listened to the brief static burst, then glimpsed Silas throw him a thumbs-up as Homestead Air Force Base rogered back they were clear to aid and assist Counterterror Measures, what was known in their circles as ThreatCon Delta Black. He knew that they were already cleared by Metro-Dade and Broward authorities, and now he was quickly informed Homestead was scrambling both the fighter jets and helicopter gunships. What was their plan? Silas told them since he was Homeland Security he would let Homestead know something in short order once they received further orders from Washington.

The skies above Miami, Braxton knew, were about to get real crowded, which meant they needed to pick up the pace. Already there looked to be a couple dozen or more Metro-Dade Bell helicopters scissoring all over the city, gleaming bladed flyspecks as far north as Fort Lauderdale-Hollywood. The light show on the streets was also pretty impressive, as he took a peek through his field glasses, watching as an EMT vehicle was pounded to fiery scrap by an 85 mm comet down Flagler, in what would be the jewelry district.

Braxton looked farther northwest, found he was just in time to find two 85 mm meteors slam into the Metromover. The HE homers pounded the upraised train around what he knew was the Produce District of Allapattah. The second and fourth cars bore the brunt, blowing apart, the silver streamlined train beginning an ungainly accordion-like fold to tumble off the elevated track. Hell, he figured if he were blindfolded and deaf he could still feel, smell and taste the terror and panic ripping from Miami Beach, to Hialeah and clear up to Opa-Locka Airport.

The four causeways in front of him, smothered in black billowing clouds, were choked for about a mile in each direction, with bodies and mangled burning wrecks littering the concrete decks like strewed checkerboards. Better still, his Arab crew had Godzilla stomping all over Lummus Park and north, with maybe ten to fifteen squad cars perforated to mangled little bonfires up Ocean Drive, the facades of three or four hotels so shellacked by cannon and Gatling fire, the way he'd just seen it he figured those untimely gemstones of renovation had reduced them to nothing but pricey beachfront homeless shelters. Their radio intercepts of all restricted and classified DEA, Justice Department, FBI and military transmissions likewise informed him that the big event was staying the course.

Miami was going down the sinkhole fast, as total

and complete anarchy, he suspected, were just around the bend.

He shifted his view to the Biscayne Towers. Three Bells were hovering over the roof, SWAT guys busy sniping at the three sources of raining death and destruction. Why one team was rappelling down while the other choppers lowered for the roof escaped him, but it was the worst of dumb-ass moves either way. The mortars with their computer links, he saw, were shot to smoking rubbish, but that was expected, going in. And unless one of those snipers had gotten lucky and disabled the anti-EM scanning box in the far south corner, their screen was still up and running. Braxton was trying to determine approximately how many rounds would be left wasted when he heard Rankin call, "Sir!"

Braxton hesitated, since there was no tone of urgency or panic in the man's voice. He was thinking about a third to a half of the loads had been used up when he lowered the glasses, cracking eyelids to mere slits just as the roof went up in a sheet of fire, what was no less in his mind and sight than the world's biggest torch getting ignited. As fiery slabs, bodies and twisted rotors winged out for eventual splash down in the Bay, Braxton watched, fairly mesmerized, as the flaming skeleton of a chopper seemed to drift out of the fireball, float for a heartbeat, then plunge. Poolside and patios of the Biscayne Towers had become an impromptu and open hospital ward for the victims of the attack. The medics tending to the sick were being belted by showering space rock, two or three uniforms knocked into the pool. They all looked like ants, scurrying from wild-fire, from his vantage point, the EM teams torn between hauling ass and stretchers or staying put. The few who braved it out with their victims began bolting a second or so too late as the flaming asteroid crashed down and squashed them like bugs.

Braxton turned and gave Rankin his full attention. "You were saying, mister?"

"Base Rhino has just informed me that PBIC is a shining star! Sir!"

Braxton checked the smile. The Pasadena-Baytown Industrial Corridor, with what was virtually a fifty-mile stretch of petrochemicals and other toxic and volatile substances, would get Houston's full firefighting, police and EM attention. Once it was discovered there was radioactive waste floating down with the demolished warehouse...

Getting better by the minute.

Braxton scanned the faces of Rogers and Morrow. "Gentlemen? Talk to me!"

Morrow held up a hand then a tight smile broke over his lips above the com link. "Black Rhino and Masto-don are a go. Spotter Teams JFK-Limo and Urban Cow-boy inform me they are full steam ahead and rocking, and better than anticipated. Sir!"

Dallas-Fort Worth, he knew, were getting similar treatment that he saw tearing through the city below. "Mr. Rogers?"

"Sir...Kong Command informs me Team String Bi-kini Gulf Sunshine has encountered a problem."

"I don't want to hear about problems, mister, I want solutions! Explain yourself!"

A dark frown clouded Rogers's face, the man bobbing his head, grunting into his throat mike. "Roger that, Kong Command. Sir! I am informed that Team String Bikini Gulf Sunshine found they were bogged down in a traffic jam involving an overturned tractor trailer and where Interstate 275 comes off of I-75 and they proceeded ahead of schedule."

Which meant, Braxton knew, they were stuck and steaming, but shooting up what was no less than a parking lot, a static shooting gallery of fat sitting targets on the interstate. Scratch Tampa, more or less, but it would prove enough to further pile up the body count, spread the terror and keep all eyes turned off them while they proceeded.

"Keep me posted!" Braxton shouted, and went back to watching Miami burn.

HE WASN'T QUITE READY to offer up one last Act of Contrition, but Paul Radfield decided he'd keep one close on tap, just in case. And he had been around long enough to know that no matter how hard a man tried to live a good life, maintain a sanctuary of right living, the insanity of the world, the evil of other men somehow inevitably found its way to his doorstep. Worse, he had been working, unsuspecting, that was, for the forces of darkness all along.

There was consolation, however, to be found in this time of peril.

The former Special Forces captain was reasonably certain he was in a state of grace, though he knew the faith stated that the way God saw things was a far cry from the way man saw them, that even the smallest transgression, the most trifling of imperfections was a glaring horror in the eyes of the divine, and to be accounted for at his particular judgment the very second the soul left the body. Not only did he believe as much, he sure counted on that very fact, and for any number of reasons, the least of which was that the wicked received their sentence as well as the just. That in mind, there really was nothing to fear, not even death, if a man lived—even sought to live—right and true in the eyes of his Maker.

His one small vice was moderate intemperance, at worst, and as far as he knew he had honored all Ten Commandments to the letter, and then some. Beyond that, there may be some floundering in his devotion as far as daily prayer went, too much concern with the welfare of his family, the pursuit of happiness, comfort— theirs and his—as far as worldly needs and material things went. He didn't want to assume best case, but there was hope he would leave this world in God's friendship.

As he burned the fourth of six CDs from the supercomputer, Radfield felt it in the air, and saw something on Mr. Brick's face he wouldn't have believed possible, considering the psychopath the man had proved himself to be.

Make no mistake that was fear in the man's eyes. Try

as he might to disguise it, what with his bellowed orders and snarled curses, Radfield knew the man was edging close to panic.

Which made him more dangerous than ever.

As the mainframe pumped out at light speed what were supposedly the darkest and most sordid intelligence truths since the Founding Fathers signed the Declaration of Independence, Radfield took in the commotion. Not even the vast expanse of the sterile vault could contain the new levels of frenzy that had only moments ago torqued up to screaming demon vibes.

The booty bags, he saw from his post in the horseshoe-shaped computer bay, had been piled across two sets of double steel bars, each about twenty feet in length. They were welded together with bars on each end, raised about ten inches off the floor by thick metallic shoes. The design made easy work for the forklifts as they hoisted them, wheeled around and rolled them a few short yards into the massive freight elevators. The steel container was being fork-lifted and hauled into the farthest and largest car. Unless he missed his guess, his recall of original blueprints outlined a canopied dock on the east end, just off ground level, wide enough to berth one tractor-trailer at a time.

They had it all figured out, well in advance. To the roof with maybe half of the loot, where a chopper or choppers were waiting, the other half of the take to be trucked somewhere, dumped, perhaps, into a waiting sea-faring vessel.

The whole operation, the heist had such a surreal quality about it, Radfield wanted to find it impossible to the extreme. Only he knew better, since he had inside working knowledge about operational security. And these men were security for the whole damn building, some of the most powerful intelligence operatives in the nation.

He popped another CD out of the drive, deposited it into the small black bag as Mr. Brick had ordered. The main computer was tied in to a series of smaller machines, black top-finish, and he wasn't surprised in the least by the colored terminals. His captor had mentioned the fact that the supercomputer housed in NATO Headquarters in Brussels, Belgium, was called 666, and that much Radfield knew to be true, though it was fairly common knowledge in both the public domain and the covert intelligence world. The supercomputer in front of him was tagged 999, and he wondered if the SOB was just looking to be clever in his own mind.

Radfield was tempted to slow the downloading pace, run a quick scroll on the blackmail leverage. Then decided the bastard would either honor his word and he would get a look at some point in the near future or...

He'd be dead.

Hope. That was all he had.

Mr. Brick, he heard, was bellowing for his grunts to move faster. Radfield popped out another CD, racked in another, watching the men in black as they began filling more bags with stacks of hundreds. What were they going to do with all that money anyway? he wondered.

He could be reasonably certain they weren't about to clip ten percent off the top and donate it to some charity or church. They weren't going to build hospitals, homeless shelters, feed a village, clothe the naked, educate or defend the poor. They were about one hundred percent pure taking, and for their rotten reprobate carcasses. Their hope, then, was in this world. It was in creating some puffed-up pleasure zone of wretched excess where they could mindlessly indulge themselves, eating, drinking, fornicating most likely, buying, in short, whatever their heart's desires, all the requisite toys that went with garnering human respect, the envy of others so that they could exult themselves as gods among mere mortals. Each goon had become no less than an individual fiefdom in his own eyes, living only for himself, everyone else be damned. In some respects, what he bore witness was capitalism at its worst.

Greedy. Grubby.

The green light flashed on beside the CD tray. He was pulling out the last CD when he saw Mr. Brick rolling his way, towing the T-WBM president by the elbow. The operative was barking into his tac radio, but the dark expression on the man's face told Radfield there was trouble.

He didn't have the particulars, but Radfield had seen the six shooters vanish through the revolving doors minutes ago.

"You got those CDs burned yet, Radfield?"

He was holding up the small black bag when, choking down at least two smart-ass one-liners about the man's sudden agitated mood, Mr. Brick suddenly turned and began ordering a four-man team to fall out and go check the Gold Room. As they rushed off with their MP-5s, Radfield heard every gut instinct screaming at him the building was under siege by the good guys. It suddenly occurred to him they weren't really all that prepared, as far as any heavy firepower went. Arrogance may be their par for the course, considering they marched in, took down and sealed off the building with no initial resistance, but now that he thought about it there were no grenades, no plastic explosive, no rocket launchers to hold back any determined armed force of size and means. If there were more than standard-issue subguns and side arms all-around then Radfield had to believe they were up top, on reserve and holding ready for the big bail.

Mr. Brick moved into the horseshoe, barking at three shooters on his left wing to get those bags into the freight. "Give me that bag. On your feet."

"What about my copy?" Radfield asked, rising.

The operative grinned, shrugged, then pulled out one of the CDs. "This is no time to be testing my good faith, Paul. But, here, take it. Call it a down payment. Mighty white of me, huh?"

Number three and four snappy comebacks were on the tip of Radfield's tongue, as he took the CD and dropped it in his coat pocket, when autofire rattled beyond the revolving doors. There was a split second of paralysis through the marauders, Radfield looking toward the doors when a massive explosion thundered, a roaring cloud of debris and fire that all but obliterated the revolving doors and hammered through the deep end of the vault. The former Special Forces captain was diving for the deck when he caught a glimpse of what was left of the op's four-man team. They came sailing down through the vault, spattering and smearing concrete along the way.

For the first time since he'd left home a little over twenty-four hours ago, Paul Radfield smiled. If he didn't know better he would have sworn hope had arrived.

CHAPTER TWENTY

There was all due concern on the way down, any number of hanging questions that couldn't be answered. Sensors and cameras, booby-traps and roving hardmen and so forth. Every step, in short, fraught with peril, the Executioner was primed to cut loose with his M-16/M-203 combo as he hugged the concrete wall, advancing toward the light and the sound of muffled voices raised in what sounded like shouted orders, twenty yards or so distant. He was twenty paces and easing around the corner where the wall began to bend, scanning, listening, wondering how to proceed when the enemy made the decision for him.

They were shadows, four total and armed with MP-5s, as they shoved their way into the black-tinted revolving doors. For the life of him, the soldier couldn't figure out why the engineers had implemented what appeared almost a grotesque caricature of security.

No matter.

Bolan held back on the trigger of his M-16. He wasn't prepared to thank the architects yet, but the four-some was momentarily stuck in those glassed-in spindles, cartoon figures that looked as if they couldn't decide what to do. The Executioner helped them out of their dilemma, sweeping the line of 5.56 mm tumblers down the doors, right to left, glass shattering, armed figures falling back. Bolan hosed them back the other way for good measure. They were howling like banshees, whether in pain or surprise the soldier couldn't tell, but he had the special C-4 package out and up.

It was a five-pound block, wrapped in thin nylon, the red light already on, as the soldier hurled the package by its plastic handle. They looked set to come charging through, three still in play by his judgment, but Bolan was falling back, the radio remote in hand. He hit the activate button and announced his presence in no un-certain terms that he had come to blow down the house. Smoke, mangled strips of metal and shattered beds of glass blew past the soldier's position. He gave it a full second, wheeled around the corner, M-16 out and searching for live ones. A short raking burst of autofire punching into the smoke, just in case one adversary was rising or in the general vicinity, and Bolan heard all the croaking, coughing, shouting coming from well beyond the pall.

The Executioner counted three or four heads, wea-pons trained toward the demolished opening. The hard-force was taking cover behind a row of pallets that even through the thinning smoke the warrior could detail the shape of dollar bills, the color of money.

Bolan drew a bead on the source of their hopes and dreams, tapped the M-203's trigger and sent a 40 mm buckshot round hurtled on to begin devouring all that glittered in the eyes of these savages.

"I BET THAT HURTS."

Lawhorn had fingernails dug into the man's ear, the hard but fleshy part just above the lobe. Grinning, he twisted, pulled and yanked Mr. Tracht III off his knees, then held him out, squawking, begging, flapping his arms, his overpaid, overpromoted, overindulged seven-figure trophy and human armor. Someone watching, Lawhorn thought, would have thought the guy just had red-hot nails driven through his nuts, his pink little sac to then be slow-roasted over an open flame. What a puking sissy! A little pain and guys like Mr. Tracht III bawled like newborns who only wanted to go back into the womb! But that, he knew, was the problem with girly-men. Oh, sure, they sat in boardrooms, on cushioned thrones, in posh settings where the room temperature had to be their exact liking or they had little premenstrual bitch fits. These puffed-up empty vessels like Mr. Tracht III, all wrapped up in big fat money they generally stole or didn't earn by anything even remotely notable or noble they had done while dictating their terms to those who marched out and did the real and dirty work for them.

They were ogled and praised wherever they trod

hand-tooled leather shoes, proclaiming their personal grandeur if only to stoke the envy and resentment of those they secretly and often openly despised as poor, all of life's losers to be ground up in their money machine or bend knees before them.

Oh, and yes, he admitted in his heart of hearts he wanted to be one of those guys. Only there was a difference between him and the standard-issue boardroom girly-man or CEO as wide as the Grand Canyon, as extreme as one end of the universe to another. Donald "Brick" Lawhorn was a warrior, a tough guy, the last of the dinosaurs, a real man in an age of wimps and eunuchs in silk suits with little more to back them up than their stock portfolios, their billable hours, their diamond pinkies.

And since Mr. Tracht III fell into that particular category, wailing up a storm and looking set to lose his bowels, Lawhorn made full and good use of his limp worthless carcass.

Lawhorn sounded off a deep bass chuckle, more out of delight and to stoke his human shield's terror, as he spied the flaming star that marked the autofire of his mystery badass, somewhere now to his one o'clock as he maneuvered Tracht into position.

And not a second too soon, he discovered, as he glimpsed the projectile streaking out of the clouds and locked on for the last of the pallets.

He heard then saw some of his guys shooting their way off the freights, streams of MP-5 weapons fire peppering the cloud and shredded guts of the doors, but he left them to it, squeezing his eyes shut for what he knew would be pure hell on earth he wasn't all that sure he would escape unscathed. He wheeled, ear in hand, hauling the bank president in tight, just as the load blew. He bit down his own curse as what he suspected were razor-sharp bits of shrapnel tearing through his men by pallets. He was damn near afraid to turn back and have a look.

He did anyway.

Tracht III was grabbing at his arm, the wails shrilling up another few decibels and endless now, one barrage after another. It was every bit as bad as Lawhorn had feared, the smoky air swirling with flotsam, chewed bills fluttering to the floor, his guys down and out and thrashing around like gutted fish. Understandable their hands were empty of weapons and thrown over their faces, since it looked like their eyes had been ripped out of their skulls by the ground-zero, point-blank impact.

"Get those freights out of here!" Lawhorn roared at the shooters bunched up in the three freight openings, weapons out and fanning. A few rounds went zipping down the vault and Lawhorn was forced to hurl a few vicious oaths into the repeated order.

If the bastard had another buckshot load ready to rip, if he was already letting grenades fly...

As if reading his mind, the mystery one-man wrecking crew hit what was left of the money piles with another blast.

Bellowing a curse, as Tracht III screamed and began to crumple at the knees like he was about to faint away,

Lawhorn caught a glimpse of a head rising above the end of the supercomputer terminal. That was an MP-5 cutting through the drifting cloud. He was wondering if that was one of his guys, still in the fray when—

Radfield turned on the subgun fire.

As rounds ripped into the bags behind and beside him, one of his guys sounding off with a stream of curses about the potential damage, Lawhorn directed a barrage over the shoulder of his human shield, twisted even harder on the ear and pulled the man with him into the elevator.

THE EXECUTIONER SWEPT OUT of the cloud, senses choked with the stink of death, ears chiming from the blasts and steady barrage of weapons fire. Radfield, he saw, was hurling a blanket of subgun fire down the line of freight cars, but the doors were already slamming shut. If he scored it would be pure luck, but stranger things, the soldier knew, happened.

In fact, they already had.

Movement to his right, and Bolan spotted the moaning bleeder, crabbing through the raining whirlwind of money. Hands that were shredded to the bone by shrapnel were raking in his MP-5. The Executioner pumped a 3-round burst up his ribs, nailing him to the floor.

"Radfield!"

Bolan ducked back, hunched low behind the shredded end of a money stack that was just high and thick enough to maybe absorb a few rounds if Radfield fired in panic and raw adrenaline.

"Hold your fire!" the Stony Man warrior shouted.
"Who are you?"

Bolan eased toward the edge. "Justice Department."

"Where's the rest of the cavalry, Justice Department?"

"I'm the cavalry."

The response was a grim chuckle. "For some reason, I'm not surprised. Not when I consider what I've lived through and seen this past day or so."

"I'm coming out. You need ID?"

"I'm looking at all the ID I need, mister. Strewed out, chewed to hell and gone all over this damn vault. And I'm thinking you're a little more than your standard Washington G-man."

"Meaning what?"

"Meaning I hope you're on the level. Meaning I hope you're not going to waste my ass first chance you get. Meaning I hope you're not just some freelance black op looking to cash in."

"I don't have time to convince you one way or the other, guy. You point your weapon at me, you go down, end of dance. That's where I'm coming from, and that's all you need to know."

"Okay. I got it."

Bolan stood and stepped out into the open, bills fluttering to the floor between him and the chief of Manexx Security. "What's your story?"

"Story? It's a horror story. These bastards kidnapped me from my home in Houston as of yesterday morning. Told me they'd kill my wife and sons if I didn't play ball."

"Which was?"

"Reprogram the security system, recode every door, every elevator, to lock the place down. Since I was instrumental in laying it all out in the first place…"

"They came to you."

"You got it. They had me work in an EM screen that would block—"

"All incoming and outgoing calls."

"I already figured you for a man with experience."

"Then you know where this is headed."

"To the roof."

Bolan gave the man a quick once-over, read him as the real thing, which meant he was stand-up and would go the distance in this or any fight, as his service record indicated. Whether he did it to see his family remain alive and well or out of a sense of right and wrong was moot to the soldier. Bolan needed action, and results, fast. "Is it reachable from the elevators on the next floor up?"

"You're not going to ask what this is all about?"

Bolan nodded at the green shreds strewed at his feet. "I already have a pretty good idea."

"Would you believe they just made off with a billion dollars—or near a billion—in what were slush funds earmarked for this country's war on terror?"

"The longer you stand there telling me what I already know, the chances are they will take off and disappear. And now that you've jumped ship…"

"Right. I just put my family in their crosshairs."

"Maybe not."

Radfield reached down, hauled a laptop from the shattered hull of a smoking computer terminal. "Lead the way, Justice Department. I hope you realize you take us to the top floor they'll be ready and waiting."

"I'm way ahead of you."

"MOVE IT, LADIES, move it! We're on the clock! This is not a South Beach club where you are some celebrity signing autographs for your female groupies! This is not some grab-ass stroll down Miami Beach staring at the string bikinis! Get your asses in another high gear and now!"

Braxton was pumped to a new level of previously unknown fury and tension. He couldn't decide if his superheated mood was owed to the sight of all the booty bags being hauled up the ramp of his Chinooks or…

It seemed beyond the realm of possibility, but something dark and angry was tugging at all his gut instincts that the trouble under the roof was more than mere coincidence.

He bounded off the ramp, MP-5 gripped tight, though he'd passed out the grenades and the Multi-Round Projectile Launcher, clipping a few fragmentation rounds to his webbing. There was no sense in kicking himself now, but it looked like a bad mistake to come in, silent and swift, opting for straight subterfuge and high-tech wizardry, armed with nothing more than subguns, autoshotguns and side arms to grab what was the biggest bank heist in U.S. history.

Lawhorn was, he saw, and for reasons he could

safely deduce, taking his sweet time on the long, slow march across the floor. The president of the Trans-World Bank in tow, Lawhorn kept looking over his shoulder at the freight elevators and with a look of grim expectation that fueled the flames of anger in Braxton. It galled him that his man in charge of Miami operations had waited until only a few moments ago, while rising to the top with their money, to inform him of the situation. It was true that no operation could ever be expected to stick to the script, A to Z, but the man's sudden negligence bordered dereliction of duty.

Braxton gave the blue skies above a long search, pondering how to deal with both Lawhorn and the present crisis, if, in fact, what the man had just told him was true. With rotor wash pounding his senses, it was impossible to hear any sudden approaches that would signal more trouble beyond the building. His three Black Hawks were in a holding pattern above the roof, monitoring all countermeasures that were being taken by Homestead and local law enforcement, but Braxton was suddenly getting an itch between his shoulder blades that warned him the easy part was long since over.

Braxton waited until Lawhorn pulled up, barking at Tracht III to shut his mouth.

"I'd put a couple of men on that VIP elevator."

"You would, would you?" Braxton growled.

"Hey, the son of a bitch, he came out of nowhere."

"One guy?"

"That's what I told you, damn it."

"And I notice that our Mr. Radfield is no longer with us."

"He grabbed a weapon and began spraying us in the freights. That's the last I saw of him."

"With your mystery shooter?"

"You want to go down to the vault and check it out, be my guest."

"And you lost how many pallets?"

Lawhorn hesitated, scowled. "Four."

"We'll talk about it later."

"What's to talk about? If you're thinking about docking me some of my end…"

"And you lost how many men?"

"Maybe half our crew."

"Call it twenty shooters."

Lawhorn bared his teeth. "I hope you're not thinking what I think you are."

"Now you're a mind-reader? What am I thinking?"

"That I'm running my own agenda. That I held back on four pallets. That I'm lying to you."

Braxton bobbed his head, maintained a neutral expression. He had already considered the possibility that Lawhorn had engineered some back-stabbing game of his own. For one thing, Braxton was having great difficulty swallowing this tall tale about one shooter suddenly showing up and—

Braxton went rigid. He felt his jaw go slack as certain dirty images filtered into his mind. "Describe your mystery shooter?"

"Tall. Dark. All-pro."

Braxton looked up at the sky, as if answers would come from above, stared next at the silver doors at the far southeast end. He was looking at the light panel above the elevator car. That particular car was reserved for VIPs, those who had access cards—or working knowledge of how to bypass the circuitry with master security codes.

That would be Radfield. And since he was on the loose…

Even at a distance, Braxton spotted the lights flashing from the first floor. Lawhorn was following his stare then cursing when Braxton bellowed at his bag handlers, "Myers! Cullinan! Gavin! We have company coming on the VIP car! Move out!"

As they sprinted across the floor, MP-5s in hand, Braxton noticed the lights flashing—eight, nine—then saw the slung Multi-Round Projectile Launcher bouncing between the shoulder blades of Gavin. The sight of that weapon froze him, as some premonition began to urge him to get the hell on his Chinook and bail.

"Sir! The car stopped!"

"You care to give them a hand loading the other Chinook, Mr. Lawhorn?" Braxton snarled, growing angrier as he strode for the pile of bags, noting that maybe two to three dozen still needed to go up the ramp on his chopper alone, holding himself back from calculating the total loss of four full pallets.

Braxton then heard Gavin shout from his end the car was moving again, spotted his shooters grabbing cover behind the empty crates, Myers aiming his MP-5 over the top of a couch in the lounge area.

"The bastard's coming!"

"You think, Mr. Lawhorn?"

Braxton was reaching for a bag, snarling at what was left of the work force to pick up the pace when he heard the bell chime signal him the doors were opening. He felt the chill and hesitation of men moving in fear and uncertainty from two hundred feet and change away, began turning to see what was happening when the explosion ripped from the car and sent yet more of his shooters flying in a tangle of broken limbs and screams of shock and pain.

CHAPTER TWENTY-ONE

Durzheb Thoulzric was dazed, confused and terrified. If feelings were facts, he figured he was way past being in a world of hurt, and in every sense. It felt as if every step now ventured was nothing short of a slippery toe-hold on the edge of a carousel, and with nothing but blood streaming into his eyes, the infernal ringing in the ears…

What had happened? Where was he exactly?

They had gone down somewhere just north of the Art Deco District Welcome Center, he thought, and he was pretty sure he was the only one left. In fact, looking back, he was certain of it, since nothing armed, angry or bloodied stumbled from the smashed and smoking heap that had, up to then, proved itself nothing short of hell on wheels.

It was just him and his M-16 with the attached grenade launcher and a few spare clips and 40 mm rounds snug in his waistband, stuffed in the pockets of his wind-breaker.

That was the good news.

Staggering on, hacking on smoke and spitting out flecks of glass from a mouth filling with bloody spit-tle, the last thing he remembered before the missiles slammed into them was the flood of infidels being mowed down as they stampeded from the park and across Ocean Drive, the hotel facade and its lobby to his immediate left being decimated by cannon fire, ca-banas and canopies and shredded mannequins of human beings being tossed about as they were plunged through their gigantic meat grinder.

That seemed an eternity ago, as pain knifed up and down the length of his body like a thousand daggers heated over an open flame. Every bone felt torqued from the marrow out, every muscle stretched to its lim-its, and on fire, it seemed.

He didn't know precisely what had stopped the war bus in its tracks, but he now made out a familiar sound that was sort of a cross between a whine and a peal of thun-der before he spotted the sleek fighter jets blazing across the blue sky, winged black or silver bats, just off the beach. Squinting, fisting blood out of his eyes, he peered through the open space between the palm trees. There looked to be six of them, roughly a thousand feet up and streaking over the water, heading north, if his senses were any-thing near accurate, considering what he'd walked away from, the burning jelly he now felt hung for limbs. Where there were, however, that many fighter jets in the area…

He wiped more blood and sweat out of his eyes, tears of pain and rage, it felt, not far behind as the fire swelled from some heated core in the center of his brain. He didn't have much time left, that much he knew, as he heard sirens wailing from blocks over, closing fast. Worse, he was sure someone was following him, right on his back. But it felt more like a presence, as he checked the flaming shells of six or seven Miami Beach police cars down Ocean Drive, scanning the carnage, the sheet of fire that crackled down the front of the wreckage for uniforms with guns.

Bodies, he saw, were sprawled from one side of the street to the other, some of the bloody figures moving, or slithering, rather, like snakes with broken backs, a few pitiful-sounding pleas for help clawing the screaming pandemonium all around him. He scanned the rooftops of the hotels, thought he glimpsed a helmet and a sniper rifle, maybe two or three, but trying to see anything clearly through the haze of blood and the sweat stinging into his eyes...

There! That sudden sensation of an overpowering terror of dying but that felt more like a living presence was yet again breathing down his neck, reaching out with its ice-cold touch. Was that laughter he heard through all the racket of human beings screaming out in terror and pain? Sound being warped by the ringing in his ears? Could he even trust his senses?

I'm afraid there really are no seventy-two virgins waiting for you or any of the others, sir, but I must congratulate you and your friends for work well done here.

He flinched, crying out, searching for the owner of the voice. Nothing!

I must say, I do admire the single-minded tenacity of you jihad boys. Holy war? Bah! Do you know how ridiculously easy that nonsense makes my task? You near rob me of any pleasure I derive from what I do. If not for the end result, I would bring down untold misery on your heads myself for the impertinence and presumption alone!

He wheeled all the way around the compass, certain he'd just felt that long skeleton finger tapping him on his other shoulder. Vacant space! Sure he was going insane, his paranoia most likely causing him to hallucinate, he found he was clear of any immediate threat. Nothing, he found, but the hordes of his enemies scattering all over the beach, racing down the sidewalk, darting between parked or abandoned cars, hiding behind trees, benches, seawall.

Something was terribly wrong. Something was stalking him, he couldn't see it, but he knew it was there. It was cold, malevolent, raging.

He froze for a second, would have sworn some black shadow, massive and indescribable as anything resembling a human being, had just fleeted, like a giant black bolt of lightning, right past his eyes.

Where was the laughing voice? Did it come from within? From without? Both? Neither?

Was it taunting him? Cajoling? Encouraging? All? None?

Between the throbbing fire in his skull, the maddening and resounding gongs in his ears, the way in which the world warbled, in and out of focus, he knew his senses were shredded. Between the blasts, the tumble, the airborne launch from the wreckage, the subsequent slam to earth, no doubt he was suffering from a concussion, succumbing to shock, or worse. It seemed all he could do just to stay on his feet, keep moving, hold the world together on a fuzzy axis, wondering if he could even trust any sight, any sound or if something from deep within the shredded agony and fire of his soul was reaching out with pure terror, dread, foreboding.

It was a wonder, Thoulzric thought, he was even still alive. How he managed to be thrown from his seat and out the door, clear of the war bus, finding himself with an M-16 in hand and stretched out between two vehicles, the twenty-five pound vest of wired plastic explosive snug in place, the radio remote box in his box and in working order…

It is almost time to go, Durzheb. Your comrades are waiting. And they're keeping your seat nice and warm.

Thoulzric screamed, rolled around the compass. There! The hulking black figure, what looked some monstrous animal or beast, wanting to take shape, but vanishing before he could determine what it was.

There!

He triggered a short burst in panic then saw it was only three or four women, chopped down by his barrage, flimsy clothing flying away with their blood and flesh. Their shrill screams swept away by the relentless barrage of blaring horns, panicked shouts, the sirens and the growing bleat of chopper blades from somewhere above all the chaos.

Suddenly, out of nowhere, it seemed, he found the small detonation box in his hand, sirens sounding near on top of him, voices shouting in anger, what sounded like boots drumming his way.

Go on, Durzheb. Do it! You hate these people! And you are right to feel the way you do! Take courage now! I have been with you all the way, I have had your back, I have seen your struggle. I feel your pain. This is your last chance!

He felt his finger on the button, glimpsed the red light, flashing, telling him he was good to go.

He knew they were near, mere yards away, as some invisible force outside his body, it seemed, put pressure on his finger.

What's this? Are you some tottering old village hag with no conviction, no spine? Will you go out like some sniveling worm? Do it!

He did.

Engulfed in the fireball, he heard his screams, loud and clear, as he was lifted and hurtled away then found himself soaring off at what felt like light speed into some vast and gaping dark hole.

PAUL RADFIELD stuck to the game plan. He hugged the corner of the bottom rail, waiting while the big Justice Department man took a slender steel pick and began fiddling with the lock.

They were screaming and shouting up a hell-storm as

the Justice Man eased the door open a few inches, the M-16 poking through the narrow space. The ploy was simple, and neither one of them expected to fool the enemy.

A ten-pound block of C-4 plastique had ridden up the rest of the way while they'd gotten off, two floors down, the surprise tucked in a corner of the car. Watching the lights for a lingering moment before hitting the stairs, Mr. Justice had waited until he was sure the package was delivered, as Radfield could well imagine their fear and confusion before the explosive gong resounded. How many had shuffled for or into the elevator, peeking in, all around, up and down, before they realized it was too late and the Justice Man blew open the gates of Hell in their faces with his det box?

Radfield was about to find out. It had been some time since he'd fired a shot in anger, but the past day of chewing on nothing but fear and anxiety, terrified for the lives of his family, taunted, threatened, while clinging to the flimsiest shreds of hope.

He had the MP-5 in hand to lead his charge up the stairs. He had snagged spare clips on the way out of the vault, Mr. Justice seeing fit to hand him three fragmentation grenades, four-second delay fuses once they were armed. It was pointless, he knew, to wonder about the big guy, but he moved like a seasoned pro, hard, experienced, always scanning, full combat senses jacked up.

Like he'd done this a thousand times before.

What's more, the big guy hadn't even glanced at what money remained intact down below. Had to be a nice pile in the fat seven figures still sitting in the vault, but there was something about Mr. Justice that every fiber of instinct shouted to Radfield he was above the things of the world, as far as money, pleasure, comfort.

Whoever he was, he was committed to the task at hand, good versus evil, plain and simple, no room for doubt, for gray, for hesitation. He was a warrior who knew what he was about and what he intended to do.

And if he was a G-man...

Radfield checked the grim chuckle, as Mr. Justice, apparently satisfied with the layout he'd sketched out, went through the door, M-16 blazing.

Time to do his part.

He heard the return fire, coming somewhere deep to the west end, from where the rotor wash reached his ears like the opening peals of a thunderstorm. How many shooters? What about the hardware? Where were they? Hunkered and hurling rounds from just yards beyond the door, or far across at the deep west edge of the warehouse helipad? Were they boarding choppers, more concerned now about a quick getaway with their stolen loot than holding hard and slugging it out?

Whatever the case, knowing it was about to rain bullets, blood and death once again, Radfield followed on the Justice shooter's heels, peeled to his left, ready to crank.

The MP-5 found two targets running their way, no sooner was he two or three steps onto the main floor, with what looked another duo of men in black pulling up the rear, but hesitating like they were deciding. Between fight or flight, from where they stood the latter made more sense.

It also stripped the enemy of any edge they thought they had.

He was a split second behind the big guy's searching autofire, MP-5 stuttering, putting him in the game, no holds barred. Chalk it up to searching to bring back the good old active duty edge, but Radfield got his head cleared. With plenty of adrenaline, anger and hope oiling the limbs, he pitched in and helped mow down the first two armed jackals. Then he began tracking on for more live ones, hoping to end it, here and now, so he could return full focus on what was really important.

IT WAS EITHER INSTINCT, earned by blood and balls, or some deep primal terror of inevitable truth boiling up from the raging mass deep within that told him the clock had just struck midnight.

And Donald Lawhorn didn't know whom or what to curse first, the list was that lengthy, that dark, that submerged in what he feared was nothing short of the pure dung of abysmal final failure. At the top of the A list was Braxton, the man who called the shots, beginning to end. He was already up, up and away, his Chinook, of course, being the first off the pad and now climbing fast and hard for the blue sky of evacuation and freedom, and the sting of the guy's cleverly crafted implied accusations was still ringing through his mind, stoking fire on top of fire. Then there were the loads themselves, and judging by what he saw heaped on the floor behind him on his CH-47, Braxton had claimed the lion's share for his ride, which meant his own end wasn't only light a few dozen bags but his force of worker ants was slim pickings, to say the puking least. Which meant his six grunts were still muling the last few bags up the ramp.

Which gave the big bastard in black and Radfield a few extra seconds to gather a second wind and—

They came out of the cloud, the sight of what they wielded and had aimed his way freezing Lawhorn in the hatch. He began to scream at the three-man flight crew to get them up when he heard the autofire rattle from across the floor. He bellowed aft for the ramp to get shut but found it already closing, the last of the bags dumped on the floor beside a cowering Tracht III. Lawhorn looked back out on the floor just as he heard, "Wait!"

There were two of them, Braxton's guys, and Lawhorn sounded a vicious curse over their lack of guts, this brazen display of dereliction of duty. He had the inclination but not the allotted time or he would have shot them himself. The yellow hyenas were cutting and running, instead, he thought, of holding their ground, fighting the two SOBs behind them. For their cowardice—justice served up, as far as he was concerned—they were scythed down with converging streams of weapons fire that seemed to punch a line of holes in the smoke and whirlwind of debris that used to be the open lounge.

Lawhorn saw pure red, as he already knew what was coming, clinging, though, to hope, but that seemed to be fleeing him like so much vapor in a strong gust of wind. Had the gutless jackals even turned and fired back for two or three seconds, drove them to cover at worst—had Braxton been halfway considerate or less greedy and seen fit to give his chopper equal time—had they been armed with more than what had proved nothing but peashooters down below instead of relying on pure arrogance, stealth and new age battle tactics that involved computers and access codes and straight greasing…

Belay all that whining noise.

Had not one big nameless bastard in black acting like he was on some personal crusade of vengeance and wrath and right, sent to them like the Angel of Death and who barged his way into the damn building in the first place…

Lawhorn threw a burst at the duo, but the MP-5 was thrown off its mark as the Chinook lifted, so hard he had to grab a strap to keep from being knocked out the door. He cursed, strode across the fuselage, snatched Tracht III off his rear. If it was over for him…

"Wh-what—what are you doing?"

"Faster!" Lawhorn bellowed through the open cockpit hatch, shaking Tracht III like a wet dog and holding him up to the doorway. "Those two sons of bitches are going to blow us all clear to Cuba!"

Tracht was roaring in his ear as Lawhorn looked down and saw the big SOB lifting that M-16 with its fixed grenade launcher, but it was Radfield who caught his eye and sent the ball of rage and frustration and despair plunging straight into his bowels.

"We're going to Hell, Mr. Tracht!"

"No!"

"I bet you think you're going to Heaven!"

"I don't want to die!"

"Nobody does, you silly bastard, but here we go!"

They were ascending, clearing the edge of the roof-line, going up, the sky burning so blue it made him squint, when Lawhorn bellowed a curse at the sight of the first two 50 mm HE rounds streaking from the Multi-Round Projectile Launcher, rising at what seemed light speed, locked on, magnetized comets.

And Lawhorn would have sworn he saw the former Special Forces captain smiling a nanosecond before the first missile plowed into the side of the fuselage.

CHAPTER TWENTY-TWO

"He called himself Brick. World's biggest tough guy, to hear him tell it. Nonstop mouth would have made any talking head look quiet and tame in opinion in comparison. But he was a stone-cold psycho. And I have to tell you, Justice, that's one evil son of a bitch I've never been so glad to see get toasted and sent on his way to Hell."

The Executioner looked at Radfield.

"Appreciate you, by the way, letting me help to bury that bastard. Tracht was unfortunate collateral damage."

The guy was holding on to the Multi-Round Projectile Launcher, still pumped to kill, if the soldier read the anger in the eyes, the set to his jaw right. For a second, he would have sworn the former Special Forces captain was ready to dump a round or two more over the retaining wall and down into the pandemonium around the flaming ruins heaped in the middle of Brickell.

Tracht was another unfortunate victim, with the body count climbing. But Bolan had bigger problems to contend with now, and more cannibal game to hunt.

It was impossible to take in the mayhem, the extent of the destruction in a few short moments, and the soldier was on the clock. He searched the skies, which were thick with rising plumes of black smoke, looking for his own Black Hawk among what was an aerial traffic jam of gunships and fighter jets in the skies above Miami. Smoke and aircraft, he saw, and as far west, north and south as he could determine. There was enough raging racket with the sirens alone, but with all the stampedes, countless victims stretched out or limping along for blocks as far he could see in all directions, with fires blazing from storefront windows, and with flashing lights…

Anarchy.

And nothing short of martial law, the soldier knew, would restore it all to anything that resembled law and order. And beyond the here and now, what became of the nation?

Whatever the grim future, it was clear to him, as he turned and scanned the air traffic over Biscayne Bay and Miami Beach where the thickest of palls were rising, what had happened, and why.

The Invisibles, or whatever they were called, he thought, had orchestrated a major terror attack.

To steal money.

While using the madness that had slammed Miami and outlying vicinity like a giant asteroid, and to cover their getaway.

There was no point scouring the skies for the savages, he decided. If they were, in fact, Homeland Security black ops, then they would be armed with every secured and classified frequency across the board. Scanning while most likely announcing to whomever it may concern who they were, that they were part of counterterror measures. Taking orders from Washington. How could they be of immediate assistance? Or maybe they had another cover story, something that involved hostages perhaps in the Trans-World Bank of Miami.

Oh, there would be fallout. Official heads would roll. Senate investigation, what would prove a feeble attempt to calm the public hue and cry that would sound a rage and that may well erupt various segments of American society into civil unrest.

If that hadn't already begun.

If it came to light that the architects of this massive terror strike were homegrown and official intelligence operatives who were supposed to be doing their damnedest to keep another 9/11 from happening.

And if other cities had seen a similar terror torch lit…

"I assume you have a plan, Justice?"

Bolan glanced at Radfield, then stared down at Brickell Avenue.

It was raining money, and more than a few citizens shoved aside their own fears. The warrior wasn't sure he could much blame them under the circumstances, but the money, he knew, that was the key.

Follow the cash.

How?

The Executioner didn't answer Radfield's question as he considered how to proceed. One Chinook was in the wind. Radfield seemed to think some of the load was trucked off the premises. Figure the bad guys had lost something in the neighborhood of a third, call it three hundred million in cash showering the street.

"Plan?" Bolan mused, hefting the assault rifle. "I'm going after them."

"Then, maybe this will help put you on their trail."

Bolan looked at the shiny disk then took the CD and slipped it in a pocket. He listened while Radfield explained its worth, according, that was, to the late and unlamented Mr. Brick.

"I haven't had the pleasure of looking at what's on it," Radfield said. "The way it sounds, though, if the bastard was even telling a half-truth, what you have there may well be your key. Only…I wonder."

Bolan waited while the ex-Green Beret mulled his next words. He heard the rotor wash a moment later, then, looking to the southwest, he found his Black Hawk vectoring his way.

"I wonder if what I just gave you is the key to stopping this madness…or opening up the gates of Hell to the who, what and why that's behind what happened here today."

The Executioner couldn't help but wonder about that himself. He had been down this dark road before, where the traitors slithered out of the rocks, the sewer, the shadows. They went for themselves. They went for money. They didn't give a damn who or how many they murdered and maimed, how their evil ambition, ful-filled, it looked, at least for the time being, would leave behind...

Bolan clenched his jaw as the Black Hawk found just enough space to his left to land.

As far as the Executioner was concerned, there was no hole remote enough on the face of the Earth for the enemy to crawl into and hide, no place far enough away, short of the ends of the universe, for the perpetrators of this mass murder and mayhem to run from what he in-tended to be no less than hard justice.

"Let's get you on your way home to your family, Radfield."

The ex-Green Beret showed Bolan a weary smile. "Amen to that."

"I WOULDN'T START popping the champagne corks just yet."

"Champagne? You're kidding, right, boss?"

"Not a swinging package, here, Sarge, would dare drink any Frog piss."

"Is that a fact, ladies?"

John Brendon bobbed his head, frowning, a few choice and scathing remarks on the tip of his tongue, but decided to let them have their chuckle. Considering how they'd sweated out the day in what was no less than one test of titanium-strength nerves after another...

Maybe they'd earned a breather, a laugh or two. Then again, they were hardly home free and sailing. The fin-ish line was still a long ways off, halfway around the world, in fact. And just thinking about it conjured any number of dire scenarios.

But he had to thank his lucky stars they'd come this far. Getting out of the Biscayne Towers had been shave close enough, forced to gun down two rent-a-cops in the parking garage on the way out. Then the traffic snafu, pretty much as expected, his guys with the point and trail vans monitoring the scaled-down tractor-trailer's progress, diddling with secured frequencies and forced to bark away some of Homestead's finest during the slow crawl out of Miami. It got a little better once they dropped onto U.S. 1, but not by much, since half of the town seemed to be evacuating for the Keys. Delay was factored in, as was their layover. Something like four hundred islands strewed along the 150-mile chain that made up the Keys, and which was the sport-fishing capital on the planet.

The fifty-foot cabin cruiser had been there and waiting at their private marina in Marathon Key. That put them in what was the Middle Keys, between the Seven-Mile Bridge to the west and Marathon Airport to the east, the Gulf of Mexico and the emerald waters of the Atlantic Ocean on their north and south flanks. From there it was a quick scoot to their next destination, the Caymans, where a cleaner was on standby and ready to start the washing process before they trooped down to Venezuela to board a classified CIA bird where at least two duffel bags would be handed off to the local Company goons.

Brendon wasn't ready to join in all the merriment of

the troops in front of him, but give it another day, two tops, and he could start counting hundred-dollar bills to lull him to sleep at nights, as, of course, he was sandwiched between two four-figure-a-night courtesans. The very vision of that alone got the blood pumping. He had to grin, as he recalled the parting shot of his ex-wife, railing how he would never know a halfway decent life without her on his arm. Or back.

Oh, but the future was full of gold, promises, pleasure.

No, it would be pure Heaven on Earth, now that he thought about it.

That they had come this far was all due to solid planning, steely nerves and resolute action. It helped, too, that they were on the inside of the young Department of Homeland Security, having been granted carte blanche to pretty much play their own hand in the War on Terror. Talk about a sucker punch, a hammering right cross that would knock the lights out back in Washington. A part of him had to fight the urge to call the DHS director to tell him to send some gofers to take a look in the vault, but he would allow Braxton the honors at some point when all was safe, secure, snug.

He lit a smoke, hefting the MP-5 higher up his shoulder. He took a long look around the rec room and galley, felt the grin wanting to stretch his mouth. Every available inch of space, it seemed, was claimed by the black nylon bags of booty. Roughly three hundred million was stuffed into the oversize cut-to-spec belowdeck living quarters, floor to ceiling, with more bags stashed into two large cargo holds engineered to order.

Security. That was the order of the night.

The camouflage netting was draped over the truck, which was shoved into some pretty dense prehistoric vegetation up the trail, but there was something about the Black Hawk he'd been informed about and that had made a fly-over about an hour ago.

Why did the hackles on the back of his neck want to suddenly rise?

There was no contact, for one thing, from Braxton, though they had sent along the e-mail on their secured hot box to let the man know everything was going according to plan. That the skies were swarming with choppers and fighter jets was no big surprise, considering South Florida clear to Tampa and to the Panhandle and Jacksonville was under the gathering storm of martial law. But one Bell helicopter in particular seemed to have shown a little more than passing interest in their little convoy. It turned out it was the DEA, and they had to give the Drug Enforcement boys their own Homeland Security clearance codes to keep the smoke screen going.

But what if...

He was getting antsy to shove off, but he was told to hang tight until he received word from Braxton. He knew the final destination but there was still two, maybe three days to go before they landed in—

Brendon jumped, felt the cigarette slip from his mouth. He was looking at the porthole, would have sworn that sounded—

Like a body thudding to the deck near the wheelhouse!

He had the MP-5 off his shoulder, boot grinding out the smoke into the carpet when he sensed a presence somewhere near the top of the gangway. He would have sworn the boat shifted just enough to warn him somebody was on the deck, moving in but doing it real slow, taking weight off so they could sneak in, silent, swift.

Only a pro moved like that.

They were still chuckling behind him, oblivious to all else but for their visions of personal glory when Brendon saw the steel egg bouncing down the carpeted steps. He cut loose with the subgun, sprayed the hatchway then decided a quick nosedive, up and over a pile of bags, was his best bet. Eyes shut, the curse was ripping from his mouth, ringing in his ears a split second before the world erupted in a blinding flash and invisible needles were spiking into eardrums despite his best efforts to muffle the resounding gongs of Hell.

THE INVISIBLES WEREN'T as clever or as invisible as they believed.

It had been something of a fluke or maybe a miracle that the black truck with government plates had been scoped and trailed from Key Largo, watched from a distance by a DEA chopper. That Bolan was in direct contact with all local and federal law-enforcement agencies, all of which were sworn to complete cooperation via orders straight from Brognola who was backed by the full weight of the Oval Office, and with the enemy clearly identifying themselves as Homeland Security to the suspicious DEA boys…

They had tried hiding out in the open.

And the Executioner was in process of burning down the house.

Or boat, as was the case.

Confirmation—at least for the soldier—came when the same DEA team had made out the black bags being hauled down the trail to a cabin cruiser by the name of *Paradise Specter.* And which no record could be found of the boat's existence. Top that with verification that the small but tidy Mainland Marina had been seized by Homeland Security about six months ago, the three former Saudi owners now in custody.

The Black Hawk's only fly-over had picked up ten live ones on the IR screens, and from there the soldier, having spotted three MP-5-wielding shadows roving the treeline near the wharf, had bailed from the chopper on a beachhead about a quarter klick west, then gone in, hard, M-16/M-203 leading the charge. Three moving sentries were down, courtesy of 9 mm death delivered by the sound-suppressed Beretta 93-R, two more Invisibles heaped on deck near the wheelhouse.

That left five belowdecks by Bolan's reckoning.

They were coughing, shouting from below as smoke and flotsam poured out of the hatch, their senses scrambled by the flash-bang. Bolan vaulted the rail, took cover behind a small shed looming a few yards to the port stern of the cruiser. He wanted a live one or two, but decided to let the savages make the call.

Fueled by ice-cold anger, the Executioner lifted the M-16, its selector mode set for full-auto slaughter, a 40

mm buckshot load already locked in place in the M-203.
He had the ghost ship covered, stem to stern, at least
down the portside, and unless there was some way to the
wheelhouse other than what appeared the one hatchway...

They went for the straight bull-rush. Panic and terror got the senses cleared, limbs oiled, their greed and
savagery propelling them.

Nowhere to run, nowhere to hide.

Two were hollering at the top of their lungs, deaf and
blind, for all intents and purposes, but they were sweeping the wharf, the deck with subgun fire. Another armed
shadow lumbered into view, eyes bugged with the light
of fury, snarling like a pit bull, but hunkering close to
his vanguard, allowing them to take the first round of
sudden death while he felt out the situation. Judging the
way he panned the beach and the wharf, falling behind
what were human shields, Bolan figured his vision was
clearing—or he'd spotted the flash-bang just in time.

The Executioner swept the screaming demons first,
the line of 5.56 mm tumblers tearing into them, belly-
first, gutting them like fish on the deck. They were
twitching, hurling out gore all over polished teak and
white fiberglass when Bolan saw another head popping
into view, the MP-5 shuddering ahead of the hardman.
The gunner was sliding away from his toppling comrades when the soldier tapped the trigger on the M-203,
aiming for the boxlike covering over the hatch. It blew
apart as if it was nothing more than a bale of wheat
shoved through a thresher. There was a brief scream, but

Bolan was already turning his sights on the man in black who was sailing over the rail. He was down, the brute impact with the wharf jarring the MP-5 free to twirl away, off into the water.

The Executioner broke cover, gave his compass a full sweep as he closed on the sounds of a man in pure agony. He checked the boiling pall over the deck, garbage and pieces of wet flesh spattering *Paradise Specter*. He gave the cannibal writhing on the wharf a quick search, head to toe.

The guy was diced to red ruins, primarily on the back where he'd cut and run a second before their world blew up yet again, but it looked like he'd make it.

At least live long enough, Bolan decided, as he freed a pair of plastic cuffs from a slot in his combat vest, to answer a few questions.

The Executioner decided there would be no let-up, no easy, no promises made from there on out.

There were other savages on the loose.

Homegrown serpents.

And nothing short of trampling every last viper, the Executioner thought, from the cannibal stretched out before him, to wherever the hunt took him next would satisfy justice.

CHAPTER TWENTY-THREE

Torture.

There were those, both military and civilian, Mack Bolan knew, safe and snug and well out of the line of fire who did the talk-show circuit, who did the cocktail hour, who did the book-signing parties and wanted to announce before an admiring, infatuated and less-than-knowledgeable public that inflicting pain on those who were deigned clear and present menaces to the free world never worked. That it produced less than solid intelligence. That the victim crawled into his own shell and spilled out anything and everything and just to get the pain to stop, that it turned U.S.—Americans and her allies—into barbarians, demons, savages just like the enemy.

Really?

At one time, the Executioner might have agreed with the pundits, the shining star ex-brass-turned-celebrity and all the so-called experts, but the world had long since changed, and for the worse, and well before 9/11. With an enemy growing daily more bold, more defiant, more demonic, and with each mass slaughter of untold innocents, with every horrifying bloody success they claimed infernal glory to, with the looming threat of WMD always lurking in the wings, tactics had to shift. Or all may well be lost in the good fight.

Torture, the soldier thought, was, yes, born out of man's lower, darker nature, designed to cause pain for pain's sake, to exact revenge, to stir up sadistic pleasure. Usually all that might be true, certainly in the cases of those who didn't know how to apply the right amount and for the sake of justice while countless innocent lives hung in the balance.

Not so he.

And Bolan would have gladly put the question to the naysayers, the experts, the talking heads as to why, then, were the extremists, the terrorists, the worst of the worst of the world's garbage heap always shipped, quaking in terror and begging for mercy, to the Egyptians, the Pakistanis, the Israelis for interrogation.

Because those people got results.

The Executioner wasn't about to turn his own dirty work over to anybody. How, in all good conscience, in all steadfast steely warrior reason, in all courage could he?

For only the second time since the campaign began he had a prisoner, and one, he was sure, who was far more important, carried more clout, had more answers than a thousand late and unlamented Drobblers.

Bolan had the man in waist-deep water. The black op was struggling like a one-ton swordfish hooked and getting reeled. With the guy's hands cuffed behind his back and forced to his knees, with the Executioner wadding up his shirt between the shoulder blades and with the cold anger the soldier felt over the day's events, nothing but raw strength, adrenaline and a sense of dire urgency turning his own body into a slab of pure grinding heavy steel...

He gave it forty seconds by his watch, waiting until some of the fight left the black op, then Bolan brought him up. He let him suck air, hacking out water and spittle for a few moments, think about his next words.

"It's just you, me and a whole lot of ocean."

"You can't...do this..."

Bolan forced him back under. There was blood flowing from where the guy's mid to lower back had been shredded by buckshot, nothing life-threatening, but the soldier knew the water was literally rubbing salt into those open wounds, giving him pain to ponder on top of being drowned.

Thirty seconds, and Bolan brought him up, shook him and snarled in his ear, "Who's above you and where do I find him?"

"I want a deal!"

"Your life, that's all you have left to bargain."

"I'm Homeland Security, pal, John Brendon. I'm what they call Black Brass at the E-Ring, you'd better check that before you dunk me again!"

"You better sound off with more than name, rank and serial number. The next time I put you under…"

"I want a deal or you can go ahead and shove my dead carcass out to sea. I don't give a damn."

Bolan knew the guy spoke the truth, and that he didn't care. Time to shift his approach a little.

"Best guess," Bolan growled. "From South Florida to Texas, how many people you Invisibles figure you murdered today, or left maimed for life?"

"What? Hell, I don't know…" Fear shadowed Brendon's face as he seemed to think about it. "A few… thousand…"

"Closer to ten thousand, dead, wounded and dying, and still counting. And if you helped release some biological agent…"

"No, no, that wasn't part of the plan."

"So why are Miami, Tampa and Dallas-Fort Worth under quarantine? Why are civilians falling ill?"

"It's an Adamsite compound. A derivative of vomit gas."

"I know what Adamsite is. You're telling me those people have nothing to worry about?"

"That's what I'm telling you, and I say no more until I hear I get a deal. I mean, full immunity, the whole sweetheart package. If not, go on and kill me."

"That's not my call, giving you a playboy-type all expenses paid lifetime stroll through Witness Protection."

"Then get me someone with clout."

"That would be me, guy. You talk and I'll see what I can do."

"I talk and then you kill me, is that your can-do?"

"What's the alternative, if you don't go ahead and take your chances my word is no less than gold?"

Brendon growled, shook his head, cursed.

"Is that a yes?"

"Yeah, damn it."

"I'm listening."

"Your word is gold, huh?"

"Pure gold."

"ONE GUY. Washington sends one guy from the Justice Department here to Afghanistan to help us with our little terror problem over here."

"Well, I didn't quite come here all by myself."

"Right. Those six MIBs out on my apron, I almost forgot. You'll have to excuse me, Special Agent Cooper of the United States Department of Justice, while I peruse these orders again, and a little askance, I may add, especially in light of what's happened back home."

"Take your time. But don't take too much."

The Executioner ignored the narrowed look Colonel Sander Williams shot him as he took a straight-back wood seat in front of the man's desk. The office was tight but Spartan, nothing but a radio console, a computer terminal and a big map of Afghanistan and neighboring countries on the wall in the man's HQ. While the CO of One Base Specter began perusing documentation—stamped with a presidential directive, with another batch of will-do orders from CENTCOM and both of which were as official with the highest authority as anything this side of stone tablets handed off to Moses by the Almighty—the Executioner clacked a lighter and fired up a rare cigarette. He gave Williams a quick once-over from behind a cloud of smoke. The way the mission had shaped up, it went without saying the Stony Man warrior wasn't trusting too many folks beyond his own handpicked black ops circle. Two wars under the good colonel's belt and since Gulf One, with enough covert work that raised a few eyebrows at the Farm, but Bolan had to start what he intended to be the full, final and bloody finish somewhere.

When in doubt, go through the front door. Sometimes the soldier even knocked, first.

It had been, what, the soldier thought, roughly forty hours since he'd nearly drowned some answers out of Brendon before dumping him off in the laps of Brognola's people in Miami? To say a lot had happened, to state that he had put behind chaos unequalled back in the U.S., to claim he was tired, angry, frayed, weary from jet lag in the classified flight of the Gulfstream C20...

Gut check.

And as he did those same guts knotted with cold anger but a concrete resolution he knew would carry him to the finish line, one way or another.

For starters, the United States was under a semblance of martial law, meaning pretty much no shots so far had been fired on civilians, though some rioting and looting had broken out in the poorer sections of Miami, Tampa, Houston and Dallas-Fort Worth. There was much understandable panic spreading from coast to coast that a bio-weapon had been unleashed on those cities, but all the President's Men were marched out before the press to state that the CDC had confirmed those who had fallen ill were victims of an agent that resembled a very potent tear or vomit gas. Fear not, sick but not dying. Before the homefront powers-that-be even got around to wiping an ocean of egg off their faces, they were mixing truth with half-truths, glossing it over with speculation loosely based on facts so far gathered, stating the attackers were believed to be Muslim extremists, that all the perpetrators had been caught or killed, and any still on the loose would be held accountable, and in no uncertain terms.

They were blurring the big picture, shading the truth, and with good reason, as far as Washington was concerned.

That Bolan had been given the nod from the Man—carte blanche, no holds barred—told him one thing.

It was his game, to win or lose. As a deniable expendable, an Invisible in the intelligence machinery himself, he was allowed to take the necessary action, without Washington taking the blame should he fail, be captured or killed, and his role was brought to the world spotlight by the enemy. Par for the course, the politicians, the intelligence community were running for cover as Brognola had related the facts to the President as put to him by Bolan.

There was plenty of panic to spare in Washington, the way the soldier understood it. Meaning if the public became aware that a major terrorist offensive had been launched on America and its citizens by the very people they paid to protect them...

That was somebody else's nightmare to deal with, but the soldier had to admit he didn't envy the suits on the front lines of damage control.

What he had was a list of names, and facts, more or less confirmed by Stony Man, Brognola and their various sources and cutouts.

What he had was sat imagery and an unscheduled landing of a classified C-130 that had somehow flown out of Miami not more than an hour after Bolan had seen the bad guys abscond with their haul of Uncle Sam's slush funds for the War on Terror.

A little more grunting and head bobbing, and Williams finally flipped the papers down on his desk. As he fired up a cigar, he looked at the bruises, the scratches, the black sutures on Bolan's face, temple, neck. "You sure you're up for this?"

"Don't worry about me."

"Says there, I'm supposed to give you full and unconditional cooperation. Says there, you are to have free and ready access to all my intel, my own people, my aircraft, my outlying special ops bases, my in-country contract players. Says there, I am to ask no questions, write up no after-action report under any circumstances. Says there, I'm on a strict need-to-know."

"Sounds like there's nothing wrong with your reading skills."

Williams blinked, a scowl dancing over his lean face, the white scar on his forehead appearing to pulse for a moment.

"I want the last orders and known whereabouts for those names mentioned in your orders. I'll want the Black Hawk and the Spectre."

"You want the Spectre? You're going to be a few hands short of a fourteen-man crew…"

"I'm aware of that. You pick who goes. I also want one of your Chinooks and a Humvee winched to it. I want you in here and standing by your radio at all times to receive any additional orders, until I return."

"Anything else with that shake and fries?"

"Yeah. Be forewarned. Your guys, if they don't follow orders, and my people pick up the first whiff of a problem, there'll be the gravest of consequences."

"Save your threats."

"No threat."

"I have a pretty damn idea good why you're here, Cooper, or whatever your name is. You think Specter Squad engineered what happened in the States."

"It's no longer a matter of what I think."

"I see."

"Do tell. What do you see, Colonel?"

Williams puffed on his cigar. "I see you here to hunt down these men, special ops who have been over here for years now, waxing bad guys, men who have gone way above and beyond the call of duty. If the brass—hell, the whole of the American public back home—knew what they've done, how many scumbags they've waxed and captured and wrung the truth out of and thwarted God only knows how many terror attacks, they'd be on bended knee, kissing their asses, weeping out an ocean of grateful tears, blubbering praise and thanks and paying homage to these warriors until kingdom come."

Bolan grunted. The Colonel was either one of them, or he had his head buried in the sand.

"That's it. A grunt? What the hell? You just going to arrest them, drag them back to the States, scapegoats to hold up for the politicians? I think you're looking in the wrong direction, Special Agent Cooper. Not that you're asking my opinion, but I think somebody in Washington has their head buried up their ass, but that's standard procedure for suits and geeks..."

Bolan blew smoke past the man's face, then dropped an icy stare on him. "Colonel. Let me be clear. I'm not here to arrest or embarrass them. I'm not here to take them back to the States."

Sanders bared his teeth around the cigar. "Son of a bitch."

Bolan stood. "One other thing, Colonel. If it turns out you're dirty..."

"You rotten son of a bitch."

"I won't be arresting you, either."

CHAPTER TWENTY-FOUR

"What?"

"Four hundred mil."

"What?"

"And some change. And we counted it again, sir, just like you asked. Bundles to bags. Weighed them each—bags, that is—and I don't think our computerized scale with the program that was installed for our specific purposes would steer us wrong."

Allen Braxton felt his legs buckle, and it wasn't from being almost forty hours in the air. No, the computer wouldn't lie, which meant, in haste and panic, he'd cleared the roof at the Trans-World Bank with far fewer bags than at first anticipated. He asked Crawford the exact number of bags so he could do his own math. When he heard the number, he felt sick, and it wasn't due to jet lag, any number of eternal minutes chewing on nerves while waiting on some apron in Spain then

Turkey. Beyond what amounted to little better than chump change in his mind, the fear and anger was quickly being owed to more what he didn't see, didn't know, and which was bringing on the fresh wave of nausea, paranoia, the concern mounting to the point it seemed as if any second now he would step right off the edge of the planet.

"It gets better, Braxton."

He shot Black Dog a scathing look, wondering if the special op was trying to be cute. "Better?"

"Our Iranian friend is going to be expecting his merchandise. In fact, I've already arranged it. About sixty minutes ago, way back when I got you cleared for landing."

Instead of answering Black Dog or looking at his own trio of money-counters, Braxton worked on his cigarette, shuffled off to the side where he helped himself to the bottle of whiskey on the shabby wooden desk of the commander of Specter Squad.

Black Dog appeared to grow tight with controlled anger. "And now you tell me there's word from your people in the Caribbean that your boat still hasn't docked. And you saw one of your birds get blown off the roof on your way out of Miami. All this leads me to believe we are no longer on our own clock. So. You want to talk about bum steers?"

"What the hell's that supposed to mean?"

"It means what it means."

Braxton broke Black Dog's stare, pulled straight from the half-empty bottle. Half empty, he thought, as he stared at the dark liquid remaining. Just like their heist. He wanted to scream in rage, as he felt the trembling hit his limbs like he was standing smack-dab on a fault line. They were all looking at him, ten of Black Dog's commandos, grim, and armed, angry dark creatures of stone standing in the flickering shadows cast from the kerosene lanterns. What was left of his crew was down to fourteen guns, maybe half still with the transport plane outside the crumbled walls of the remote and abandoned village, weapons ready, fanning what was no less than moonscape, rugged hills slashed with gorges, plateaus, caves.

No-man's land.

Nowhere. That's exactly how he felt.

Assume the worst. Brendon's load had been seized, or there was the off chance he'd simply boated off with his end, sailing, yes, into the sunset. Say it was the latter, and in that case that was just plain stupid, since what they could've deposited in various accounts would've multiplied in interest alone, and with any number of deals that could be struck with drug cartels, arms dealers...

In light of attrition—or anyone's AWOL status—Braxton supposed that was the only good news.

Four hundred million and change. Split, then, about forty ways, he'd still walk off with ten mil. Grinding his teeth, he wandered a dark stare over the bags piled against the walls in the large stone hovel. He figured if he went ahead and took two of them right now...

"I can't sit on this much money for too long, Braxton. I got you in-country, we used my contacts along the way, as advertised. Problem is, I can be sure we are under the microscope. AWACs. Space eyes. You name it. No matter how well I cover the bases, there are too many ops floating around from where this began to just across the border—well, maybe you see our dilemma. And I still have about ten million promised out, maybe more depending on who comes running out of the shadows with their hands out. It gets better."

"Will you stop saying that?"

"There's money not included into your safe passage to the Far East."

Braxton took another deep pull from the bottle. Along the way, he had acquired an M-16/M-203 combo, and he was wondering how smart it would be, how good he was...

He killed the idea as soon as he saw how Black Dog's mongrels were spread around the room, watching him closely, shoulders tense, assault rifles and one big Squad Automatic Weapon in the hands of some Goliath.

"So, we divide up the haul and go our separate ways," Braxton told Black Dog.

"It isn't that easy."

"How do you figure that?"

"That ten million I mentioned promised out..."

Braxton felt his heart thunder in his ears. "Comes out of our end?"

"It's negotiable."

"Negotiable? Stick that noise! Are you forgetting I was the one who put this thing together?"

"No."

"Then show a little respect, and gratitude."

Black Dog lit a cigarette, paused. "Hold your horses, Homeland. When I said negotiable, what I meant is that I need your help with the Iranians."

"I see. You're going to squeeze them for some cash before you give up the plague and the vaccines."

Black Dog shrugged. "That's the only way to recoup some of what was lost, the way I see it. Now. I move the merchandise to a spot I have on the other side of these hills, tuck it deep in a cave, rig a few nerve-shakers, as in landmines. I contact our boy and have them meet us there. Tell them, plain and simple, this one isn't a freebie, sorry about that, they'll need to cough up— Well, let's call it thirty mil."

"And if Amarshar takes exception to your demand?"

Black Dog chuckled, smoke funneling out his nostrils like some fire-breathing dragon. "What do you think?"

"You want us on board as extra shooters."

"Just in case."

"What about the gold mine of what the United States military-intelligence industrial complex intends to do over here within the next ten to twenty years?"

"The CDs, you mean? Taking over the Saudi oil fields before they dry up? Unleashing a controlled program of genocide on the Muslim populace in about six different oil-producing countries?"

Braxton patted his combat vest. "This info is straight from what they wouldn't consider any less than the Devil's mouth. It couldn't be any better if Mohammed came down from the mountain and handed it to him."

"It's a carrot, all else fails, I'll grant you that. Right now I need an answer, Homeland. In or out?"

He seethed at the very idea he would have to risk his life, and now, against Islamic rabble.

A 101 bitter regrets wanted to stoke the fires of rage and frustration. The plan, for the most part, had gone off without a hitch. Sure, a score of bodies and untold mayhem had been strewed in their wake, but that had been anticipated. Sure, it would come to light that the very same operatives who were security for the nation's slush fund on the War on Terror would be fingered for the heist, but that was factored in from the beginning. Still, he hadn't counted on more than half of the billion-dollar haul to get lost, seized, or whatever. Lost money was just that. And that's what disturbed him most of all. He had been hoping—no, craving—for twenty to twenty-five million off the top, more depending on casualties along the way, of course, and whoever was waiting in the wings to be greased but who could be dealt with in prompt and bloody fashion.

Black Dog was right—they weren't just on an opposing black op's clock, they were, in all likelihood, being hunted. Assume worst case, which would be Brendon or one of his crew getting bagged, squeezed for information, squawking, pointing the finger of blame their way—in this direction.

"Look, Braxton," Black Dog said, an edge to his

voice, "I hope this isn't where we all turn buzzard on each other and start tearing out the choicest entrails."

Braxton scoured those cold lifeless eyes. "How many men is Amarshar bringing to this little get-together?"

"My guy at the border told me thirty to forty. Could be more, since he didn't check in the back of two GAZ transports."

"GAZs? Hell…"

"It gets better. They've got Technicals with Russian LMGs, a couple dozen RPGs."

Braxton bit down the curse.

"You think I'm happy about this? My ass is hung out over the fire more than yours. I've got CENTCOM, CIA, DIA, NSA to keep watch of all over this little slice of Hell tucked up against the Iranian border. It's nothing short of a miracle I even got the first load of plague to the Iranians, and maybe somebody somewhere already knows something about that, for all I know."

"Meaning what? You let me walk right into crosshairs that are fixed on you and yours?"

"I can never be one hundred percent positive either way, Braxton. Okay. So the clock might strike twelve. This is the goal line, pal. The brass ring, right there parked against those walls. Take courage. Show a little faith. If you're so inclined, pray. Didn't you learn anything from all that quality time you spent with your Christian friends back in Montana and Idaho?"

Braxton checked the scowl, the angry remark as he detected the subtle shift in tone, leaning now toward threatening. Greed made even the staunchest of allies unreliable, untrustworthy when all hope was on the verge of being dashed, and someone was going to get left short-changed and holding the dung end of the stick. What to do?

In or out? Stay and fight or take his cut and walk out the door?

He was considering the moment some more, Black Dog shifting from one boot to the other, blowing up a smoke storm, then decided to take his chances and just stroll out the door when the decision came to him.

"We've got a problem, Black Dog."

Braxton had the assault rifle off his shoulder, as there was no mistaking the urgency in the commando's look and voice.

"Actually, sir, we've got two problems."

THE FORMER TALIBAN STRONGHOLD was called Jamman Hektayr. Right after 9/11 when the bombs began raining on the thugs of the landlocked nation about the size of Texas, a good number of the regime scurried for the mountains bordering Pakistan to the east and south, and where various warlike tribes were sympathetic to their flight from American justice. Others scampered into the waiting arms of their northern Muslim neighbors, Turkmenistan, Uzbekistan and Tajikistan, when the Americans picked up the scent or the mullahs figured life in hiding and freezing at high altitudes wasn't the easiest way to go. Some of the smarter and more well-connected mullahs, though, had read the tea leaves and saw the brightest prospects for life and liberty were best sought somewhere near or over the border with their like-thinking and West-hating Iranian brethren.

The end result of all their best scheming, Bolan saw—giving it a second but quicker scan through the ghost-green haze of his NVD goggles as he topped out the narrow gully and set his sights on the target about forty feet across the rocky shelf—was a vast graveyard of bombed-out hovels, a smashed hill of stone that marked the mosque, and the blackened rusty shells of what appeared two Russian T-72 tanks and a smattering of demolished vehicles of undetermined make.

How long ago the ghost village had become a remote outpost for the so-called Specter Squad depended on whom Bolan believed. Whatever the truth—and the soldier had been around long enough to know that no matter what the finish he'd never have all the facts, and maybe even a few of the guilty would slip the net—it was spruced up with radar and satellite dishes and antenna that marked the Command and Control hovel, then a concrete runway laid out to the northwest in recent times and where the C-130 that had been tracked all the way from the coast of England was now parked. It took some digging, some wrangling on down the line with some presidential threatening to CENTCOM, the CIA, NSA and DIA but Bolan had names and faces of the snakes in hiding here.

Usually it was far easier than that to determine who, what and where the bad guys were. Dark truth be told, more often than not the soldier couldn't even begin to count up all the opposition he had taken out over the years who actually lived and thrived, as bold as brass testicles, right out in the open. They always used their money for armor, believing that and simple intimidation and spreading the fear of the devil in all parties concerned and on both sides of the law made them bulletproof, and above the rules everyone else played by.

Ask any cop not on the take, he thought. Ask any judge not being greased or skewing laws as he created morality and truth in his or her own eyes, ask anyone who had the power of the law on their side and the same sad story would be retold so many times it would shake the faith of the most stalwart, right-living, principled man-warrior-soul to the point where he had to wonder if the world was maybe down to a few good folks that could be counted up…

The way of the wicked—it was all about money, power, pleasure, taken, stolen or seized to the extreme, and at the expense and the suffering of the innocent, the not-so-innocent and anybody else who crossed their path and didn't bow down in homage, respect, groveling or could be used to further serve their agendas. And as much as the Executioner believed in the good fight for the innocent, the peacemakers and those so inclined to obey the law of the land it damn sure seemed the longer he was around that a darkness was fast spreading to all corners of the planet.

Which was, unfortunately, he believed, why his particular skills were in demand, now more than ever.

And starting, yet again, in this desolate little pocket

of northwest Afghanistan, in the cold shroud of dark night in the gnarled lunarscape foothills of the Paropamisus Range about three hundred miles due west as the buzzard flew from Kabul and just to the northeast of Herat.

If there was any doubt about what he was about to do, the shadow at the edge of the ledge that overlooked the northeast corner of the ruins confirmed it.

Black Dog.

And that was all that the Executioner needed to hear, though he had done the gist of the prior conversation.

The commando sensed the threat looming on his six as he signed off. There was just enough tension in the shoulders, the guy putting on a pretty good act, like he was going to go back to the infrared glasses, when Bolan drew a bead on the back of his skull with the sound-suppressed Beretta 93-R.

Then he scooted.

The guy was quick, good, a pro, darting hard to the side, seeking quick sanctuary behind a wall of rock, but the Executioner anticipated the move, gave him some lead and pumped two 9 mm Parabellum shockers through the temple.

One down, crunching up in a heap, twitching out the final spasms.

Bolan quickly bridged the gap to the body, then scanned the shelf, Beretta seeking fresh victims. IR reads on the Black Hawk that had dropped him off on a ledge about two hundred yards down and to the east before searching the hills and keeping him posted for roaming shooters may have turned up one lone sentry, and his own handheld heat-seeking unit may have backed that up...

But the moment of truth had an uncanny way of always being ready to change when he walked up to the edge of the crocodile pit.

Like now.

Crouched and concealed, his back covered by the wall of rock his victim had sought and lost, the soldier shed the NVD headgear, filled his hand with the infrared binoculars and scanned the play.

The Chinook, lights out, was a black speck on an even blacker horizon, moving at a slow clip of about fifty knots to the south, two klicks out, as though the crew was suspicious and undecided. But the big transport bird had not only just dropped the package, gathering a curious crowd now of eight hardmen, it was still getting plenty of attention from the enemy.

Panning west, the Executioner found he was just in time to help the enemy in that direction greet the arriving convoy. There were Technicals, Russian transport trucks, and black turbaned fighters enough now disgorging and armed with AKs and RPGs to damn near make Bolan smile. The C-130 was parked on the special ops runway, north of the gathering hyenas, the enemy far enough from what was coming that Bolan didn't have to worry about any bio-agent getting blasted into the air. A few moments later, and the warrior spotted maybe twenty-plus armed shadows weaving a slow march through the rubble to parlay with the extremist horde.

Or, Bolan hoped, worse.

Which would be the cannibals eating each other alive, saving him the trouble.

The Spectre, he knew, was in the neighborhood, holding a southerly vector, ready to lower the boom on his word. As far as any death from above, Bolan had gotten lucky on the way out of the colonel's HQ. Much to Williams's chagrin, the soldier had borrowed a Predator drone, fitted with a Hellfire, while one of his blacksuits from the Farm stumbled across an Apache gunship while touring the premises. And since the man in question had logged some sorties during Gulf One in the tank-slayer, had played a hand in mopping up the Republican Guard on the ill-fated Iraqi Highway of Death...

Why wait?

Another search of the eight-man force walking toward the black nylon bag, and Bolan found his man.

Or, rather, one of them.

The guy's name was Braxton, and he didn't look all that eager to leave the cover of three Humvees, as he held his ground on the far side of the lead vehicle, head rolling around the compass. It had taken some digging, more threats...

It was the first time he'd laid eyes on the savage, but Bolan knew the look of a guilty and cornered animal.

He knew the face of evil.

The Executioner slipped the M-16/M-203 combo off his shoulder and set it down on his right flank. Then twenty-five pounds of pure killing power came off the other shoulder, filled his hands. He did some quick computations, factoring in the breeze at his back, trajectory, distance to targets.

It felt like old times, the sniper skills flaring to life.

Just like riding a bike.

The big piece was good for two thousand yards, more than a mile, well within the five hundred yard range he'd require.

Bolan took his tac radio and patched through to his blacksuit in charge of the Spectre. "Striker to Grand Slam."

"Grand Slam here, Striker."

"You read my position?" the Executioner asked, waiting as the blacksuit checked his screen to make sure the transponder was still green.

"You're good to go, Striker."

"I've got about fifty to sixty hornets that need swatting. They're buzzing but holding tight, all for you at the west side of Ghost Town. Same orders as before. Ghost Town proper still belongs to me, unless you hear otherwise. Bring it on, Grand Slam."

The blacksuit copied, passing on the ETA.

Two minutes and counting.

The Executioner watched as his half of targets stopped about twenty yards from the air-dropped gift. They were suspicious, and he couldn't blame them for that.

Far worse beyond confusion and hesitation was coming for the savages, as Bolan palmed the small black box, thumbed on the red light.

A quick watch check, a sky sweep...

Then the Executioner settled the M-107 .50-caliber rifle on the bipod, switched on the mounted infrared scope and stretched out on his stomach.

CHAPTER TWENTY-FIVE

"That looks like…"

"One of our bags."

It wasn't much more of a mutter, but the words that came out of his mouth might as well have resounded in his ears like a thunderclap. As Braxton felt the hackles rising on the back of his neck, he searched the broken foothills that loomed on his left wing, the M-16 fanning the broken rock, certain that was more than just shadows scudding under the moon and clouds in the green world of his night vision.

It felt wrong.

And simply because it had all gone off with very little sweat. Years in the making, every base covered, every move checked and triple-checked, from grooming the SOR crud to greasing the right people above him in the shadows. The operation itself, impossible on paper, had gone down with virtual flawlessness, silky-smooth. And now…

For some reason, the panic was rising the longer he stood there, seven of his men shuffling toward the bulging nylon bag, the chute still billowing as a gust of wind blew over the plateau, displaying the drop for all of them to see.

Like it was a trophy.

Or bait.

They were made.

If so, then where was all the opposition, come to clean their clocks? Why wasn't the sky swarming with choppers, fighter jets? Why was it so still, quiet, calm?

"Go on!" Braxton barked at his guys as about half of them froze a good distance from the bag. "One of you open the damn thing!"

Patton showed the most courage or curiosity, as he crouched over it, hesitated. Then Braxton heard the zipper. Patton was a few moments too long, hunched and looking stupefied. Why did that bother him so? If it was only money…a taunt…

Then Braxton saw the man pull a bundle from the bag, hold it up. He was about to snarl for Patton to confirm what he already knew when he heard one of them cursing. That was enough for Braxton, as he heard the warning Klaxons resound in his skull, instinct pulling him back and hunching beneath the Humvee's door when Patton's head disintegrated in a dark cloud. He heard the peal, positive it came from somewhere up the slopes—where else, since it was open range to the south, east and west—then another decapitation blew up before his eyes. With the only cover the Humvee, with no clear fix on the invisible sniper, Braxton knew the survivors, scrambling to head his way, were fat ducks.

Braxton was reaching behind to pull open the door, heard autofire ringing out as they tried to cover their cut and run when he decided to look back, determine just how bad it was, how his guys were faring.

It didn't look good at all, as he found himself just in time to watch a dark mist erupt from the backside of another killing shot, the body launched off its feet, sailing on for what looked ten yards but was in reality only a few feet.

Braxton froze, torn, dangling over some furnace blaze between rage, frustration and fear, then the night blew up in his eyes, the blast so bright and fierce he screamed against the dazzling brilliance as it flared in his night vision.

HIS REAL NAME was Mel Forrester, and he knew Afghanistan like the back of his fist—the land, people and the politics of war. He should, since he'd been there since right before the end of the Russian debacle. What he knew was that the more something changed, the more it stayed the same. He really didn't need to take history lessons in ass-whippings from the Persians, the Brits or the Russians for anybody to inform him that any foreigners who thought they could stake out some turf here and settle in for a long-term vacation was either a fool or a naive dreamer.

He was neither.

What he'd done over the course of almost two decades was make contacts, play all sides, and earn a nice little nest egg, profits courtesy of arms sales and heroin. Since war was life and his life was war, there was nothing and no one waiting back home in the States. No sweat, since there was no one to mourn his passing, then there was no one to share what he still intended to be the sweet retirement of some long bloody covert years where he knew nothing much would ever get resolved or remotely better in this neck of the woods.

He led his men to the convoy, taking in positions, numbers, the M-16 held across his chest but ready to rip. He braked, maybe twenty yards from the line of Islamic fighters, landing smack in the middle of the Muslim force. A few assault rifles and cone-shaped warheads fixed to RPGs were poking around the back edges of the transport trucks. Those were big DshK Russian machine guns in the beds of the Toyotas, and the shadows weren't swinging them their direction—yet—but Forrester sensed they were ready to cut loose on a drop of sweat.

Amarshar, he saw, cradling an AKM, stepped up, his men parting to give him room. "Is this what you call bringing the mountain to Mohammed?"

"I thought I would save you some trouble, Black Dog. As you can see by the transports, I am ready to pick up what you promised."

"There's been a slight change in plans."

"Really? Such as?"

"We need to renegotiate our contract."

"It has been almost two days since my men were

martyred in your country. I have waited long enough. Give me what you promised or—"

"If I see one AK, one RPG swing my way, I start blasting."

"Then you die."

"Go crazy. Somebody once told me I was never meant for this world anyway."

"You were made for Hell."

"And I guess you think you're going to go soaring off to Allah's bosom, floating around Paradise with your seventy-two virgins, and, which, I bet, are all non-Muslim beauties?"

"You have a tongue like the devil you are."

He weighed the odds, threw a look over both shoulders. Four to one, at best, and with three of Braxton's guys and three of his own men back in their command post, guarding the store...

He thought he heard a familiar noise, somewhere in the black heavens, coming from the south. It sounded like the first rumblings of thunder before the tempest. A moment later, as he glimpsed Amarshar and other Arabs looking up, he was sure he wasn't suffering from auditory hallucinations.

That flying battleship was an AC-130 Spectre.

Only the explosion that ripped into the heart of the Muslim army came from his blindside.

Forrester would have given full savage vent to the curse tearing from his mouth, but the next thing he knew something came winging from the core of the fireball, slammed off his skull and doused the lights.

IT WAS BEYOND INCREDIBLE, so unbelievable, in truth, Braxton wasn't sure whether to scream, laugh or wail and gnash his teeth. He couldn't believe it was all going to end here, like this, bloodied and mauled, alone with the stink of more of his dead troops in his nose, with a bag of his own money blown up in his face—what had been staged for his benefit, he was sure, get the nerves frayed to the bone. As though whoever the bastard—and he was sure it was the same SOB who'd been sniping his guys from the hills—was having some fun with him.

Or sending a message that it was all over but the crying.

He gritted his teeth against the fiery waves of pain, checked the huge gash down his leg. Let it bleed, he figured. Pain was the least of his problems right then.

If only he had bypassed Afghanistan. If only the damn Iranians hadn't showed when they did. If only Brendon had made contact to let him know something. If only…

It seemed as if some angry or sadistic fate had conspired against him. Dangling the brass ring in his face, letting him grab it, no less, but only holding on for just so long. It was as if he was allowed to make all the right moves, keep chugging, keep killing, keep running, and just so that same fate could bring all the players in question together, same place, same time.

It made no sense. It wasn't right.

All he wanted, damn it, was his rightful slice of the pie! Some peace and quiet, much earned, much deserved, considering how many lives he and his Invisibles had saved from the scourge of terror and from an unknowing and ungrateful American public. He was owed, at the very least, a few million! And since nobody seemed inclined to step up and offer him what he was owed, he had taken it. It was only money, after all, Uncle Sam could always print some more; they did it every day.

If not for rage and the overpowering urge to kill, to survive, he would have missed the black spear hurtling out of the sky, from the east. That was a Hellfire, spit from an Apache gunship, that had ripped apart the Humvees. Little good did quick feet and knowledge of the enemy's firepower do him now, since he was scraping himself off the ground, hearing a thousand-and-one bells going off at once in his ears, wondering how long he'd been under. Sucking wind, the stink of burning gas and blood further melting his senses to jelly, the world revolving in some nauseating spiral—

What was that?

It looked a tall shadow, armed with an assault rifle, sliding between tongues of fire, and coming from the north. Braxton wasn't sure he could make out who or what it was beyond any doubt, since blood and sweat burned into his eyes, obscuring vision, and the way the fires danced there were shadows leaping everywhere. He knew, though, that was money raining down with flaming warped debris of the Humvees, as a shredded strip fluttered up to his face and pasted itself to the blood on his cheek.

The question now was, where did he go? More important, what to do?

The sky was strobing to the west, the sounds of thunder and explosions so loud the very din seemed to shake the earth under his boots. What was no less than a full air assault...

He jumped at the sound of autofire, the sharp cry of pain, followed by a heavy silence he couldn't mistake for anything other than another one of his guys, wounded perhaps, and just getting waxed. The shots came from the mangled shell of a fiery Humvee, it sounded, at some point on the other side of the pall of black smoke. He was thinking he spotted movement when the answer hit him.

The village! The C-130!

Run!

Then another barrage of thunder slammed his senses. Feeling tears of rage burning behind his eyes, as he glimpsed more bills floating to earth, he looked toward the rising fire storm to the west. It didn't take much effort to pinpoint the source of all that destruction, as he quickly decided, cursing, that any hopes he had of reaching the hovel, grabbing up a few bags then simply rolling off in the Hercules was a no-go. The Apache was strafing from the south, unloading its 30 mm Chain Gun, cutting loose with two Hellfires while Spectre dropped the sky on Black Dog and the Iranians. He couldn't see the action, as it was blocked by the rolling mounds of rubble where once stood the Taliban village, but judging by all the screams, what looked like stick figures and flaming meteors shooting like so many fiery geysers high into the air—

The tall shadow seemed to materialize right before his eyes, to his one o'clock, as if the smoke had breathed the armed figure forth from the night. Braxton hesitated for a split second, as he found his stare riveted on the icy blue eyes framed in the black streaked face. Eyes that seemed more like orbs of pure fire than anything human, but there was something about the man he thought he recognized, or maybe it was the stare that burned back, telling him something about himself, as if the shadow had known him all along.

And he was judged.

The distance was twenty yards, nothing too great to overcome, but where he hesitated in bringing his assault rifle to bear the shadow's M-16 was already flaming.

EPILOGUE

The Hellfire from the Apache had saved him the effort on four of them, though one of Braxton's brigands needed a burst from his M-16 to finally send him on his way to face his maker. Even with the .50-caliber rifle swiveling at will on the flange between the bipod and weapon, and despite all his skill and experience as a sniper, it wasn't feasible to pick them all off from his sniping perch. And since Bolan had planned on moving in for the up-close and personal touch before he hunkered on the ledge...

They were down and done, as of fifty-three minutes ago, a final four draped over their booty in the main hut where the soldier had moved in on them through a back door and while they were peeking out the front, a bag in each hand, figuring out their next move.

Black Dog, a.k.a., Mel Forrester, the Iranian extremists, what were believed a few Taliban fighters who had been holding out hope across the border, for the most part, strewed in various bits and pieces and puddles of slick ooze and entrails over a wide stretch of barren earth where the Spectre and the Apache had nailed it down for the soldier. What was left, he knew, was somewhere out there to the west, charging hard, by foot and vehicle, for the border or the hills, but as Bolan saw the Hellfires streaking like flaming spears from the Apache and the Spectre hammering out the Bofors thunder, he knew they wouldn't make it.

The black horizon out yonder seemed to jump, a curtain of lightning, as each hit lit up the plateau. Ironic, or maybe it was divine justice at work, he thought, but the very same warbirds he was sure Specter Squad had used in the past to tear up half of Afghanistan and probably beyond had been the very same instruments of their own demise.

Funny how that worked.

Cosmic justice?

The will of God?

All the bad guys coming together, right time, right place? Or wrong time, wrong place, depending which side of the dividing divine line a man stood on the Cosmic tracks?

That gave him pause, as the Executioner walked away from the south end of Jamman Hektayr. He heard the Black Hawk as it swept past, that team now going into the C and C hut to help load a few dozen black bags, after, that was, the HAZMAT team secured the Armageddon Plague.

All done?

He wasn't so sure.

The Executioner cut a wide berth around the slaughterbed where a few bills were still swirling in the breeze or riding the smoke. There would be those, he knew, who would bemoan such a deplorable trashing of money, about six million in cash to be exact. That was their problem. And since greed and twisted ambition was what the whole bloody mess was all about from the beginning, that and unloading some undetermined bioagent into the hands of extremists...

He looked at the three CDs he'd plucked off Braxton. According to Radfield—and Bolan had debriefed the man for a good hour before getting him shipped back to his family in Texas—Braxton had cleaned the brains of the 999 Supercomputer in the Trans-World Bank. And, as Radfield had suggested, the soldier had perused the CD he'd given him while transcribing the data back to the Farm over secured e-mail.

Bolan pocketed the CDs as he stepped further away from the dead, the clean-up, the plague.

There were big names filed away on what was supposed to have been blackmail leverage for Braxton in case the heat came scorching after him. Big, big names, both present and retired, and two who had not sought reelection. There were names, famous and infamous, bank account numbers, dates, facts and figures as to various and sundry shady deals that had gone down over the past three decades involving dictators, tyrants, drug cartels, the sale and shipment of everything from uranium yellow cake to centrifuges to backpack nukes to the enemies of the free world. Whether or not it was true, well, it bore some serious investigation. Especially the named bigshots in the UN oil for food scam, which Bolan decided to look into personally. Then there were the long-since dead, named as co-conspirators in everything from Roswell to the Kennedy assassination. There were CIA plots that involved genocide...

Bolan took a deep breath of clean cold air.

The pain shot down his spine where he'd taken another two hits to the Kevlar vest in the hut. Now that the adrenaline was subsiding...

Invisibles. Sons of Revelation. The Armageddon Plague. Black ops gone bad. He had to wonder what would have happened had he declined Brognola's offer to look into the murders of two FBI agents. He wasn't one to start patting himself on the back, and how could he, in all good conscience? Scores of innocent civilians lay dead or dying in five different U.S. cities.

The com link crackled with Snowstorm's voice. The blacksuit informed Bolan the container holding the plague still looked sealed, undamaged and was being moved into the Black Hawk. The money was being loaded into the Chinook. Bolan copied, told Snowstorm to pick him up when they were done.

Going home, the soldier thought.

The Executioner wasn't sure what waited on the other side of the Atlantic, but he could count one thing.

Tomorrow would arrive.

And his War Everlasting would march on.

JAKE STRAIT

THE DEVIL KNOCKS

BY FRANK RICH

HELL IS FOR THE LIVING

It is 2031, the hellscape of the future where chemical and biological cesspools have created everybody's worst nightmare. In the corner of hell known as Denver, Jake Strait must face a bounty hunter turned revolutionary in a flat-out race for the finish line, where even victory will place him in double jeopardy.

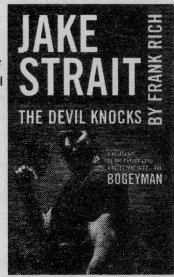

Available April 2007, wherever you buy books.

GOLD EAGLE

GJS2

STARFIRE

Panic rocks the White House after an unknown killer
satellite fires a nuke into the Australian Outback—
a dire warning from an unknown enemy.
Stony Man is on the attack, racing to identify
the unknown enemy and using any means to
destroy it. As anarchy and mass murder push
the world to the edge, Stony Man hunts down
a threat no power on earth has yet faced....

STONY MAN®

*Available
April 2007
wherever
you buy books.*

Or order your copy now by sending your name, address, zip or postal code, along with a check or
money order (please do not send cash) for $6.50 for each book ordered ($7.99 in Canada), plus
75¢ postage and handling ($1.00 in Canada), payable to Gold Eagle Books, to:

In the U.S.

Gold Eagle Books
3010 Walden Avenue
P.O. Box 9077
Buffalo, NY 14269-9077

In Canada

Gold Eagle Books
P.O. Box 636
Fort Erie, Ontario
L2A 5X3

**GOLD
EAGLE**®

Please specify book title with your order.
Canadian residents add applicable federal and provincial taxes.

GSM88

TAKE 'EM FREE
2 action-packed novels plus a mystery bonus

NO RISK
NO OBLIGATION TO BUY

SPECIAL LIMITED-TIME OFFER

Mail to: Gold Eagle Reader Service™

IN U.S.A.: P.O. Box 1867, Buffalo, NY 14240-1867
IN CANADA: P.O. Box 609, Fort Erie, Ontario L2A 5X3

YEAH! Rush me 2 FREE Gold Eagle® novels and my FREE mystery bonus. If I don't cancel, I will receive 6 hot-off-the-press novels every other month. Bill me at the low price of just $29.94* for each shipment. That's a savings of over 10% off the combined cover prices and there is NO extra charge for shipping and handling! There is no minimum number of books I must buy. I can always cancel at any time simply by returning a shipment at your cost or by returning any shipping statement marked "cancel." Even if I never buy another book from Gold Eagle, the 2 free books and mystery bonus are mine to keep forever.

166 ADN EF29   366 ADN EF3A

Name	(PLEASE PRINT)	
Address		Apt. No.
City	State/Prov.	Zip/Postal Code

Signature (if under 18, parent or guardian must sign)

Not valid to current Gold Eagle® subscribers.
Want to try two free books from another series? Call 1-800-873-8635.

* Terms and prices subject to change without notice. N.Y. residents add applicable sales tax. Canadian residents will be charged applicable provincial taxes and GST. This offer is limited to one order per household. All orders subject to approval. Credit or debit balances in a customer's account(s) may be offset by any other outstanding balance owed by or to the customer. Please allow 4 to 6 weeks for delivery.

Your Privacy: Worldwide Library is committed to protecting your privacy. Our Privacy Policy is available online at www.eHarlequin.com or upon request from the Reader Service. From time to time we make our lists of customers available to reputable firms who may have a product or service of interest to you. If you would prefer we not share your name and address, please check here. ☐

James Axler
Outlanders

CLOSING THE
COSMIC EYE

Rumors of an ancient doomsday device come to the attention of the Cerberus rebels when it's stolen by an old enemy, Gilgamesh Bates. The pre-Dark mogul who engineered his own survival has now set his sights on a controlling share of the cosmic pie. Kane, Grant, Brigid and Domi ally themselves with Bates's retired personal army, a time-trawled force of American commandos ready to take the battle back to Bates himself, wherever he's hiding in the galaxy, before the entire universe disappears in the blink of an eye.

Available February 2007 wherever books are sold.

Or order your copy now by sending your name, address, zip or postal code, along with a check or money order (please do not send cash) for $6.50 for each book ordered ($7.99 in Canada), plus 75¢ postage and handling ($1.00 in Canada), payable to Gold Eagle Books, to:

In the U.S.	**In Canada**
Gold Eagle Books	Gold Eagle Books
3010 Walden Avenue	P.O. Box 636
P.O. Box 9077	Fort Erie, Ontario
Buffalo, NY 14269-9077	L2A 5X3

Please specify book title with your order.
Canadian residents add applicable federal and provincial taxes.

GOLD EAGLE®

GOUT40

AleX Archer
FORBIDDEN CITY

A stunning artifact holds the key to an untapped power of global destruction.

While working on a dig in the California wilderness, archaeologist-adventurer Annja Creed uncovers evidence of a tragedy linked to Chinese miners from the days of the gold rush. Lured by legends of gold, betrayal and a vengeful Han Dynasty overlord, Annja travels the Orient Express and encounters adversaries who will stop at nothing to stake their claim to a fabled lost city that promises doom for those who dare to reveal its evil power..

Available March 2007 wherever you buy books.

GOLD
EAGLE ®

GRA5